# TWO OF A KIND

1st edition Copyright © 2023  Sean P. Gaughan

The right of Sean P. Gaughan to be identified as
author of this work has been asserted by
him in accordance with the Copyright, Designs
and Patents Act 1988.

All characters in this publication are fictitious
and any resemblance to real persons, living or dead,
is purely coincidental.

All Rights Reserved.
No part of this publication may be reproduced,
stored in a retrieval system, or transmitted, in any
form or by any means, electronic, mechanical,
photocopying, recording or otherwise, without
the prior permission of the copyright owner.

ISBN: 9798852721914

# TWO OF A KIND
Sean P. Gaughan

## CHAPTER ONE

"Are ye getting out of bed yet Agatha? Ye don't want to be late for Mass." It was the acerbic voice of Bridget Nelligan coming from the back bedroom overlooking the sea. Reproof and condemnation were qualities ingrained in her methods of communication when dealing with the general clutter of humanity. She expressed a modicum of warmth only when conversing with a priest or some other pious being. And it was just a modicum; warmth was not a part of her nature. There was an element of inbuilt unpleasantness about her; she was in fact a long thin streak of unmitigated misery, it had to be said.Even towards Agatha she was reserved, distant even, having had little to do with her until the request to provide her niece with accommodation had so recently been thrust upon her.

Until a few weeks ago Bridget herself had occupied the slightly larger front bedroom of the tumbledown cottage overlooking the lane and the distant mountains. From it she could keep a jaundiced eye on the unvaried activities of the few neighbours who lived round and about. She'd vacated it with only a little reluctance, in favour of Agatha, who had moved in to lodge with her when she'd come up from Geesala to take an assistant's job at the post office in Glenowen.

Bridget had viewed the mountains for nearly thirty years, ever since she herself had come to live in the cottage when she'd had to leave the convent because of poor health. Her older brother had owned it then, and had let her move in with him, as she had nowhere else to go. He left it to her when he died the following year. Bridget didn't really mind changing bedrooms. She liked the view over the sea from the back of the house as much as that of the blue distant mountains in front of it, and could now watch over her cow in the small field in which she confined it. The cow was in fact still a heifer, and must have been the oldest unmated cow in the West. Bridget had inherited it as a calf, along with its mother, when her brother died. She had kept that cow until a while after lactation ceased, then sold it to a man in the next village. When the calf matured, she could not bring herself to introduce it to a bull; copulation and birth being things that were quite abhorrent to her. So the calf remained something of a pet, and she ignored its plaintive mooing over the fence when it could see other cattle – including, sometimes, a bull – in the fields nearby, or being driven down the lane in the morning and evening past the house. Bridget's few scrawny hens were also denied any scrap of pleasure a rooster might have brought to them. She would never own a cockerel. She said she couldn't stand the early morning crowing, but in truth, it was the flagrant sexuality of the male bird that Bridget couldn't cope with. She'd once, a long time ago, stood talking with old father Doran outside of the town, when a rooster had mounted a hen atop of a dung heap and loudly crowed the while about his conquest. She had not known where to look, and had thought she would die of shame at having witnessed such a scene. The priest had not endeared himself to her with his casual observation that, 'He seems to have made a friend.' That remark served only to confirm what she had always believed: men were a bad lot.

The peace and privacy were even greater at the rear of the cottage than at the front, although the front garden opened only onto a quiet, unpaved lane used almost entirely by local people walking from the scattered settlement to their fields or to their turf bogs or to the tiny township of Glenowen just a few miles away. Bridget liked privacy. She was wary of people, especially men, and would have gladly stayed forever within the convent walls had not the austere conditions so utterly debilitated her. Although she did not relish the thought of having her niece living with her, she did not mind her taking the larger bedroom. She expected Agatha to have books and clothes and things – whatever a seventeen - year -old girl might require, and thought therefore that the slightly larger room would be useful to her.

Bridget had agreed to accommodate her niece only with a significant degree of trepidation, and then only because her younger brother in Geesala had almost begged her to take his daughter. Bridget was afraid of young people; they were too forward these days; knew too much, or thought they did. They didn't take as much notice of their elders as she thought they should. There was no telling what they might get up to. But she could hardly have refused her brother's request. The position at the post office was the first job opportunity his daughter had been offered, and without lodgings in the area she would have been unable to take it up. And to some extent Bridget acknowledged to herself that she owed him that, as she herself had benefitted by being willed the cottage when it might have been more fairly left to both of them. But something else that had concerned her at the time was her brother's mentioning that two or three local lads in Geesala were showing too much interest in Agatha, and he'd be glad to get her away from there. Bridget wondered if that might suggest some reciprocal interest on Agatha's part. Surely, if a girl were pure enough, as she ought to be, and made that plain to everyone, the lads wouldn't bother her. Bridget, when she herself was young, had never experienced that sort of problem. No one had paid her any such attention. These things were beyond her comprehension and a source of great consternation to her. Any untoward goings-on between the sexes appalled her. Even what married people were said to get up to made her shudder.

Agatha had been equally unenthusiastic about going to live with her aunt, but she had little choice if she wanted the job. And she wanted it desperately. She hoped one day to be able to get out of the West and to see the city lights. Dublin and its many pleasures loomed large in her dreams, but you needed the money to make a start there, as well as a reference saying you'd done a bit of work somewhere and knew what you were about.

She had met Aunt Bridget only a few times in her short life and had visited the cottage only once before. She knew she had been in the nuns, and Agatha's experience with that lot had not been too good. One or two of her peers at the convent, who intended becoming nuns themselves, had enjoyed the schooling they had received. They had been given special attention, and were always having praise – unwarranted praise in Agatha's opinion - heaped upon them. Whereas she and the rest of them, apart from being taught the 'three Rs' in a desultory fashion, were generally regarded as nuisances at best, fit only for becoming household skivvies. And Agatha herself was less well regarded than most of the girls. The nuns said she was too forward in her ways, too careless in her dress and general deportment, and given to looking at boys too much and in an unbecoming manner. She'd get herself into all sorts of trouble before long.

At the sound of her aunt's voice Agatha awoke suddenly from a troubled sleep. She had been dreaming feverishly of apples and serpents and people who were not wearing clothes. Agatha had some hazy recollection of what had once been explained to her in the vaguest of terms, several years ago, as something to do with a tree, The Tree of Knowledge, she thought it had been called. She hadn't been interested then, but she was now. She was totally intrigued by some of the voluptuous scenes she'd encountered during her nocturnal adventuring. She was in a state of excited bewilderment, having never fully grasped the meaning of events in the Garden of Eden, and was a little moist to say the least. Indeed, it would have hardly been stretching the point to say that she was in a bit of a lather. She turned her head guiltily from left to right and back again, as if checking that there were no witnesses to her colourful exploits. How on earth could these wanton wanderings come upon her so often when she was sleeping, and herself as pure as virtue itself?

Still half asleep, she answered her aunt: "Yes Auntie Bridget, I'm awake. I'm getting up now."

She lifted her head slightly and looked out over the patched counterpane in the direction of the window, where yellow daylight was seeping in around the edges of the faded curtains, revealing the flaking lime-wash and the crumbling plasterwork. She sat up slowly, making sure that the shoulders of the drab flannelette night gown were securely in place and the neckline nice and high, in case her aunt might enter the room at any moment. Then she rolled down the threadbare sheets carefully with one hand, at the same time pulling the hem of the gown down around her calves with the other. Only then, demurely presentable, did she swing her slim legs out, knees held tightly together, over the side of the bed. Old habits, instilled by the nuns, still affected her, although they were rapidly losing their grip, and were definitely at odds with her hormones, which these days were strongly asserting their influence.

Agatha could hear her aunt rattling about in the kitchen, so fears of her entering the bedroom diminished. She stood up and walked over to the window, and, taking hold of the edge of the curtain at eye level, she created the smallest chink in its armour to look out upon the peaceful lane. The protection of her modesty was further ensured by a heavy net, once white, but now grey with age, which covered all of the glass; Aunt Bridget had not taken chances where modesty was concerned.

Pulling back the curtains fully, Agatha then removed her nightdress to let her overheated body cool a little after the imagined exertions of the night, at the same time pulling a chair across the door to delay any entry should Aunt Bridget come to check on her. She returned to the window to look out again on the deserted lane. Suddenly the lane was no longer un-peopled; the car of Father Padraig Nolan, coasting at walking pace, came into her view. For the second time in a week Agatha asked herself how a priest as young as Father Nolan could possess a car. Very few priests did; only the occasional older one, whose legs were giving out and for whom a parish collection had raised the funds to buy him some ancient jalopy to help him get round his scattered flock.

Nolan was new to the parish, she'd been told, arriving only a few months before herself, fresh from the seminary outside

Dublin. He was hugely attractive and had sophisticated city ways, or so said the slightly older, more experienced women of the town. However, there was not a man in the place who had a decent word for him. Agatha judged herself unqualified to venture any such observation, although she could not fail to see, indeed, she'd acknowledged to herself on several occasions, that he was wonderfully handsome. She wished she had the experience, whatever that might mean, of these older women, to be more able to gauge his 'sophisticated city ways'. She would have liked to have been on friendly terms with such a man. A pity he was a priest, she felt, but even if he weren't, she didn't know how she'd set about catching his eye.

Nolan was, no doubt, on his way to say the later Mass of this sunny Sunday morning. Why he was so far out from the church and the presbytery at this hour was inexplicable, unless calling on the sick perhaps. He was driving slowly, the better to enable his lively blue eyes to scan the bedroom windows of the houses. Perhaps hoping, she wondered, that a female parishioner, not too particular about her modesty, might be letting her feminine attributes be glimpsed by passers-by. Agatha watched him, and saw his gaze travel towards her. He was looking straight at her, she felt. Her initial instinct was to close the curtain, but immediately she also felt that she'd love him to see her. She knew that the net effectively concealed her figure from him, unless sunlight revealed a faint outline of her form. But that he would surely see as innocence on her part. Tremulously she held her pose. A *frisson* of excitement pervaded her whole being. The wicked sense of concupiscence was exhilarating; she shivered with wanton pleasure.

She wondered what sort of man it was that would be inclined

to enter the priesthood. He'd have to have great patience and understanding; be tolerant of lesser people than himself. He'd have to be nice to the mammies, who'd always be asking him to show interest in the latest addition to their tribe; at the same time turning a deaf ear to the profanities of the daddies when the same squealing creatures were getting on their nerves, adding to the headaches purchased in O'Neill's bar the previous night, and in need of a good clout to quieten them. Sure, wouldn't such a man make a wonderful walking- out-with friend, if he hadn't given himself to the Church. But then again, such a person would have a certain purity about him, and the inner strength to enable him to resist all temptations of the flesh. That would be a drawback in a young man. There would be times when you'd need a man to have a certain stiffishness about him, and not of the upper lip variety, so perhaps the qualities that made a man a priest curtailed his usefulness in other ways. How could priests marry people and talk about the union of the flesh, she wondered, and not want such an experience for themselves. They must be men of great fortitude, living saints, almost.

She moved back across the room to the wash- stand next to her dressing table, still quivering, and amazed at her immodesty but flushed from head to toe with the thrilling feelings it had given her. The icon of the Virgin Mary, with a votive candle beneath it on the table troubled her a little, standing there as she was, just in her skin. Having rinsed her hands and splashed her face with cold water from the ewer, she towelled herself slowly. She then addressed her visage to the mirror of the dressing table to reassure herself that she was no less attractive than she had been the night before. In the last couple of years, she'd had many lads showing an interest in her, and they weren't all lumpish gossoons and spalpeens. Some had been mannered, good looking, with a bit of class about them. So, she knew that she had something about her, but she was still unsure of quite what it was, or how she should use it. She knew, of course, what the lads were after, and that knowledge excited her, but she had no intentions of losing her allure by being too free with any favours. Not yet anyway.

The mirror had been purposefully girdled by a remnant of the same ancient net that obscured the windowpane, so that Agatha could see only her face, the outlines of her body being effectively veiled. This unusual arrangement had been contrived by her aunt all those years ago when she first came to live in the house. In the convent there had been no mirrors, vanity being seriously discouraged. On arriving at her brother's house, she had inherited the worm - eaten dressing table, which must have stood in the room for years. Too embarrassed by her womanly form to look at herself in the glass, she had netted it almost to its top, leaving just enough to be able to check if her hat was on straight before going to Mass. All this was perfectly understood by Agatha, being well-versed in convent lore. There had been no need to talk about it when Aunt Bridget had shown her the room. She herself had done something similar in her early teenage years when she was becoming embarrassingly aware of her own developing figure. And hadn't it developed at such a rate, a total transformation in almost no time at all; bumps and bits popping out all over the place. The nuns at her school had strongly condemned revealing the outlines of the body, and Agatha had reluctantly done her best to conceal hers at the time. Nowadays, she was well-aware of her splendid curvaceousness, and often lifted the net to admire it, although she usually threw a headscarf or some bit of cloth, even her underwear, over the icon of the virgin whilst she did so.

The net draping the glass was starting to sag somewhat, being held in place only by a length of knicker elastic which engirdled the mirror. This had done sterling service in the upkeep of stout voluminous undergarments but was now well past its best. Aunt Bridget had looked in through the window of Maddigan's, the drapers, only the day before Agatha arrived, with a view to replacing it. She was looking to see if old Mrs. Maddigan herself was in behind the counter, in which case she would have entered the shop and purchased a yard and a quarter of new elastic. However, the owner was not in sight; only the two floozies, Breda and Deborah, who worked there part-time – if you could call their attendance work – and she was not going to lower herself by asking *them* for knicker elastic. Those brazen hussies, she felt, would wear only the flimsiest of under-garments, if they wore any at all. She shuddered at the thought. She was not going to give those two gossipy bitches something to talk about all day, and then tell half the town about it. No; she would bide her time until she might catch Mrs. Maddigan on her own. But after Agatha had taken the room, Bridget had forgotten all about it.

Agatha reached for her chemise, which was hanging over the corner of the mirror, adding to the obscurity provided by the bit of dusty net. A button on the neck of the garment had snagged the net, and, as she pulled, the elastic holding it expired with a sigh; there was not a twang left in it. Chemise and net fell in a pathetic little heap upon the floor. There she stood, revealed entirely in the glass. Taut, creamy, voluptuous young flesh, exposed from the thighs upwards, right up to her lovely head of golden red hair.

Wasn't it wonderful? The nuns had said it was improper, lewd, even, to dwell upon the outlines of the body. To veil it discreetly at all times should become a habit, a way of living that one should permanently adopt. It was good for the soul they said. It kept one from thinking of the sins the fulsome flesh might lend itself to, although Agatha was not entirely sure what, exactly, such sinning entailed. This dogma had always been at odds with her natural inclinations. No wonder she'd always been in trouble with the holy mothers.

"Are ye getting up yet Agatha?" her aunt, shouted again, sternly this time. Agatha, lost in her thoughts, almost jumped out of her skin, thinking that her aunt was about to enter the room, although she had never intruded before. "Yes, Aunt Bridget, I'm coming, she shouted, rapidly spinning away from the all-revealing mirror. Whereupon her foot caught the handle of the chamber pot, which she'd omitted to return to its place under the bed, and had not seen in the gloom, sending it rocking, and spilling some of its contents over the cracked linoleum. In her embarrassed confusion her pure little Catholic mouth, before she could chasten it, gave vent to the most unholy vocabulary for someone who had been about to receive Holy Communion. "Oh shit!" she hissed, in a loud whisper. Then: "Holy Christ – I've just cursed; Oh, help me God, now I'm blaspheming. What is it I'm saying? Holy Mary Mother of God, save me."

The sin of blasphemy now hung over her like the sword of Damocles. The swear word wasn't so bad, a venial sin at worst. But taking the Lord's name in vain was serious. And how did she stand with taking unbridled, lustful pleasure from looking at her own body. And just in her skin. Might that be a mortal sin? She hardly dared risk receiving Holy Communion now; she might not be in a state of grace. She'd told her aunt that she would abstain from breakfast, fasting in order to receive Communion, so she couldn't eat now. To do so would take some uncomfortable explaining. And she'd been to confession only a couple of days ago. Now she'd have to confess again and hope that Aunt Bridget didn't ask her about it. She didn't want her thinking that her niece was an incorrigible sinner who spent all her time in the confessional. And what if the new man, that blue eyed Father Nolan, was hearing confessions the next time she went, and he probably would be. The old priest, Father Doran wasn't likely to be doing it. Now in his eighties and on his last legs, he seldom did more than take the first Mass of the day, and then his bladder often didn't hold out and he'd have to take himself off for five or ten minutes in the middle of a sermon. And when he returned, he'd usually forgotten where he was up to, the congregation champing at the bit the whole while, thoroughly pissed off with listening to his senile ramblings. And even in earlier days, apparently, when he used to hear confessions regularly, the whole community knew your sins because you had to shout them out to him to overcome his deafness. Some said that he'd been taken off confessions, except when they were desperate for a curate, because of this. It had been noticed that the mortal sin rate was diminishing considerably, as people would dare to confess only their more trivial misdemeanours after Paddy McBride half-killed Owney Farrell when he'd loudly confessed to putting his hand up the skirt of Paddy's wife, Nellie. All of those who had listened in on this revelation were left wondering as to how much encouragement she'd given Owney, as she was known to be a very welcoming sort of a woman and Owney was a shy, retiring sort of a man. Yes, it would undoubtedly be Nolan; he was the one doing most of the duties now. The problem was it was him the last time. She knew he wouldn't be able to see her in the darkness of the confessional, but he might recognize her voice and remember that he'd listened to her only recently, and wonder why she was back in the box so soon. And she could hardly bring herself to tell him what had caused this profane outburst, her wanton nudity in front of the mirror and the feelings this had aroused in her, the immodest intrigue of total nakedness, the sheer delightful abandonment of looking at one's self just in one's skin, and gazing brazenly at him through the window-net whilst completely naked, and thinking what an interesting going out together friend he might be. How could she tell him any of that? It might inflame him, on the other side of the curtain. He was a man after all, and men, she had been told, were easily inflamed. Apparently, they somehow couldn't help themselves in that respect. This was not going to be straightforward. It might have been easier if she'd simply insulted a protestant, or even robbed a bank - so long as it was not the Bank of Ireland of course, but only one of those oppressive English banks. One could expect forgiveness without too much penance for those natural sorts of human failings.

\*

Nolan found nothing on which to feast his libidinous eyes. This place was not Dublin after all, the women were a lot different there.He continued on his way towards the church. He slowed the car when he saw a group of youths in front of him, all of whom, much to his dismay, he recognized immediately. They were staring into a deep cleft in the face of the cliff that hemmed in one side of the mountain road as it twisted its sinuous way towards Glenowen. Set back within the cleft, which opened to the sky, was a single huge rock, about one and a half times the size of a man, and of a vaguely human outline, insofar as there was a piece at the top of it that stood higher than the rest, almost like a neck between two shoulders, and that piece then widened out a bit into a roughly cuboid form, which in a poor light – very poor – might just pass for a head. If a lonely traveller were to come that way at night and catch a glimpse of it by moonlight, it might give him a bit of a fright, as if he'd seen one of those predatory giants that were said to roam the land on certain nights of the year; especially if he was on his way home from O'Neill's and had a drop too much taken. But it had been there almost forever and had always seemed part of the mountain itself. Set around the entrance to the cleft, and spilling out onto the road, narrowing it considerably, was a cluster of smaller rocks. Clearly, a fall of rocks from higher up the mountain had very recently occurred. This was not at all unusual; small boulders fell frequently, and, very occasionally, some the size of a sheep or even as big as a cow thundered down, requiring the concerted efforts of several men to wrestle them across the road and roll them away down the hillside and into the bog below. Traffic through the glen was so sparse that no one had ever been injured, although some nifty footwork had been required from time to time, even though the narrow escapes had always been attributed to 'the grace of God.' The rock falls were generally accepted for what they were: a natural phenomenon that had to be endured, albeit with a wary eye; they were not attributed to the Almighty. However, this latest occurrence was attracting more attention than usual.

Nolan stopped his car and got out. "What is it you're looking at?" he asked the motley assembly. "You'll be late for Mass if you don't get a move on." The thought of offering any of them a lift was as far from his mind as the likelihood of his solemnizing a mixed marriage.It did them good to have to walk a few miles, pick up a couple of blisters, maybe. Good for the soul. A bit of suffering did no one any harm. So long as it wasn't himself. He didn't much care for the company of any of this bunch of ignorant gossoons and he was well aware that they were not overly enamoured of him.

"Wilya look at dat, Father." said the ginger-haired, freckle-faced lout of a lad Mick Mullarkey, waving his hands expressively at the monolith in the grotto.

"What is it I'm supposed to be looking at?" growled Nolan. He detested Mullarkey; he saw him as a cocky young know-all who in fact knew nothing.

"Can ye not see the face of Saint Patrick there, Father? There, on that big lump of rock that stands away from the cliff."

Nolan studied the rock. He could see there was something different about it. It had somehow changed since the last time he'd seen it, but he could not have said in what way. He passed by it almost every day and had never taken much notice of it. He'd had no reason to scrutinise it until now. Then he saw what Mullarkey was getting at. A falling boulder must have struck it during the night, smashing a small piece away from it and exposing paler, un-weathered stone close to its top. If the rock had been a man, the newly exposed area would have been roughly where a face should be. Nothing else had changed; the monolith was still a couple of feet higher in the centre than at the outer edges. These could, he supposed, be regarded as 'shoulders', if one was really determined to find a human shape within the rock, with the lighter-coloured patch now resembling a face. Well, it very faintly looked like a face. He wouldn't have made the connection himself without the dubious and unwanted guidance from the cretinous Mick Mullarkey. It had certainly required someone with a vivid imagination to point it out to him. And Mullarkey, the impudent young bastard, had that all right, rakes of it. But why it should be the face of Saint Patrick that he thought he detected, Nolan had not the faintest idea. But then, Nolan knew well, the minds of any of the Mullarkey clan were best not looked into.

"How would I know it's Saint Patrick? I've never seen a likeness of him. But I take it you have?"

"No Father; they didn't have cameras in those days. But you can tell it's him right enough, because of all those snakes around his head."

Nolan seethed inwardly, but bit his tongue. The insolent spalpeen; didn't you just want to punch him in the face? Wasn't it only the night before last that he'd scutched the back of his thick ginger skull with the flat of his hand when he'd caught him and Tim Murphy out the back of the dance-hall, where they were relieving themselves through the rails of the fence, with the white-faced cows mooing at them across the moonlit field. Nolan's first concern had been whether or not it was merely their bladders they were relieving, as Mullarkey was making obscene comments about the anatomy of Breda O'Bryan. Which surely had to be hugely exaggerated, another example of Mullarkey's wondrous imagination. Although Nolan couldn't be altogether sure of that, being not well acquainted with such matters. And now here he was, the lout, looking him straight in the eye, his flat face resembling a potato that had been clouted with a shovel, the two great nostrils on him like entrances to an empty rabbit warren. Here he stood, shamelessly, spouting utter garbage like a pagan, and expecting Nolan to be taken in by it.

He focussed his attention on what Mullarkey claimed were snakes, as much to take his mind off the tempting thought of throttling the imbecile as for the unlikely possibility of agreeing with him. At first, he couldn't envisage anything of a serpentine nature. Then he realised that the stupid youth was referring to the straggling roots of shrubs and small bushes and mountain ferns that had been exposed by the landslide, some of which now hung around the supposed head of the apparition.

"It cannot be Saint Patrick then, can it?" said Nolan. "Saint Patrick drove all the snakes out of Ireland. Did you not know that?"

"Of course I know that Father," replied Mullarkey, in no way chastened by the priest's obvious loathing of him. "That's the very picture of him driving them out."

"You're an idiot Mullarkey, if you think I'm going to buy that one. Ah, sure you're all a bunch of heathens. Get along to the church now. I'll be saying Mass in half an hour's time."Mullarkey carelessly shrugged his shoulders, totally oblivious to criticism, and made to continue his shambling way towards the church.

With that Nolan got back in his car, and carefully avoiding the fallen rocks, continued on his way through the glen, the town below it and the sea beyond the town now coming into view. He could just make out the upturned currachs on the quayside, their black, recently tarred keels glistening like a row of lazing seals. The thought then occurred to him that if the fallen rocks were still across the road when next Saturday's bus to Ballina tried to get through, they might prove to be a bit of a problem. Ah, but sure, he was a priest wasn't he, not a council man. He was not going to make that his worry. Anyway, he'd enough concerns of his own. He was struggling to fit in with this strange rustic community to which he'd been assigned on leaving the Dublin seminary. Only the women seemed to like him, and he liked some of them, the better-off ones anyway, but for what he knew were the wrong reasons. It had been so much easier in Dublin; so many more people with whom to mingle, to derive that quiver of excitement from the smell of their perfume, their laughing eyes, their hands briefly touching your sleeve, maybe even lingering momentarily before moving on. Such fleeting dalliances passed unnoticed there, unlike here, where every man appeared to be watching your every move. Nolan was seriously doubting his fitness as a priest. He did not have a forgiving nature for a start. He'd too many strongly-rooted dislikes of certain types of people, and not just the likes of Mullarkey and his ilk. As a young buck in Dublin, before entering the seminary, which he'd done somewhat belatedly, having been deeply unsure about it, he'd mixed and moved easily amongst city society, his middle-class background easing him effortlessly into groups of people who were like himself, without his realizing just how exclusive they were or how discriminating he had become. He barely acknowledged those whose demeanour did not instantly meld with his own. Fleeting, superficial relationships with the others were all right then, but not now. Whether you were a priest or not, in this small community you had to get along with everyone, but at the same time give them an example as to how they ought to live. The way of life of these people was so far removed from what his had been that he hardly knew how to communicate with them. He seriously wondered how he was going to sustain this living.

## CHAPTER TWO

As he drove on towards the church, Nolan's mind wandered back to Mick Mullarkey's obscene fantasies the other night concerning Breda O'Bryan's unusual intimate attributes. She was becoming a bit of a slut, it was true, and her only just after leaving school. Her mother needed to be told about her; ought to be instructed to keep her in a bit more, especially at night-time. That unenviable task of telling her might become his. But he would have to nerve himself to tackle Norah O'Bryan; it was a thought he didn't exactly relish. Sure, weren't they a difficult tribe altogether, the O'Bryans? You couldn't knock any sense into any one of them. As a family, instilling religion, common sense, or anything else into them was a hopeless task. Ned O'Bryan, the father, was in the pub all night and every night, where he could down a pint of porter in three or four gulps. And before his right hand had slammed the empty glass back on the counter the left hand was back in the trouser pocket extracting a coin for the next one. He must be engaged in some dubious enterprise, thought Nolan, to be able to fund such profligate consumption. Yet none of them ever put more than the odd copper into the collection box, always pleading abject poverty.

Whenever he called at the house on his priestly visits, Ned was missing; and Norah, on her own he found disconcerting, to say the least. It was the way she sat him down in the only half- decent armchair the household possessed, and then took her time, quite a long time, in setting a mug of tea in front of him on a very low table, made by Ned in one of his more creative moments from a large wooden crate, upturned, with a shawl thrown over it for a tablecloth. Norah was always on at Ned about improving it. "When are ye going to put a set of legs under this feckin' table? The feckin' dog keeps snatching the kid's food off it."

"When I drop across a decent bit of timber. And in the meantime, put the feckin' dog outside when there's feckin' food on the feckin' table."

Nolan wished that Norah would take the shawl off the table and throw it around herself, as her low and loose-fitting blouse, the only one she possessed, it seemed, always appeared to drift away from her, and her form itself always seemed to sway and undulate in his direction. He was always afraid that Norah's substantial dusky bosoms, which had a life of their own, were about to spill over and knock his tea off the table. Then, after serving him his drink, she would sit down opposite him in a chair that sagged so much she might as well have been seated on the floor. And her knees never managed to stay together for any length of time. After several minutes of that sort of conversation, which did not contain many words, and the few that Norah uttered could be open to various interpretations, he found it difficult to get up and leave in any decent fashion, and had, therefore, to accept a second mug of tea, by now the colour of bog water, whilst he attempted to compose himself by focussing his eyes behind her head, where hung a picture of Pope Pius XII, now nearly ten years into his reign of infallibility, and try to put his mind elsewhere.

Another thought, long overdue, then occurred to him: how

come the three daughters - Breda being the oldest of them – were possessed of casques of blond hair, rarely combed, which usually looked like sheaves of corn that had been hit by an Atlantic gale, when both the parents were as swarthy as tinkers, as were the two older lads of the family. Sure, wasn't 'Himself', Ned O'Bryan, often referred to as 'Black Ned' because of this? And why were the girls so tall and slender – Breda at sixteen was already much taller than her mother – when the parents and both sons would be better measured cubically, rather than in linear fashion? Ah, sure, what did it matter? Nolan accepted that genetics had never been his forte, no more than any other scientific explanation of any aspect of Life's rich tapestry. It was obvious to anyone that they were a dubious bunch altogether, and that was the best that could be said about them.

Nolan pulled up his car on the gravel outside the church, reflecting that the trained mind was a wonderful thing, an attribute that placed him above the run- of- the- mill, superstitious heathens around him. Now he would enter the church and shortly witness the wonder of wine being miraculously transformed into the actual physicality of a spiritual being.

*

The door of the church was unlocked, as he knew it would be. The lights were not yet on, and in the gloom, he could see the shaggy white-blond head of the sexton, 'Long' John Donohoe, shining like a beacon at the far end of the building. John was chalking up hymn numbers on a board fastened to the wall and had already laid out the missals for those who didn't have their own – and most did not, or could not be bothered to bring them – on a table in the porch. Sure, wasn't he a great man, John Donohoe, almost a living saint. He attended to all the parish duties and dug most of the graves in this and other parishes round and about. If he wasn't in church, then his tall wiry figure, topped by the unruly blond thatch, could be seen pedalling the old bike around the countryside, his shovel balanced across the handlebars and his pick slung across his back on a stout bit of rope. He was always, or so it seemed, either in a church or else in a hole somewhere. Sure, if only he'd had the learning, wouldn't he have made a great priest?

The church was now filling with people, Nolan robing himself hurriedly in the vestry, being a bit behind time because of his meeting with the rabble on the road.

In Bridget Nelligan's house time was also slipping by, Agatha assembling herself hurriedly, knowing now that wheeled transport would be necessary if she was going to reach the church on time.

In the church, the heathen wiseacres led by Mullarkey were entering noisily in their hob-nailed Sunday boots, looking for a place near the back, as close to the door as possible, ready for a racing start in the direction of Darcy O'Neill's bar whilst Nolan was saying the last psalms with his face towards the altar. They knew that most of the other males in the congregation would be hot on their heels the moment that Nolan had left the altar, and if O'Neill was on his own behind the counter there would be a queue, so they intended having their own thirsts slaked first.

Aunt Bridget had not felt at all well the previous evening and had doubted if she would go to Mass at all. Agatha, therefore, was thinking about the possibility of the loan of a bicycle.

"Aunt Bridget," she shouted, "I'm late for Mass. Are ye still not going yourself?"

"No. I cannot. My head is too bad." Bridget pummelled her forehead with her bony knuckles. "I can hardly open the two eyes on me. I'll have to see Doctor Kelly again for some more tablets. I think it's my blood pressure rising again. I hope the Good Lord will let me off this time."

"Can I borrow your bike then, if you haven't need of it? I've no chance of getting there on time if I walk."

"You should have got up sooner. I shouted you enough times, and I shouldn't have had to. Anyway, take it; I won't be needing it today."

In the church the last of the louts entered the pew, then decided he wanted to be at the farthest end of it, up against the wall, no doubt to conclude in whispered tones some iniquitous undertaking with the reprobate already stationed there that wouldn't wait until they were in the pub. In order to avoid treading on the feet of those miscreants already seated, he attempted to thread his way through by walking along the narrow kneeler which stretched the length of the bench. Halfway in he lost his balance, and the kneeler went over with a resounding crash against the plank floor that was raised above the flag-stoned aisle. In snatching for the back of the bench in front of him he grabbed instead a bunch of hair belonging to the woman seated there, who let out a shriek of pain as her hat descended over her eyes. In readjusting his grip, he got hold of her hatpin and shared her pain. As he fell, the lout landed heavily on the knees of another wretch, who groaned and stifled an oath, the knees having been well clouted with a hurling stick the previous day, during an ill-tempered match against a motley crew from Killala. Heads turned, but on recognizing the source of the commotion, no one expressed surprise. There were only sighs of resigned acceptance.

\*

At Bridget's house Agatha was making swiftly for the door, pushing the Sunday hat firmly on her head and tying its ribbons under the chin, hoping the breeze wouldn't lift it.

"Can you ride that bike decently in your Sunday clothes?" The acerbic tone of voice stated that Bridget considered this to be an impossibility.

"I'll be fine Aunt Bridget. Thanks."

She adjusted her lisle stockings, tightening a suspender, almost ready for the off.

"And don't be showing your petticoat, it's not decent, especially on a Sunday. And there'll be men on the road".

"I'll be all right auntie, don't worry."

"And mind the brakes, they're not too good."

"I will. I'll be careful. 'Bye now.'

Agatha wheeled the bike out of the porch. Putting one foot on the pedal and pushing off with the other, she scooted along the dry dirt road. There was enough momentum now to allow her to find the seat. Up and aboard the saddle, but only just. There was a problem. The seat was somewhat too high, the dress a little too tight. Her legs were awkwardly constrained. She stood up on the pedals, pushing hard and making some progress, but she knew it was much too far to go all the way like this. She reached the end of the rutted lane and joined the Macadamed road. It was better now, smoother, easier, but she was still too confined about the lower limbs to sit and pedal properly. Aunt Bridget's assessment of the Sunday clothes in relation to cycling was proving correct. She looked around herself; there was not a soul in sight, the countryside deserted except for a couple of cows. A few sheep were dotted distantly over the purple faraway mountains. The sound of an ill-tempered ass braying disconsolately reached her from somewhere in the green expanse. The aroma of a turf fire emanated sweetly from an isolated cottage. The countryside was empty. She reached behind her now, and grabbed a large handful of skirt, hauling it up over her pert rear. That was better. She could pedal comfortably now. She wobbled precariously with only one hand on the bars, as the other pulled up the front of her dress. Pedalling quickly now, with both hands back on the handlebars, she was making up time, the legs free at last, labouring lithely. A mile to go, downhill all the way until the last hundred yards before the short climb up into the glen. She'd have to walk that bit anyway, it was far too steep to ride. The road was still her own, still free of people. The decline steepened and her speed had increased alarmingly, but she was loving the thrill. Gosh, this is daring, she thought. Her head tilted upwards, eyes spying the white gulls high overhead, jarring the air with their raucous screams as they raced the restless winds to the rocky shore. She felt at one with them, such freedom; such unfettered hedonism, rolling along swiftly like the billowing sail-white clouds above, at one with the green pasture, with the yellow-decked gorse and the dark distant hills. She could scent the sea now, almost tasting the salt on her lips. She felt different somehow this morning. More vibrant, more alive. Different from how she'd felt at any time since she'd arrived at Glenowen. Aunt

Bridget and her miseries were forgotten for the moment. Agatha's pulse was racing, her face flushed with exhilaration. Her wild red-gold hair was blowing back, streamed by the wind over the brim of the hat. The bend before the hill was coming up. She banked the bike into it, freewheeling fast. "Oh shit!" she muttered to herself. "Holy Christ!" She saw the rocks all over the road. The brakes were useless and disaster seemed inevitable. Hold your nerve, she told herself, avoid the drop; find a way through. And then she saw, to her huge embarrassment, the old hermit Peter Keighley with his donkey cart, who was picking his way through the debris from the other side. He was leading the ass by its halter, and looking right up her over-exposed legs, blocking most of what little remained of the narrow road as he gazed at the sight before him His big red toothless gob hung open in motionless amazement. Then in an instant, he snatched his tattered old cap off his shaggy head, and holding it over the ass's eyes, muttered desperately to himself "Holy Mary Mother of God save us."

Agatha's feet back were back on the pedals now, but her underwear was still on display, preservation of life and limb being prioritized over protection of modesty. Taking aim for what little space remained between Keighley's cart and the rock-fall, and trying to avoid the drop into the bog on the other side of the road, she tucked in her elbows and went through the gap with barely an inch to spare. But now she was veering dangerously towards rough ground. The bike bounced over the ruts, the slack chain rattling off the sprocket, pedals spinning uselessly. Then back onto terra firma. She leapt off the bike and ran with it into the start of the hill, trying to put as much space as possible between herself and Keighley, who stood frozen like a moonstruck calf, still mesmerized by what he'd just witnessed. Does he have no regard for the Sabbath, she thought, working like a heathen, going out to cart turf on a Sunday, and then feasting his eyes on a women's legs. Surely, the man has no sense of decency!

She walked swiftly on up the hill, still trying to run with the bike, so great was her embarrassment. She kept her head down, hoping Keighley wouldn't call her back to admonish her. She was breathing hard with the exertion, all earlier excitement gone. The only thing in favour of her reputation, she remembered, was that Keighley the hermit hardly talked with anyone, living in isolation as he did with his cow and his ass. So, what he had just witnessed might not be broadcast.

*

In the church the lights were being turned on by Donohoe and the doors were closing.Nolan made his entrance from the sacristy, walking with great solemnity towards the altar. A few latecomers were squeezing in guiltily by opening the doors just far enough to admit their frames, trying, in vain, not to attract attention to themselves as the wind slammed the doors behind them, causing everyone to turn around. They tip-toed sheepishly to whatever space they could find. A certain amount of noisy footwork took place as the established occupants shuffled sideways, closing up churlishly to make room for the stragglers. There was a good bit of muffled coughing, and spitting into revolting handkerchiefs – mostly, anyway, into handkerchiefs- and the occasional fart.All part of Sunday morning normality. Nolan's keen ears were soaking up the sound of it all. He'd become well used to it. Every Sunday the same; always some lazy bastard who couldn't get up in time for Mass. Always some who'd imbibed too much at O'Neill's the night before and were now voiding their excesses into the rest of the congregation. He particularly detested the ones who stationed themselves close to the door with thoughts of Guiness rather than God on their minds, and who were always ready to slive off to the pub when they thought he wasn't watching them. The previous incumbent must have allowed this form of blasphemy to develop, he felt, and he intended to stamp it out. What with coming in late and leaving early, sure, they were hardly attending Mass at all. He'd lectured them from the pulpit about it a couple of times already, but it had made no difference. He might yet have to tackle them about it individually in the confessional. He knew who the chief culprits were.

\*

The service had been under way for a couple of minutes. Nolan was hitting his stride and the congregation was getting in behind him on the responses. Well- practised, they mouthed the Latin as if they understood it. Nolan was setting a good pace, much to the satisfaction of the drinking fraternity. If he didn't spend too long on the sermon - and he wasn't inclined to, he liked an early finish as much as any of them - they'd be into O'Neill's place in good time.

The door opened again, just wide enough to allow the slender but curvaceous figure of Agatha to enter. Flushed and breathless, having run up the hill and abandoned the bike behind a wall, she now felt exposed as a sinner. She closed the door behind her as quietly as she could, but it creaked badly, causing various heads looking for anything of interest, to turn in her direction. She dipped her fingers in the stoup and crossed herself with holy water, her eyes nervously scanning the fetid rows of tightly packed bodies, looking desperately for the chance of a seat to squeeze into. Seeing none, she was forced to stand with her back to the wall amongst the greyhounds waiting to be first out of the trap and away in pursuit of the hair of the dog the moment Nolan turned his back to them and began the last psalms. And just at that very moment didn't the man himself turnaround from the altar, and didn't his eyes instantly light upon her? Oh, such bad luck, such acute embarrassment. She felt she'd die of shame. Fortunately, a friend from the post office spotted her and silently beckoned her to come in on the end of the crowded pew she was occupying.

Nolan made a mental note to speak to Agatha about her late entrance. He'd no intention of reproving her. She hadn't, to his knowledge, been late before; there must be a good reason for it this time. And it would be a chance to get to know her. He'd noted her shy attractiveness when he'd been in the post office, but because she worked mostly in the back room, not on the counter, he'd been able only to smile at her from a distance and it would be so much nicer to talk to her. He'd heard that she, like himself, was a newcomer to the community, And perhaps she might be a little lonely, so for him to assure her of his priestly concerns for her well-being would not be a bad thing.

*

The service over, the church was emptying fast. The women would soon be getting their heads together to exchange scandal, the men escaping from any part they might have played in creating it by heading across the road to O'Neill's. Darcy O'Neill was already topping up the line of half-filled glasses he had standing on the counter. He'd done his duty already at the earlier Mass and had then pulled his place back into shape after the usual Saturday night's shenanigans.

Agatha made her way towards her aunt's bike, thinking about the long walk home she would have if she couldn't get the chain back on the sprocket. She pulled the machine out from behind the wall where she had, in her haste, thrown it, and began to make her way down the hill, walking slowly and pointedly glancing at the chain as if bewildered by its slackness. She had no wish to try rectifying it herself. Aunt Bridget, miserly in most things, was unusually liberal with the oil-can. She felt that a chain ought to last almost as long as the bike itself if kept well lubricated. Agatha had no intentions of getting her hands lathered in oil, which would inevitably transfer to the handlebars and then her clothing. Fortunately, two ragged barefooted urchins came to her aid. Their squalid appearance would scarcely be worsened by a drop of oil; in any case, that could be outweighed by a penny-piece for their assistance, if such might be gained.

"Yer chain's come off, Miss," one of them informed Agatha helpfully, in case she hadn't noticed. "Would ye like us to get it back on for ye?"

"I'd be glad if you could," she replied.

"We'll have it on in a trice. It'll be grand in no time."

Despite their tender years the lads were well experienced in making things work. One took hold of the saddle and lifted the rear wheel clear of the ground, whilst the other poked a short stick he'd found at the side of the road under the chain, all the while turning the pedal with his free hand until the chain engaged with the sprocket. The job was completed in the trice he had predicted, and without a trace of oil touching his hands.

"There y'are miss. As good as new."

"Thanks a lot. Let me see what I have in my purse."

"Ah, sure yer all right, Miss; twas nothing," said the lad, although his eager eyes were fastened on to Agatha's purse like a stoat's teeth on a rabbit's throat.

Agatha knew that her purse was almost empty; she'd put a few coppers into the collecting box. The purse itself was almost a rag. She'd had it since her twelfth birthday, but she couldn't afford another. She found a couple of half-pennies in the linty corners and proffered those with apologies. She felt childish and small and foolish for having no more to give. But the lads seemed satisfied; they'd have willingly done it for nothing.

She cycled home in a more decorous fashion than that of her outward journey, there now being more people on the road, and she was, in any case, still embarrassed by her encounter with Keighley and his ass, and more keenly aware that one never knew what might lie around a corner.

When she reached the cottage, she found Aunt Bridget had returned to bed, leaving the breakfast pots still on the table. She went out and fetched a bucket of water from the well and began to wash up, feeling relived that she would not be asked about the Mass.

## CHAPTER THREE

Monday morning began with an assertive knocking on the Nelligan's door. It was Nolan: paying a visit, working on a hunch. The hunch being that the pretty girl that he'd seen working in the post office and also standing at the back of the church was indeed, like himself, new to the area, and might be staying with Bridget Nelligan. Someone had said to him that Bridget was not on her own anymore. That fact alone pleased him. Some of the old women he visited were lively enough. Even the deaf ones that he had to shout at he could stand for twenty minutes or so, as long as they were affable and made a good pot of tea. But not Bridget. He'd visited her only once before and she hadn't taken to him, nor he to her. She'd wanted only to talk about her life in the convent years ago, and such limited recollections bored him stiff. All nuns bored him, a priggish, self-righteous bunch. And although she'd made a pot of tea, she'd offered him nothing to go with it. A nice bit of balmbrack, well-buttered, wouldn't have gone amiss. So, if she wasn't on her own now, there was less of an obligation to visit her. Unless, perhaps, her new companion, if it really was the girl he thought it might be, could benefit from his attention.

As for Bridget's assessment of Nolan… well, it wasn't great. She'd not found any particular fault with him, although she'd searched hard enough. No, it was more to do with the fact that those women who spoke well of him were not her kind of women. They were lacking in overt piety, talked about matters that should not be spoken of, and as for the practise of them, well, that was awful, too terrible to imagine. Therefore, in her eyes, they were a dubious lot. So, to her, Nolan was dammed by their praise.

From where she was standing in her kitchen, Bridget couldn't see who was knocking the door down, so she shouted "Come on in will ye, before ye have the door off its hinges."

At that moment Nolan was distracted by someone in the lane shouting "Top o' the morning t'ye Father," so he failed to hear the grudging invitation to enter as he continued to hammer away, whilst turning his head to return the greeting. It was the schoolboy Mikeen Scully, who wasn't in school, and was riding by on a donkey. He was sitting sideways, chewing a straw, and wishing it was a woodbine between his lips.

"Why aren't you in school? Michael," shouted Nolan, knocking again. "I'm looking after me mam, Father. She's not too well," answered Mikeen, quite unperturbed by the priests question.

Bridget was annoyed by the banging, and began wiping her hands clean.

"Don't worry, Aunt Bridget, I'll go and see who it is" said Agatha, making for the door. Both she and Bridget were hoping that it wouldn't be some tinker woman asking for a jug of milk, or a bit of bread, or some eggs. You could never get rid of them until you'd given them something; they'd put a curse on you. And anyway, they'd rob your turf pile whether you gave them anything or nothing.

Agatha opened the door and there was Nolan, face to face with her, his fist uplifted in mid-clout. His face broke into a huge smile; his hunch had paid off.

Agatha gasped with momentary horror at the sight of the

oncoming fist, and then with surprise and embarrassment as she remembered standing naked in her room with only the net curtain between them when Nolan had driven slowly past the house. Had he come about that? Then she recalled that she'd been late for Mass the same morning, and he'd seen her enter the church.So perhaps he was calling to chastise her for that.Before she could find her voice, Aunt Bridget was behind her. "Oh, it's you Father, come in, sit yourself down. You shouldn't have stood there knocking. Agatha, put on the kettle, I'll butter us some bread in a minute. Oh, this is my niece, Father. Her name's Agatha. She's up from Geesala. She's staying with me for a while."

Agatha went off into the kitchen whilst Bridget settled Nolan into a chair and pulled up another for herself. Nolan would rather have had Bridget going off to make the tea, but that hadn't happened, so he braced himself for more torpid tales of convent life thirty years ago. However, Agatha soon returned and sat with them, so he quickly focussed his attention on her, forestalling Aunt Bridget's intended reminiscences.

"Have I not seen you before, somewhere, Agatha?"he asked, not wishing to imply that he'd observed her in as much exciting detail as visits to the post office would allow, and less than he would have desired. And that he'd thought about her quite a bit, and not altogether in the way a priest ought to think. Agatha felt an immediate sense of relief. He obviously had nothing to admonish her for if he couldn't remember if or where he'd ever seen her.

"I don't know, Father. I've only been here a short while. I hardly know anyone yet. I'm working at the post office in Glenowen. You might have seen me there."

"Yes, possibly so. I go in there quite a bit. I must say you're a little bit out of things here. It's nice and peaceful but there's not much for a young person to do." Bridget frowned at this. She felt that young people did too much, at least too much of what they should not be doing. And any activity which gave pleasure was not to be indulged in.

"If you could get into Glenowen itself, there are things happening occasionally. I organize dances from time to time at the church hall." This was not what Bridget wanted to hear. Dancing was a very dubious pastime; something good Catholics ought not to indulge in. It could easily lead to sinful behaviour.

"I think I'd like that, Father. I might meet a few more people that way." Nolan immediately realized that she might meet the likes of MickMullarkey, Tim Murphy and the rest of the dubious crowd with whom they were associated. He'd have to make sure that didn't happen. Aunt Bridget was thinking along the same lines. She could hardly believe that a priest was suggesting such dangerous activities to a naïve young girl. As far as she was concerned, the road to hell was lined with dance halls and the lewd, licentious behaviour that went on inside them, although, of course, she had no first-hand knowledge of such things. She had never set foot inside a public house or a dance hall and she knew she never would. All Nolan's suggestion had done was to confirm what she already believed: that he was the wrong man for the priesthood and the women whom she'd heard speak well of him clearly must be as dubious as he was. She'd always had her doubts about them. The Lord Save us, what was the world coming to?

Bridget tried to steer the conversation back to her time spent in the convent, which led to Nolan preparing to steer himself out of the door at the earliest opportunity. He'd achieved the objective of his visit. He'd introduced himself to Agatha, and had opened the way, he hoped, for further converse. A pity though, that she was lodging with her aunt. The first time he'd met the woman he hadn't liked her. Now he knew, without a doubt, that he disliked her. And he could tell - it wasn't difficult - that she reciprocated his animosity. Bridget also wished that she'd never acquiesced to her brother's request to house Agatha. She'd seen the look on Agatha's face as she'd gazed, doe-eyed, at the priest, and she recalled her brother saying that the lads in his village were paying unwarranted attention to his daughter. Bridget felt that the attention might have been based on well-founded expectations. This was worrying; she was too old, too set in her ways, to cope with the wantonness of bohemian youth.

Agatha was almost quivering with excitement. Father Nolan had been so nice to her. He had a certain poise, a charming manner, a sophisticated easy-going confidence. It was no wonder the women of the place spoke well of him. She could not understand why most of the men had so little time for him.

## CHAPTER FOUR

It was a clear, starry night. A slender moon illuminated little but the vague outline of the crooked road Colm Mullarkey – father of the potato headed Mick Mullarkey and a whole tribe of gossoons and hoydens– and his friend Joe Murphy, a slow-witted, naïve kind of man, were taking in the direction of Glenowen and Darcy O'Neill's public house.

"How's your grandson Seamus doing now Colm? Is he sleeping any better?"

"Ah, sure he is," replied Colm.He's fine now. Sure, there was nothing wrong with him in the first place. He's outgrown the crib, that's all. He's a couple of years old now you know, or thereabouts. I can't quite remember when he was born. Anyhow, his feet were up against the end of the crib, and he couldn't straighten his legs out. It's no wonder that he wasn't sleeping. I'd told Sean to knock out the end of the crib, but the idle bastard hadn't bothered himself to do it."

"So, what's happened then, why is he sleeping now?" asked Joe.

"I fixed it myself. I took a hammer to it a couple of days ago" replied Colm. "Knocked the end clean out of it. Now Seamus can stick his legs out as far as he wants to. He'll be all right now. Happy as Larry, he is."

There was silence for a while as Murphy pondered this explanation. "Won't his legs hang down a bit as he grows?" he finally enquired, being not entirely devoid of intelligence.

"I suppose they will in time," Colm answered, having not considered this perfectly valid point before. "Ah, but sure, there's no hurry; his dad can put a couple of planks under them before they do."

Murphy found this explanation entirely satisfactory and they continued on their way, Mullarky lobbing a desultory cobble at an inoffensive donkey hanging its head over a gate, and, a few furlongs further on, the same again at a Kerry cow quietly chewing the cud. It's not easy to see a black cow on a dark night, but Mullarkey had the eyes of an owl and the hearing to match. He could detect the tinkle of a six-penny piece falling from a pedestrian's pocket and veer across the road to scoop it up and into his own without breaking his stride, so his missile easily found its mark, sending the docile creature thundering into the darkness, bellowing angrily. But sure, there was little else to entertain a traveller on a country lane at that time of night. And there would be little happening at O'Neill's pub for the next couple of hours at least, until the lame fiddler from Blacksod got a few pints inside of him and struck up a tune. Then Breda O'Bryan might start up doing a bit of a shimmy and showing her legs, providing her father Ned was in the other bar at the back, and she well out of his sight. And then someone would say what a slut she was becoming, and she'd hear him, and throw a glass of beer over him. Some young buck would jump to her defence, hoping, perhaps, for favours later. And then some kind of a set-to would ensue. A table might go over, and O'Neill would raise hell about his broken glasses, and send for Garda Dan Doyle in the next house down the road. Sergeant Doyle was a great one for the roughhouse. He'd wade into the thick of it, laying about him in all directions at once, cracking heads and breaking noses with his baton. But when all was over, he'd return home and resume whatever it was he'd been doing, as if nothing had happened. He'd never dream of summoning a man to court, and, in the morning, would pass the time of day with last night's adversaries as if they were old friends.

Another reason why Darcy O'Neill always welcomed the garda into his pub at any time was because Doyle was not a man who interfered with free trade just because the government had set statutory licensing hours. He never passed comment on the times O'Neill kept, not even when he served customers until seven in the morning. Sure, a man had to make a living, didn't he? There was no need to make life harder for him than it was already. Especially when he'd pass a ball of malt out the back door to you in grateful recognition of your cudgelling someone who'd been troubling him the night before.

As Mullarkey and Murphy rounded the bend before the hill into Glenhowen, they could just about discern the fallen rocks that strewed the road. "They say there's the face of Saint Patrick on the side of that cliff," said Joe Murphy.

"There is right enough," replied Mullarkey. "My lad Mick seen it, and he pointed it out to the priest."

"And what did Nolan make of it?" asked Murphy.

"He told Mick he was a feckin' heathen eejit," said Colm.

"He didn't say 'feckin' did he?" gasped the mildly spoken Murphy.

"Well, maybe not. But that's what he meant to say. But anyway, it's Nolan who's the eejit. If he had a brain in his head, he'd have it broadcast in the newspapers, and then we might soon have a shrine in our midst like at Knock, or Croagh Patrick, and we'd all have money made out of the pilgrims who'd come to it. And then there's that big shallow rock pool on the other side of the road. Nolan could bless the water and we could have all the cripples in the land dipped into it and them leaping out like hares, all cured of their affliction. It could make this the richest place in Ireland."

"Sure there's no depth to that pool is there?" enquired Murphy, peering into the gloom where the water reflected the moonlight. "Ye cannot poke a stick into it more than a few inches before y're into thick mud."

"It's deeper than ye might think," replied Mullarky. "I've seen it empty and cleaned out."

"Y're a great man, Colm; I'm always amazed at what ye know. How did that come about that it was emptied? I've never known it to be any different from what it is now."

"Can ye remember, about twenty–odd years ago, there was a farmer named Hennessey, lived the other side of the mountain? Had a wife named Annie- Kate."

"I do remember," said Murphy. "They were both great drinkers."

"They were, and the drink was the cause of the pool being emptied."

"How was that?" asked Murphy, his torpid brain slowly telling him there surely could be no such connection. He was certain that whatever other results alcohol brought about, and he'd seen quite a few of them of them, it could never have caused a pool to be drained. Mullarky paused and surveyed the pool, picturing a night from twenty years ago.

*Two of a Kind*

"They were returning home from O'Neill's one night, and she'd too much drink taken …"

"She must have had a fair drop taken then. She'd the stomach of an ox on her, and could drink stout faster than the brewery could produce it," interrupted Murphy.

"She could. But this particular night it got the better of her and she puked into the pool and lost her spectacles, as well as the set of false teeth Hennessey had just had made for her."

"And they emptied the pool to look for spectacles and false teeth?" said Murphy, dubiously.

"Well, Hennessey had paid big money for the teeth and he wanted them found."

"They've too much money, these farmers."

"Aye, they have, right enough." Murphy turned his back on the pool that glistened like black treacle under the moon, and resumed his stride.

"But why did he spend so much on the teeth? I didn't know he thought that much of her."

"He didn't! In fact, he belted her in the gob for losing them." Murphy nodded approvingly.

"I suppose that was his opportunity, the mouth being empty. He'd hardly want to risk breaking them when she'd got them in. But what was so special about them? Could he not have just got her another set made?"

Mullarkey, revelling in the authoritative role of narrator, raised a finger to emphasise the crucial point:

"Amn't I about to tell you? She'd asked him to have gold fillings put into them to make them appear more natural. She had a mouth like a bucket and it must have looked worse when it was empty of teeth, all gum and tongue, so he went along with it. And he thought the gold would be a sound long-term investment, should he ever fall on hard times."

"I didn't know that gold could occur naturally in teeth," said Murphy, pondering deeply upon Mullarkey's reserves of wisdom, and wishing he'd a few more teeth himself, regardless of what metal they might be made. He fingered his remaining fangs tentatively. He was fairly sure he didn't have any gold in his mouth. Or perhaps he did. He'd look in the mirror in the morning. He could see now why people took up dentistry as a profession; it was like mining. From now on he'd pull his own teeth when they were giving him trouble. "Anyway, what happened?" he asked.

"The next day Hennessy paid a few bob to three school lads to have them empty the pool. Two of them waded in, mud and water up to their waists to begin with, and spent the next two days bucketing and shovelling the muck over the side and away down the hill. They'd stationed the third lad a bit down the hill with a rake, and he pulled the dross apart as they threw it towards him."

"Did they find the teeth?"

"They did," said Mullarkey. "But not in the pool. They'd fallen beside the water, along with the spectacles. They were in the heather all the time, close to the road. But without the spectacles she was as blind as a bat, and in any case, they were both dead drunk at the time, and wouldn't have found their own arses with both hands, so neither of them had any idea where they'd fallen."

"Wasn't that wondrous that they should find them," said Murphy. "That's almost a miracle in itself."

"I suppose it was a bit of luck. Anyway, Hennessy gave her another quick clout before she'd got the teeth back into her mouth for causing him to have to pay the lads to empty the pool for nothing."

"Were the spectacles all right?" asked Murphy.

"No, the glass was broken. But one of the lads liked the frames. He said they gave him the appearance of an intellectual and made him look like James Joyce, so he gave Hennessy a few coppers for them and wore them for a long time afterwards. But the pool, when it was cleaned out, was about twice the size of my pigsty, and three or four feet deep. It's the shape of a scallop shell, just a natural hollow in the rock. If a pilgrim were standing in it taking a cure, he'd have the face of Saint Patrick looking at him from across the road, with the hills behind, and a view in the other direction across the heather and down to the sea. That view alone would make you feel better, even if it didn't cure you."

Murphy's brain, always working in arrears, had locked on to the long departed Hennessys, and momentarily he'd lost the thread of the narrative about the pool.

"What happened to the Hennessys, Colm? They haven't been seen in years."

"Sure, didn't she die soon after that, and he moved away."

"He needn't have gone to all that trouble and expense over the teeth then," said Murphy, "but of course, he wouldn't have known she was going to die, I suppose."

"Oh, he didn't lose money over it. The price of gold had gone up, so he sold the teeth to Annie's sister. She said they fitted her face perfectly, and that they were always something to remember her sister by."

"Ah, sure they always know how to make money, farmers do."

A long silence ensued whilst Murphy slowly steered his mind

back to the original point of the discussion. He ponderously contemplated the problems of turning the place into a holy shrine that might attract pilgrims and develop the mercantile benefits that might come with them. Then he asked Mullarkey, "How would the people taking the waters avoid exposing themselves whilst getting in and out of the pool?" Murphy would never countenance any glimpse of nudity. He had his standards.

"It could be managed; a fence could be put around it somehow, and a shed of some sort put alongside for changing out of your clothes. That problem could easily be resolved if only Nolan would apply himself to it. But that's where the problem lies, of course. Ah, sure, that damned priest has no business head on him at all"

Murphy gave further consideration to the idea of fleecing pilgrims, trying to balance it with giving reasonable value for money, as it were, to ensure the place developed a favourable reputation which would ensure its long- term prospects. "But what if they were not cured of their afflictions?" he asked. "After all, you couldn't expect to cure every last one of them."

"That's made no difference at Lourdes," replied Mullarkey. "That place is thriving, and has been for years."

"But some of 'em do get cured there," said Murphy. "Kathleen McCarthy did. Before she took the waters she walked like a hobbled cow. Now she swings her hips wonderfully and runs around all over the place."

"They do say she had legs of different lengths before she went to Lourdes," said Mullarkey, but with doubt in his voice.

"That would have accounted for the way she used to walk I suppose," said Murphy.

"One was said to be two inches longer than the other," continued Mullarkey.

"Which one?" enquired Murphy.

"How should I know? Anyway, what does it matter?"

"I was just trying to remember did she lean to the left or the right when she walked, that was all."

Murphy dwelt on the theory of the differing leg length for another minute or so, before asking, "Who do you think measured them?"

"I dunno," said Mullarkey. There was another long pause whilst Murphy's brain ticked over. "It wouldn't have been McNally, would it?" he eventually asked.

"McNally?" said Mullarkey. "Theo McNally, the schoolmaster? Why would he have had a ruler up her skirt?"

"Oh, I dunno. I just thought it might be him. They do say he's very precise with figures."

A couple of minutes silence followed, broken only by the tapping of their heels on the stony ground, as both pondered the mercantile potential of the place. "You're right Colm," Murphy finally said. "Nolan isn't up to the job. It's a pity they deported Father Tom to Cork. He'd have made something of it."

Ah, Sure Tom McGrath was a different man altogether," agreed Mullarkey, with enthusiastic fondness of the memory of the priest. "He had his head screwed on right. He could turn a penny–piece into a pound note any day of the week."

"It was a great shame indeed that they moved him," reiterated Murphy, sadly. I suppose he didn't do himself any favours by importing that big black Studebaker from the States. It must have stretched the parish funds a bit."

"I don't know how that was paid for that," said Mullarkey, "but he was never without money. He'd always stand his round at O'Neill's. Anyhow, I heard he sold it at a profit to a racehorse breeder in Cavan. If he'd succeeded in convincing the bishop that he was only buying it as a hearse for the parish's benefit, so that they didn't have to rely on McGarrigle's broken-down horse-drawn contraption to bring the dead into the church, he might just about have got away with it. And he did say he would run the nuns about in it - and I believe he would, he always took good care of them."

"Ah, sure the bishop was another one who had no head for business," said Murphy. "But anyway, he's getting past it now. He'll be retired soon. I wonder who we'll get in his place?"

"I've heard mention of a Monsignor O'Flaherty from Dublin coming in our direction when the present man is gone," said Mullarkey. Murphy's slow brain was still mulling over the erstwhile Father Tom and his legendary abilities. "They say Father Tom was good at curing women's infertility," he ventured.

"He did seem to have that about him," agreed Mullarkey. "A good many women conceived after asking for his help."

"I wonder how that came about?" said Murphy.

"It does make you wonder," said Mullarkey. "Ah, but sure the old ones were hard to beat; they were up to all the dodges."

They were now ascending the hill into Glenowen, when Mullarkey spotted a weak metallic glint as faint as the light from a glow-worm, which appeared to be coming out of the ground at the far side of the road. He crossed over and then advanced cautiously towards it, picking his way carefully through rocks and scrubby foliage. Murphy followed him. A sliver of moonlight was reflecting off a chromed bicycle bell. The bike itself was down in a deep ditch with only its handlebars level with the road and mostly covered with bracken. Mullarkey, on his knees now, reached down, grasped it by the crossbar, and hauled it out, pulling it onto the road, where he proceeded to bounce it up and down on its tyres to see if they were pumped.

Murphy was peering at it through the darkness, trying to see if he might be able to discern the possible ownership of the machine. "Whose d'ye think it is?" he asked Mullarkey.

"It's mine now," came the terse reply. Mullarkey walked back down the hill for twenty or thirty yards, pushing the bike, and dropped it down into an equally deep ditch on the opposite side of the road to where he had discovered it. He then scrabbled about for some cover. Finding a small rowan tree nearby he broke off its lower branches and threw them on top of the bike.

"That's just what I need for going to Mass on," he told Murphy.

"I thought ye already had a bike?"

"No. It's banjaxed. I ran it into a gatepost coming back from O'Neill's. I buckled the forks and the front wheel. But this one will do me fine."

"Won't someone recognize it?" enquired Murphy.

"Not when I've given it a lick of paint," said Mullarkey.

They continued on up the hill towards O'Neill's pub. At the house before the pub the huge mongrel hound of Garda Dan Doyle, both of whom were noted for their savagery, was trying to get its massive head through the bars of a big iron gate that had once formed part of a prison cell. The size of its head suggested mastiff was a substantial part of its imperfect pedigree. The dog clearly intended taking the legs off the two of them. Mullarkey, totally undaunted and never averse to conflict, aimed a few good kicks at it between the bars. The cur, being well-practised in battle, whipped it head back out of the way each time, snarling ferociously. Then, it managed to anchor its jaws on the toe of Mullarkey's boot, sat back on its haunches and attempted to drag him through the bars. Quick as a flash, Mullarkey grabbed the upper bars of the gate with both hands, and with the free foot, booted the hound in the face, making it release its grip. Withdrawing both legs with alacrity, he went across the road and scrabbled about. Finding a hefty lump of granite, he returned to the fray. The dog wisely took off around the back of the house.

Sergeant Doyle, disturbed from his supper and wandering why the dog was taking so long to get on top of whatever the situation was, went over to the open window. He saw the reason why: "Mullarkey! Fuck off! Before I get out there and stiffen ye," he bellowed. The dog, sensing its masters support, hurtled round from the back of the house towards the gate, just as Mullarkey, by way of a valedictory gesture, lobbed his missile in its direction. Only the hound's lightning reflexes, as it pirouetted out of the way, saved it from being brained by the airborne granite. For the second time that night it retired to the back of the house and Dan Doyle went back to his bread and cheese.

Mullarkey and Murphy walked the last few yards to the pub, Mullarkey totally unconcerned by the flapping toe of his boot and his big toe sticking out of the hole in his sock. His woman would have difficulty this time finding enough of the original wool to put yet another darn in it.

Darcy O'Neill had been watching all this with great amusement from the back door of his pub. He was well used to Mullarkey's often colourful entrances to his establishment; this one was nothing unusual. He also made almost as many inglorious departures; usually head-first down the steps at the back door with O'Neill's boot making its well-practised trajectory towards his arse.

Mullarkey ran up the steps and in through the front door with all the agility of a goat, and in no way impeded by the flapping boot. The brief altercation with Guard Doyle and his slavering canine was now well out of his mind as he concentrated on whom he might touch for a drink. He was immediately exchanging colourful greetings with the regulars, who then pointedly turned their backs and resumed converse amongst themselves. They had by now almost filled the place in an attempt to find seats before the fiddler arrived, and did not want to end up buying drinks for Mullarkey.

"Am I to get them in yet, Colm," asked Murphy, wondering if he'd given Mullarky enough time to trick a drink for them out of some stranger, but then realized that there were no visitors in the place. They were all locals, too well acquainted with them both to fall for buying them drinks.

"If ye like, Joe," said Mullarkey. "I'll get the next one." That statement would be fulfilled only if he failed to get in with a crowd from another settlement who hadn't heard of him -which was highly unlikely, his notoriety was widespread - and thereby acquire a free drink, before slipping away whilst people were pondering whose round it was next. He then spotted his eldest son, Sean, father of the erstwhile leg-cramped infant, Seamus. Hoping that Sean might have a shilling in his pocket, he rapidly made his way in that direction.

"Bejasus, I haven't seen ye in dog's ages," he said, pumping

Sean's hand in a manner reminiscent of Stanley greeting Livingstone. "I thought ye were still away"

'Dogs ages' equated to little over a week, although that was quite a while, given that they usually saw each other several times a day, living as they did in hovels only a quarter of a mile apart. Sean had been working with a road mending gang on the other side of the county. The foreman of the gang always liked to have Sean if he was short of a regular man, as he was tireless with pick and shovel and would come at a moment's notice, as he was generally doing little else. Sean could do the work of two men, and the foreman would use him as an exemplar, berating the rest of the gang with colourful obscenities for not keeping up with him. The trouble with Sean was that when he'd earned a few pounds he'd lose interest in the job and make for the nearest tavern. There, he'd drink a gallon or two of porter, buckle a few noses, and make his unsteady way home to his cow, his pig and his hens, and tell his woman to fetch him some bread and boil him a pan of eggs. Sean liked a simple, uncommitted way of life, so he was no use as a regular road man.

"How did ye get down here?" Colm asked him. "We didn't see ye on the road"

"I biked down earlier; I've been here a while," replied Sean, his unsteady hands and spilt beer confirming the truth of that.

"I didn't see any bike when I came in. Ye've not left it where some thieving bastard can take it have ye?"

"No, it's around the corner. It'll be fine."

"But y' don't have a bike," remembered Colm. "Unless ye've bought one with ye's earnings, and knowing ye, I doubt that. It's more likely a few gallons of porter ye'll have bought."

"I came down on your bike."

"Ye did not! My bike is ruined. The forks are bent and it has no chain on it. And the tyre is punctured. It's in the stable, where it's stood for over a month."

"I fixed it, the day before I went away. Dunleavy had an old bike with a buckled wheel and no saddle. He'd been riding it without the saddle for ages, but when the wheel was buckled too, he had to lay it aside. He was going to repair it, but when he was coming home from the bog with a cart-load of turf that wild black mare of his took a fit the way she does, and dragged the cart over it. The frame was bent, so I gave him a shilling for it and put the forks and the chain and tyre on your bike. It'll do for us both to use."

"Ye could have told me. I've been walking when I needn't have walked."

"I wasn't able to tell ye. I was called away to the road gang whilst ye were cutting turf in the bog. I asked Kathleen to tell ye. She must have forgotten."

"Well, where's my bike now then? It's been taken, I'll bet, whilst ye've been in here pouring Guinness down yer throat. Sure, some thieving bastard's riding it around the hills right now."

"No, they're not. It's about fifty yards down the hill. I've hidden it in the ditch at the side of the road."

## CHAPTER FIVE

Nolan was seated at his breakfast table in the presbytery, waiting for his part-time housekeeper Noel Daly, who, for the remainder of the day, was the town's barber, to bring him his eggs and rashers. He was lavishly buttering a hunk of bread and shouting to Daly to bring him some marmalade. His mind was wandering over Mick Mullarkey's insistence upon what Nolan considered to be a very dubious likeness of Saint Patrick, or of anyone else for that matter, which the rock fall had created on the hillside. His thoughts were travelling roughly in the same direction as those of several of his parishioners, whose ears the loud-mouthed idiot had bent with his preposterous claims. Nolan knew that shrines attracted pilgrims, for all manner of reasons, and pilgrims brought money with them. And they might be persuaded to part with some of it.

He doubted whether the monolith in its present state- despite the recent surgery caused by the rock fall, and that wouldn't endure for long- was sufficiently convincing to be deemed a holy figure, and attract pilgrims from all over the land. Mick Mullarky's dogmatic assertions had left him far from impressed. But if it could be enhanced in some way to look more like a human form to which a saintly appellation could be attached, then, who knows what might result. He would give some thought to it.

Nolan knew – sure, wasn't it beyond doubt, that he had not been accepted by many (perhaps most) of his male parishioners.

## *Two of a Kind*

It was a sad fact, but one he had to face. He simply did not fit in. And, he had to admit to himself, he didn't like a good many of them, so that hadn't helped him to integrate into what was a closely knitted community, where every little fault and foible was universally known, but was also generally accepted. Not many actively disliked him, perhaps, but he had not been able to fill the shoes of the legendary Father McGrath, 'Big Tom,' as he was known. The local economy had plummeted since Father Tom had been sent to Cork, and he was still greatly missed. Any priest would have found him a hard act to follow, and Nolan was by no means outstanding in his priestly duties, so he had no chance. He knew that himself, and he knew equally well that he was finding those duties ever more onerous. This was a problem that he couldn't see a way of dealing with, but he knew it could only get worse. It was his upbringing, and his mother's wishes, rather than his own inclinations, that had led him into the trap which presently constrained him. By nature, he was something of an epicurean, or a sybarite. Sensuous, irresponsible luxury held too much appeal for him. Setting an example one ought to emulate was, for Nolan, an impossible task.

By contrast, Big Tom McGrath could do no wrong in anyone's eyes. He could deal with any situation; arrange almost anything that wasn't explicitly condemned by the Church. The fact that something might lie towards the outer reaches of the law, or even beyond its bounds, was a different issue altogether and no concern of his. Sure, he was a priest, wasn't he, not a lawyer. When Father Tom had been in charge of things, life had been good. There had been no risk of any of his flock going without food, for instance. Many a poor family had suddenly found themselves the unlikely possessors of a side of bacon, or a leg of salted pork, when they were on their uppers. It might have come from a protestant pig up north, and maybe have been procured in dubious circumstances, but that didn't diminish the nourishment in it. A half-hundredweight of flour could come your way if the schoolmaster had noticed that none of your six or eight kids had brought a bit of bread to school in the last couple of days. Even a few yards of cloth suitable for a First Communion dress might find its way to an impoverished mother to save her from embarrassment. The poor-box inside the church door had always been full to overflowing when McGrath was in charge, as the parishioners were well aware that the money was 'recycled' locally, with a bit more added to it by 'Himself' when he'd had a successful day with the nags at some race-course or other around the country. And he was a frequent winner; he understood horseflesh. Now that the rapidly declining funds were in Nolan's hands the money went to the children in Africa, and whilst no one was without pity for the African poor – and sure, weren't the missionaries doing a great job converting the poor little heathens? –but that said, charity should surely begin at home.

Another thing about Father McGrath: he loved driving, and always had a powerful car. And if anyone had a close relative away in the hospital in distant Galway who was in a bad way, he could get them over there to visit, and never seemed to have a problem procuring the petrol, although space in the vehicle, large though it was, was invariably more limited on the way home, due to a significant number of crates and parcels acquired during visiting hours.

The only person who was not sorry to see McGrath depart was Darcy O'Neill, even though he was inordinately fond of the priest.

## Two of a Kind

It was just down to the fact that that McGrath seemed somehow to be behind the trade in a powerful spirit – and it had nothing to do with the Holy Ghost – that came in unmarked bottles and substantially undercut the price of his own whiskey.

No, there was no likelihood of Nolan ever becoming a replacement for Big Tom; any man would have struggled with that insurmountable task. But Nolan felt that if he could promote the glen as a holy shrine and get visitors pouring in and spending their money, then maybe his own status within the community might rise somewhat. Any improvement would be better than none. And whilst suffering might be good for the soul, surely there was no harm in trying to raise the overall living standards of the place. Those who wanted abject poverty and self-abasement could always donate any financial gains they incidentally derived from gullible pilgrims to good causes, or crawl around the shrine on their hands and knees until they bled, or whip themselves with barbed wire, or find some other form of masochistic pleasure to indulge in.

Yes, he would apply himself vigorously - although vigour was not one of his more salient attributes - to make the most of a God-given opportunity. If the place began to thrive, and if that upturn in its fortunes could be associated with his own arrival there, he might be better accepted. That could make life more bearable, although he still would never to make a good priest, so he'd many misgivings about his future, and knew that at some point he would have to apply himself to solving that ever-growing dilemma, holy shrine or no. But, in the interim, if he was better liked, then any injudicious activity on his part might be overlooked.

Nolan had already convinced himself that the configuration

of the newly exposed rock face did indeed bear some slight resemblance to a face, and that the overall proportions of the rock could be said, if one had a vivid enough imagination, to display outlines of the shoulders and upper torso of a large man wearing a cloak. Unfortunately, the protuberance that could be called a nose was marred by what looked like a large carbuncle on the end of it, but perhaps some work with a hammer and chisel could rectify that.

The roots of bushes and shrubs of various mountain plants that had helped to fissure the rock and had probably started the old surface to split away even before the rocks had struck it from above, and which were deemed to be serpentine in appearance by the moronic Mick Mullarkey, these were another detriment. But they would very soon wither away now they were exposed to the elements, and, as the fresh rock weathered, any contrived similarity to Saint Patrick, or any other holy figure, would soon be gone. Therefore, he needed to take his chance now, if he was going to take one at all, for in a few weeks of heavy weather the 'face' of the apparition would become less visible, and anyway, people would soon consign Mick Mullarkey's pronouncements to the rubbish heap, as they usually did with the rest of his and his family's inane observations.

What was needed right now, Nolan reckoned, was a bit of general tidying up of the whole scene and then the addition of some form of suitable embellishment and a few highlights to make it more convincing as a holy figure – although he knew some people would talk themselves into believing anything, evidenced or not. And although the embellishments wouldn't last for long before the weather obliterated them, it would be long enough to seed fertile imaginations. And by then, the rock, already standing back a bit from the road, could be cordoned off with ornate but stout railings, possibly embellished with religious icons, to keep onlookers at a respectful distance. Then only those with the keenest eyesight would proffer criticism, and they would soon be shouted down; sure, didn't most people like to believe in something.

Nolan's instincts rose to the challenge. Whilst his merits as a priest were seriously questionable, his natural talent as an artist when he was a schoolboy had never been in doubt; in fact, it was precociously outstanding.

But you couldn't paint features onto a rock. That would look artificial, so some other medium was required, some natural-looking mineral colouration. Nolan had a brainwave: The previous summer his permanently sweaty feet had, in the exceptional warmth of that year, caused him to suffer a serious case of Athlete's Foot. This, in his case, was something of a misnomer, as athletics had never been his strong point, being by nature an outstandingly lazy creature. The incessant itch, which he scratched until his toes bled whenever he had the opportunity to remove his footwear, almost drove him mad, until he was forced to seek the advice of Doctor Kelly. The good doctor had given him a tin of permanganate of potash crystals, instructing him to mix a quantity of them in a bowl of water in which he should immerse his feet every day. The relief had been wonderful, the only downside being that the purple dye the crystals made, when applied to his feet, or to anything else, turned them a deep shade of brown, giving him, from the ankles downwards, a somewhat Moorish appearance. Still, better that than having purple feet, he supposed. There was no race of people in the world, as far as he knew, that had purple feet. Whilst brown feet attached to white legs would cause serious puzzlement to the medics should he ever fall unconscious and require their attention, purple feet might lead to immediate amputation. It would be unlikely that Lourdes, or any other place purportedly dealing in miracles, could ever rectify that situation.

The stuff was practically indelible. There was still a chocolate-brown patch on his kitchen floor where he'd spilt some several months ago. Therefore, permanganate of potash would be just the right substance with which to daub shadowy features on the pale, buff coloured rock to create a more convincing picture of Saint Patrick. And he always kept a tin of the stuff handy for whenever his feet started giving him trouble. This medium, he felt, would look perfectly natural on the rock; quite unlike any paint, which would crack and flake. This would slowly, almost imperceptibly, fade away. By which time half the country's population would have seen the photographs in the newspapers.

Nolan had no doubt that he was well up to the task of creating a good likeness of a face, especially where the sketchy contours of one existed already. At school he had been deemed something of a 'brush-hand', a natural when it came to art. A promising career in that area had been forecast. He might have benefitted greatly from the attentive efforts the art tutor lavished upon him, and perhaps eventually become a 'name' in the art world. That is, if only he'd stayed within the prescribed parameters as to what he should paint. His downfall had lain in his choice of subject matter whenever he let his mind stray. He'd once adorned the back of a lavatory door at his school with a picture,

## Two of a Kind

outstanding in the quality of its composition and execution - amazingly so, given that he'd completed it in minutes- and also truly memorable for being totally and utterly pornographic. And what had compounded the felony was that the face of the person who was doing what he was doing bore a striking resemblance to that of the parish priest. And what had made the situation wholly irretrievable, and it could only have been an act of God, surely, it must have been, was that the self-same priest, accompanied by Monsignor O'Flaherty, who was tipped for promotion to Bishop, visited the school on the exact day that Nolan had completed his masterpiece. And, before that day was out, the Monsignor needed to use the lavatory... Unfortunately for Nolan, he entered the very same latrine, despite the fact that there were three others to choose from. Yes, it must surely have been an act of the Almighty. How else could such misfortune have been visited upon the wretched, misguided youth?

Unsurprisingly, the parish priest, after being summoned by the relatively unperturbed Monsignor to view and comment on the obscene image, felt duty bound – not to mention being driven by seething rage –to go off and find the headmaster and to lead him to the offending door and to demand of him what sort of school did he think he was running. And did he wish to continue to run it or would he rather be a bookie's runner or a corner-boy or a lavatory attendant, because such occupations might well be the only choices left for him if he didn't identify the depraved culprit and thrash the arse off him immediately.

Nolan's undoubted talent identified him all right. No one else in the school was capable of such high- quality work, so he would have been found out anyway.

His arse was duly thrashed, to such considerable effect that he couldn't sit down for two days. The priest held the squealing youth over a desk whilst the headmaster administered the necessary correction. He would have taken greater pleasure in carrying out the torture himself, but he deemed the cane to be a constitutional weapon which should remain in a constitutional hand, although he would have preferred it if the constitution permitted the erection of a cross in Merrion Square and allowed him to attach the incorrigible whelp to it with nine - inch nails.

Afterwards, Nolan was advised to stick to landscapes and pastoral scenes, and his parents were advised to find him another school forthwith. He did, subsequently, produce some excellent landscapes, but only two years later his interest in bucolic scenes, coupled with a more 'historic' outlook, led him to create a truly unforgettable canvas of a bull mounting a cow, which he thought he might have got away with by entitling it 'Zeus at Play.' Unfortunately for him, Greek mythology was not on the syllabus, so he was duly flogged once more. At that point he began to think that his calling did not lie within the world of art, and his teachers and his mother insisted that it didn't. His mother strongly encouraged him to consider the priesthood, where, she hoped, his baser instincts might be curbed, and a more spiritual bent might flower.

Nolan's father never had much of a say in his son's upbringing. Often out of the country doing work for a firm of architects, with whom he was a senior partner, and usually out of his wife's sight when he was back in his homeland – this due to his disdain of monogamy, and her fiery temper, which was exacerbated by his misdemeanours – he had given the boy little guidance and had set a poor example of conventional living. Nolan's mother, therefore, had brought him up almost singlehandedly, although her part-time husband kept her generously suppled with money, so they both lived well. She'd once held high expectations of her son, particularly as an artist, - his talent was undeniable – but his frequent licentious lapses brought her considerable embarrassment and, she felt, would lead him to perdition. She urged him therefore, following poor advice from her brothers who both were priests, towards a clerical life.

Although, since these formative years, Nolan had apparently allowed his artistic abilities to lapse, insofar as no one had seen anything of them, in fact he'd drafted a substantial number of private doodlings which he kept well hidden. Therefore, he had no doubt that he could easily resuscitate his erstwhile skills and apply them to the creation of a reasonably convincing Saint Patrick. He would attend to this new challenge at the first opportunity.

\*

For much of the day there was very little movement of people through the glen. A few sheep were the most likely creatures to wander through and above it, along with the odd cow that had kicked off its hobble. In fact, these were a common cause of the smaller rocks falling from above as the beasts pulled out tufts of grass and moss and heather high above the road, slowly undermining the bigger boulders, which then crashed down from time to time. Nolan therefore supposed that he would have little difficulty in performing his handiwork on the saintly rock without attracting attention to what he was about. In any case, he would take with him, as well as a paint-brush and other essential accoutrements, a pocket- book of wild flowers and mountain herbs, should anyone pass by. He would then simply drop his brush amongst the scree, and, book in hand, studiously scrutinize the vegetation until they had passed out of sight around the bend in the road. He found a jar, within which he mixed with water a few spoonsful of the potash, replacing the lid tightly. Putting a small paintbrush in his pocket, he prepared to walk to the glen. Then he remembered the lumpy protuberance on the 'nose' of the figure. That was a problem; without it that part of the rock could be made into a convincing face.Saint Patrick just might have had a carbuncle on his nose, but the history books had never mentioned it. Nolan knew that John Donohoe, the sexton, kept a few tools in an old wooden chest inside the church porch, which he used from time to time for small maintenance jobs, so he walked around from the presbytery to see just what it might contain. He'd noticed that Donohoe, whenever he'd time on his hands, could be found on his knees in the church yard cleaning up a few of the oldest, moss-covered headstones with a chisel.Donohoe had several relatives buried there, one of the graves dating back well over a hundred years. The elements were slowly obliterating the inscriptions on them. Donohoe wanted to maintain his pedigree, and indeed, went to some covert lengths to extend it, so he spent time chasing out the original incisions to ensure they remained legible. Nolan found exactly what he needed: a couple of different sized cold-chisels and a small lump-hammer. Putting these into a knapsack and with his book on mountain flowers in his overcoat pocket, to which he added his missal for good measure, he began the half-mile walk to the glen, glancing around for possible witnesses to his mischief.

## *Two of a Kind*

Much to his satisfaction, the road remained deserted the whole way to the miraculous rock. When he reached it, he surveyed the road ahead, then looked back the way he had come. There wasn't a soul to be seen. He scanned the surrounding bog-land to see if anyone was cutting turf. He gave a couple of minutes to this study, as a man might be there, but resting on his haunches, back against the bank as he took brief respite from his labours, perhaps taking a bite of bread or a sup of cold tea from a bottle, and then a head might pop up over the bank and discover him. Nolan soon decided all was well, just as he had expected. The only witnesses to his intended endeavours would be a few sheep, whose heads he had seen peering from around the larger rocks above him.

He approached the rock, hammer and chisel in hand, having concealed the knapsack and the jar of potash behind a clump of heather. He was pleased to see that the lump on what was to become the nose of the saint, although fairly sizeable, had only a slender connection to the main protuberance. It should, he felt, be easily detachable. However, there was a drawback, insofar as the whole thing was quite a bit taller than he had estimated; the would-be head was just beyond his reach. Nolan dwelt for a moment on the problem. There were many rocks around, varying in size from that of a footstool to some as big as armchairs. Most were obviously too heavy to shift, but one or two held the promise of being portable. He would have to stack some of the smaller ones. He took hold of the nearest of these to his workpiece and tried to lift it. It was too heavy, and, being quite unused to physical labour, he felt the wrench in his back. He straightened up slowly, rubbing himself awkwardly. He could not give up now; the economy of the place was at stake, and, more importantly, his own status within it.

Gritting his teeth, he bent over again and tried to lift and pull at the same time. The rock moved a little on the loose shale. With a few more painful tugs he found he had moved it about a yard. Taking some deep breaths and making furtive glances all around him, he bent again to his task. He was becoming practised now and the rock was sliding more easily towards 'Saint Patrick's' feet. When he'd established it as a plinth, he tried standing upon it. Not bad, he thought, but a few inches higher would be better. Nolan looked around again for possible witnesses to his dubious activities; the coast was still clear. He had only the sheep for company, and a couple of croaking ravens overhead. His back was giving him hell, but he had to persist. He saw a smaller rock that he thought he might just be able to lift, only a few feet away. It was pancake shaped and should stand well, he estimated, upon the cube shaped piece he had just manoeuvred into place. He dragged it across, and, with one grim heave, hoisted it atop the other. Now he had a good platform on which to stand and exercise his creative talents.

Taking up the hammer and chisel he addressed the rock. A couple of tentative taps – he was never a great one with the hammer or, for that matter with any other tool associated with hard work-then a full-blooded swing at the target. The hammer struck the chisel awkwardly and glanced off and onto his thumb. "Bastard!" he cursed, dropping the tools, which first clouted his knee before hitting him on the foot, adding pain to considerable pain. Clutching one hand with the other and swaying precariously as the injured foot came away from the rock, he endeavoured to stay upright. The upper stone on which he was standing slid sideways, and, losing contact with its fellow beneath, deposited him in a heap amongst the shale and sheep turds. He scrambled

## Two of a Kind

to his feet, looking around for witnesses to his fall. Apart from the bemused stare of a raggedy ram that had escaped last year's shearing, there was still no one in sight. Ruefully rubbing the damaged digit, he flexed it gingerly to see if it was broken. It wasn't, there was only a smear of blood where he'd skinned his knuckle. He spat onto his handkerchief, cleaned the wound and then wrapped up the hand. He hobbled around, trying to ease the pain in the foot struck by the falling tools. It was hurting him as much as the injured hand, and his back was now giving him hell. Dusting the dung, moss and shale off his trousers and wishing he'd never started the job, Nolan directed his gaze back to the unforgiving rock. His spirit lifted; the lump on the nose had gone. He'd fettled it with just one blow. Thanks be to God.

He saw now the considerable difference that one small alteration had made. That part of the rock did now almost resemble a face. That mutton- headed drongo, Mick Mullarkey, was perhaps not so far wrong after all.

Nolan's artistic bent was returning to him with a certain degree of enthusiasm. Whilst he'd always had talent with pencil, crayon and brush, he'd never done much in the way of sculpture; it was too slow for him. And physically arduous. But he could see potential here, and was becoming ardent in his endeavours. If he could emphasize with the chisel what could be termed brow ridges, before highlighting them with the potash dye, the rock could well make a convincing figure.

Setting in place a better rock on which to stand, he set to work with greater confidence, despite his aching back and throbbing thumb. Every now and then a dray or trap, or pannier-laden donkey would come by, at which early sound he would drop his tools, sit on a rock and study his pocketbook avidly, pretending not to hear until the last moment. Then he would hail the driver cordially and engage briefly in superficial conversation, having affected the impression that his scrutiny of the book was of paramount importance. As each interruption disappeared out of sight around the bend, he returned enthusiastically to his task.

The brow ridges greatly enhanced by the chisel, Nolan then spotted the potential for an ear to be created, without too much effort, out of another natural protuberance. Two ears would have been better, but the rock didn't lend itself to that. In any case, one ear might have been all Saint Patrick had. After all, he'd been knocked about a bit in his time, according to the legends. Surely no one would query this small detail.

This task completed, Nolan stepped down carefully to admire his handiwork.

The roots and tendrils decreed by Mullarkey to be serpents, were already withering and losing their hold; they would soon be gone. Nolan reached up as far as he could, and those within his grasp he pulled away. If serpents were needed, he could do a better job with his paintbrush and potash. He climbed down from his plinth, put the tools into his knap-sack and concealed them behind a rock. Taking the lid off the jar, he gave the purple-coloured potash a stir with a handy plant stem and re-mounted his rocky platform cautiously. Knowing well the almost indelible properties of the dye, he intended to brush it on sparingly so as not to spatter his face with it. His first job was to highlight the brow ridges that he'd already delineated with the chisel. This was easily accomplished with swift, confident brushstrokes. Then, with most of the liquid gone from the brush, he created the hint of a pair of brown eyes. This was looking good; now for the background, the necessary adornment of the cliff-face itself, either side of the protuberant figure. Reaching up as high as he could, he painted snaky coils where the tendrils had been. At this point he paused. Mullarkey had seen – or imagined he'd seen – a Saint Patrick figure driving all the snakes out of Ireland. But with just one or two serpents rather than rakes of them it wouldn't be too difficult to create a Garden of Eden, and the figure could be, perhaps, that of the Almighty himself. But that, of course, would require at least a vague outline of two more figures, one male, one female, and they would have to be in a state of nudity, and that would be pushing your luck a bit too far, wouldn't it? Nolan knew that he was more than up to the job, I fact it would be easy for him. He'd done several interpretations of the Garden of Eden privately, just for his own pleasure. Some of them were fairly salacious; he'd enjoyed doing them. But this would be risky, just asking for trouble. Perhaps he would settle for a few more serpents around the feet of 'Saint Patrick' and leave it at that. Then Mick Mullarkey, he of the ginger head and flattened nose and the thick-lipped, vulgar mouth, could broadcast his vision to the whole of Ireland, if any reporter from the *Western People* would listen to him.

But having added several very convincing serpents to the grotto, Nolan's loins tingled with the thought of a pair of breasts upon the rock. But what if someone passed by? He couldn't do what he'd done before- pretend to be reading his book, as if he hadn't noticed the scene around him. But he'd see anyone approaching in good time - he had the advantage there.Then he'd have to hide somewhere of course.He checked for cover amongst the rocks. There were a couple of clefts he could slip in to until anyone had passed by, and if they did spot him, he could pretend to be relieving himself and they'd quickly pass on to avoid any embarrassment. He could almost guarantee the landscape would remain devoid of people a little longer. Yes, he'd chance his luck.

Within minutes his artistic hand was endorsing the scene he held in his head. A casque of hair and sensual lips were soon added to a voluptuous form; and after that, a decidedly male figure, all too obviously succumbing to the abundant temptation of Eve, stood close by. The outline of the bole of a tree with a few hastily sketched branches completed the job. Nolan knew that within days rain would wash down mud and sediment from the top of the mountain, obliterating his handiwork before it could ever be traced back to him, but the initial form would remain, and, with a bit of advertising, the glen might yet begin to attract visitors.

His task completed within a few hours, the exhausted Nolan prepared to dismount from his precarious perch. To his chagrin, a sheep, moving about the hillside fifty feet above him, dislodged a shower of small rocks. Several of these peppered him painfully as he twisted violently to avoid a larger boulder that was heading his way. His feet went from under him and for the second time that afternoon he found himself lying stunned amongst the sheep-shit gazing glumly at the sky. His hand felt wet and he thought it was bleeding. As his head cleared, he realized that in his fall he'd up-ended the jar of potash over his hand and over the sleeve of his jacket. It had soaked through the handkerchief that bound his swollen thumb. For a minute or two that didn't trouble him unduly as he lay there recovering. Pulling himself to his feet he began checking himself all over for more serious damage. He was relieved to find there was none. The jacket was an old one, and being black, the stained sleeve was not so obvious that he wouldn't be able to return home without attracting attention should he meet anyone.

He dusted himself down again, pulled the sodden rag from his hand and threw it in amongst the rocks and vegetation, along with the jar and brush, collected the hammer and chisel and made for home. He would have to keep his hand in his pocket if he met with anybody.

The only person he met with was the hermit Peter Keighley, who was walking his ass on the end of a string. Keighley often took his ass out for a walk, and sometimes his cow too. He said it kept the ass in condition when he had little work for it to do. He never explained why the cow needed a walk. In truth, it was probably because Keighley communicated with hardly anyone and just liked a bit of company when he was abroad on the lonely tracks. He talked to his animals fondly and incessantly, even to the few scrawny hens and the pig he kept, in an unintelligible patois of Irish, with a few words of the English he knew thrown in. Whether or not they made any sense of it would be debatable; very few humans did.

Nolan spotted Keighley coming up at him out of a boreen where it came off the side of the mountain and inclined upwards to join the road he was on. He was still a good fifty yards away and Nolan looked in the other direction trying to ignore him. He'd been told about Keighley; told that he must tackle him about his failure to attend Mass. Did the filthy heathen not realize that he was in a permanent state of mortal sin because of this? And if ever he should fall off a cliff or were to drown in the sea when he was barrowing kelp from the shore to manure his land then he'd no chance of getting into heaven. But right now, Nolan's main concern was his throbbing thumb and aching back and Keighley was the last person with whom he wanted to get involved. He regarded him as an idiot, a complete waste of time. But Keighley meant having him. Still in high dudgeon from his sudden exposure to Agatha Nelligan's underwear, which had taxed his various emotions to the edge of apoplexy, he intended to accost Nolan and berate him for the presence of such harlots abroad in the hills, as if the recent occurrence was entirely Nolan's fault. Sure, what were priests for if not to maintain the moral fibre of the population and keep loose women continent? Keighley had pulled his greasy cap from his head and was waving it wildly at Nolan, and shouting at him to stop, although Nolan could not make out the actual words. But he stood and waited whilst Keighley and the ass hurried in his direction, Keighley's toothless mouth hanging open and his pink pate, surrounded by long grey curls, turning redder by the second with the effort he was making. He gained ground on Nolan and finally stood before him, frothing at the mouth like a spent racehorse at the finishing line. The two halves of the British army greatcoat that enshrouded his skinny frame were held together by a string around his waist, and still bore the insignia of rank, which was why some people referred to the hermit as Captain Keighley, though never to his face of course, as no malice was intended, no offence taken. The weather being dry, Keighley did not have with him his wet- weather accoutrement to this ancient garment which clad him every day of the year, inside the house and out. This other device consisted of a rancid hessian sack, well- greased on both of its inside surfaces with tallow, which he somehow contrived to attach to the epaulettes of the coat with short twists of fine wire in order to cover the huge rent down the back and run most of the rain off when the weather was particularly inclement.

As Keighley drew near, Nolan could see the edge of something moving inside the neck of his tattered shirt. He then remembered that Keighley sometimes slipped into the porch of the church after the congregation had departed the last service of the day, and helped himself to a copy of *The Universe* if there was one still remaining on the porch table. He stuffed the Catholic newspaper down against his chest between his greasy vest and his shirt to keep out the worst of the cold Atlantic wind. They didn't object to his stealing the odd one now and then if it seemed likely that it would remain unsold anyway, so long as he didn't do it too often. The clergy were good to him like that, given that he didn't pay them any other attention. Not that Keighley was particularly attracted to *The Universe*; being totally illiterate he was only interested in its insulative properties, and for those he felt the *Irish Independent* was a better paper. He reckoned that each page was thicker and there were more of them. It was a good winter newspaper but it was harder to come by; he was always glad when someone gave him a copy. But more importantly, when he'd had good usage out of it for warming his chest, but before it became too tattered, he would tear it into strips which he threaded on a string and hung on a nail on the back of the door of his privy. He didn't like doing that with *The Universe*. Its pages were mostly covered with pictures of the pope, or with cardinals, bishops or priests, and there were always plenty of nuns portrayed. He couldn't bear the thought of a nun looking at his private parts whilst he was cleaning himself. When, *in extremis,* he was out of the *Independent* and was forced to make use of *The Universe* as lavatory paper, he carefully tore out all the pictures and hung only the print on the nail. As he couldn't read, none of that made any sense to him, so the marks he left on it were not to be taken as comments on the content of the text.

Having reached the priest, Keighley stood drawing breath noisily, and mentally composing his attack. Nolan waited impatiently, studying Keighley's wellingtons the while. They were an ill-matched pair, and Keighley had several more like them. People gave him the odd one every now and then when they'd caused irreparable damage to the other one of the pair, such as when they might put a misdirected fork through their foot after a hard night before at O'Neill's place and their hands were unsteady, or when an unpleasant dog they'd kicked might retaliate. Often, they were not of the size Keighley required, but he didn't mind if they were too big. He was an inventive man, and eventually he'd make them fit perfectly by drying out hay by his turf fire and judiciously packing it into the boots until they were exactly to his liking. Nolan had noticed a few stray stalks sticking up out of the top of a boot. He noticed also a red rubber patch on the other boot. Keighley must have cadged a puncture repair outfit off someone; he never had any money. He also had on a stout looking pair of sea-boot stockings, turned down over the tops of the wellingtons. Nolan wondered how he had acquired those; surely no woman had ever knitted for him. He didn't know that the feet of the stockings were missing entirely, long gone from years of wear. Keighley still wore the legs of the stockings as he felt they gave him an air of affluence.

Having regained his breath, Keighley threw back his shoulders, stretched himself to his full height of a little over five feet and began his diatribe. He meant to castigate Nolan in no uncertain terms. He didn't get off to a great start. Hardly a conversationalist at the best of times, when confronted by other human beings Keighley developed a terrible stammer, something that didn't encumber him when conversing with other creatures. Although he intended to tell Nolan what he ought to do about lewd foreigners who frightened him and his donkey half to death, the pressure of the moment got the better of him. In his anger he sprayed Nolan with spittle as he stammered out a confusing jumble of half-formed expletives in a tirade that lasted a full two minutes. All Nolan could make of it was that Keighley had had to sit down on a rock for a good half hour or more to recover himself because he'd had feelings he'd never had before in his life that made him think he was having a heart attack, whilst his ass had run off in terror. All this because some foreign harlot who rode a bike with her underwear on display had nearly killed the pair of them, and on the Sabbath, too. What was the world coming to?

Nolan, confused and weary, aching in every limb, assured Keighley that he'd look into the matter, and made for home. He had missed his opportunity to mention non-attendance at mass but he was so taken aback by Keighley's invective that he'd never even thought about it. And wasn't he glad now that he hadn't? Fuck him! Let him roast in hell! And didn't he stink! Holy Christ, the stench of the man! It was a good thing he'd never turned up in the confessional. That would have kept Nolan there till midnight fumigating the whole church, never mind the confessional box. Although Nolan had been spouting the parable of the good shepherd and his lost sheep from the pulpit only a couple of weeks ago, in truth, he'd never seen the sense of it. Why chase around looking for the one stupid bastard that's vanished into the wilderness and give all the other fuckers the chance to run away? He'd drop that particular parable from his repertoire from now on. This encounter had confirmed that it made no sense at all. Wasn't Keighley the living stinking proof of it!

\*

Returning to the presbytery, Nolan put the borrowed tools back in their box, and turned his attention to his damaged hand. The thumb was no more swollen than before, and might soon subside. But the hand, oh, the hand, it was the colour of his summertime feet. When he spilled the dye, he should have plunged it immediately into the nearby pool, which might have diluted the effect somewhat. But he hadn't, being too focussed on his creative deceit, and his sin had found him out and would now disclose him. He scrubbed and soaked it in the out-house sink, to no avail. The dye was under his nails and along their edges, whilst above the wrist his forearm was white. He'd have to try to buy some thin white gloves for when he was saying mass, as his hand would be very noticeable during communion. This was not going to be easy.

He heard a step behind him and turned to see John Donohoe entering the out-house, making for the adjacent latrine. He'd seen the hand, as Nolan was reaching out with it to unhook an old towel off the wash stand.

"What happened to your hand, Padraig?" asked John. "It looks a mess."

"I trapped it in the door" lied Nolan. Donohoe was not a man who would dispute other people's facts, nor advance any of his own. He kept his own counsel. He did not want anyone prying into his affairs and he kept his nose out of theirs. But he had a subtle way of letting you know when he disbelieved you.

"It must have slammed hard on you; it's darkened the whole of your hand. You wouldn't have thought it would colour it like that. I'd go and see Doctor Kelly if it was my hand."

"I might have to," replied Nolan, desperately hoping that John Donohoe didn't bump into Doctor Kelly anytime soon.

## CHAPTER SIX

The whole community was beginning to ripple with rumours of the holy apparition, supposedly sighted, and certainly broadcast, by Mick Mullarkey. At least half the population of the place considered him to be a halfwit and not to be trusted, like the rest of the family, but in a settlement where nothing happens for most of the time, any story was likely to catch the general imagination. The newspapers had not yet been near, but everyone was waiting expectantly for the arrival of reporters. Then, rumour and wild speculation would soon become 'fact.'

A few people had gone to look at the rock of 'Saint Patrick' immediately Mick had announced his discovery and before Nolan had set about embellishing it, and a smaller few of them, had concurred with him that it was indeed a miraculous likeness of the saint himself. But now a new rumour was abroad, chasing the original. It was said that someone had lewdly defaced Saint Patrick; that the side of the glen now had immoral figures adorning it. Devil's work! At this point the newshounds arrived.

Nolan was soon to be questioned by the pressmen, who were keen to have a cleric pronounce on it. The words of a priest would lend authenticity. They had failed to get any sense out of the original messenger, Mick, who was sticking to his description of only a likeness of Saint Patrick; and was genuinely unable to account for the Garden of Eden scene which now covered the rock on either side of the patron saint. For the first time in his life, he freely admitted to being completely baffled.

Nolan feigned ignorance of the miracle, other than to say that that Mick had drawn his attention to the doubtful – he emphasized 'doubtful'- possibility of the face of 'Saint Patrick' on the said rock. When asked if he could account for the difference between Mick's version of the snake- chasing saint and the present picture of serpentine embellished licentiousness, he averred that the poor misguided, naïve youth was so pure in both body and soul that he would not have been able to make sense of the scene at all. Nolan almost choked as he said it. He would much rather have said that Mullarkey was a stupid fucker who should not be given the time of day, let alone listened to. However, as a priest, he had to mind his tongue, especially as the press's probings were penetrating deeply.

In his defence of Mick's moral probity Nolan had trapped himself. The press wanted to know exactly as to which picture Mullarkey had drawn his attention; surely, he knew the difference, did he not, between rampant sexuality and the repression of reptiles? Or were there in fact two different images, and was this a divine work still in progress, with more instalments to follow? Nolan weakly offered the explanation that it had been a very misty morning when Mick had accosted him and he was already late in making his way to the church to say Mass and he wasn't too sure what he had seen in the first place. He added that Mick might have been intending to receive Holy Communion that morning, in which case he would have fasted, and perhaps he was feeling faint because of it. Sure, wasn't it awfully long walk to church for him after all, and he might have been hallucinating. And he himself was not too well at the time, because he'd recently trapped his hand in a door, and he wasn't able to concentrate on what Mick was telling him. The stained hand was presently bandaged to support that explanation and to avoid questions about its somewhat African hue.

When the news hacks asked him what he thought of the present scene – surely it was obscene, wasn't it? – Nolan replied that it seemed a fair depiction of the Garden of Eden and as a learned man he saw no harm in it, but that it was far too voluptuous for the general run of humanity, who might take a more prurient interest in it. And for that reason alone, he would see to it that it was cordoned off from general view immediately.

\*

The womenfolk of the township were greatly affected by the scene in the glen, in various ways. They had never realized that biblical scenes could be so stirring, and many were trying to beg or borrow bibles to see what else might lie in store. Whilst some of them were getting a fit of the vapours, and keeling over, others were making unfavourable comparisons with their husbands, leading to considerable marital discord and causing Nolan to have to waste his time in the confessional listening to admissions of domestic violence dished out in response to alleged shortcomings. He quickly had the undertaker's handyman knock up a wooden barrier to cordon off the recess in the rocks wherein the figure stood. This restricted close-up viewing, but left more to the imagination. If people chose to stand on tiptoe to get a look at it, then that was their sin, wasn't it? And they'd have to broach it to him in the confessional later.

Within a week or two it would be less discernible, and the locals would have lost interest anyway, but a few pilgrims were already heading this way, and might, with any luck, continue to do so for a long time. Once the hullabaloo had died down a steady trade with the pruriently curious and the innately gullible from all over the land might establish itself. If everyone's livelihood improved a little Nolan might yet find favour within the community, at least a little more than he had so far. Not that he would be connected directly with the improvement in material circumstances, but he hoped that at least the legend of the great Father Tom McGrath might diminish somewhat if the mercantile situation of the town exceeded what it was when McGrath had charge of it.

*

Agatha Nelligan walked the long road towards the glen, on her way to make another confession. She was filled with trepidation. Since Nolan's visit to herself and Aunt Bridget she had realized that he would now almost certainly recognize her voice. It had not occurred to her that in any such community as small as Glenowen it was inevitable that the voice of every inhabitant would eventually identify them to the priest. But the pretence of secrecy was always maintained within the dark confines of the confessional box, where only the shadowy silhouettes of priest and confessor were discernible. The voice was just the confirmation of the probable identity.

She was going early, so as to be the first in the box, she hoped, and out again before too many others had entered the church, who might wonder what sort of life did she lead that would require her to be back so soon after the last, very recent, visit.

There was plenty of life left in the day and she was asking herself would it have been better to have come a couple of hours later, when confessions had almost finished, and to have entered the church under cover of darkness, slipped in last, or almost so, and away quickly into the night. She continued on her way with ever-increasing unease. Only the pressing knowledge that the problem had to be faced sooner or later kept her going.

Agatha moved over to the edge of the road when she heard the distant sound of a car engine approaching from a long way behind her. As it passed, she saw that the driver was Nolan. She'd half-expected that, as he was one of the very few car owners in the district, but she was surprised that he was running late. Nolan began to brake as he overtook her; he longed to give her a lift and chat to her. She cringed inwardly at the thought of having to confess to a man she'd been chatting to minutes before, but Nolan immediately realized that she was possibly making for the church and had enough about him to empathize with her embarrassment if he should pick her up, so he accelerated without acknowledging her. Agatha heaved a sigh of relief, but she was sure he would have recognized her and would surely know her when she entered the box, even if he didn't remember her voice. And that was highly unlikely.

She stopped and considered turning back, but reflected upon that course of action and decided that she must get it over with. If she could not face him when she got there then she'd kneel for a while in front of the altar, say a few Hail Marys and Our Fathers and an Act of Contrition, then make her way home again. But she'd try to steel herself to tell him what she must. She felt that Nolan – or any other priest – would have heard a lot worse than she could tell. She'd known several Catholics who'd committed what to her mind were very serious sins, like thieving someone else's pig and eating it. Nolan's car rounded the bend and disappeared from view. A couple of minutes later she rounded the same bend where the rocks had fallen, and where Peter Keighley had taken the opportunity to study her underwear. The wooden fence, which Nolan had arranged to be hastily erected, was already falling apart. Visitors to the grotto, when straining to get a view over it, had pulled several of the boards away from the rails, so much of Nolan's handiwork was again on display. The scene that met Agatha's eyes made her blush and gasp and then perspire. She went weak at the knees, feeling the blood course through her veins, and rampant excitement mingled with considerable embarrassment made her, for the moment, quite wobbly. Then she looked around to see who else might be on the road. There were a couple of people a long way in front of her going in her direction. She stopped, waiting to make sure they definitely were walking away from her and not towards her. She did not want them to see her looking at lewd pictures. She decided that they were travelling in the same direction as herself. So they must have seen what she was now seeing. She wondered what they would have made of it. She looked more closely at the rock. She was witnessing a scene that was straight out of her dreams. There was a voluptuous body of a woman, a totally naked body. And next to it, oh my god, the image of a man's body in a similar state of nudity. She gasped again. Look at it, just look at it! The size of it! Were they really like that? Where would it all go? Surely it was too much, too much for any woman. I can't cope, she thought; this is so much like my dreams. Am I dreaming now? Can all this really be in front of me?

It was in front of her. She was not dreaming, she was liking, very much, what she could see. If a sketchy picture could arouse these feelings, what would the real thing be like?

She felt that she ought to return home, to compose herself, and go to confession another day. She turned around, then stopped. Returning so soon would attract questions from her aunt. Then she saw a man and a woman in the distance coming from the direction she'd just travelled. She couldn't face them just now, she thought. It would be overwhelmingly embarrassing. She turned again in the direction of the church. This had to be dealt with. She must get it over with.

The thought then occurred to her: Father Nolan must surely have seen what she was now seeing. He would have that on his mind and would be unconcerned with what little she had to tell him. That would pale into insignificance by comparison, and perhaps make her confession a little easier for her. She continued on her way.

On entering the unlighted church, Agatha was greatly relieved to find that she was the only person there. Those on the road ahead of her must have been going elsewhere. She wondered if she was too early; perhaps confessions hadn't started yet. She fretted. She didn't want to wait long; others would soon enter. She knelt and said a quick Hail Mary. Then she heard movement inside the confessional; Nolan was already ensconced. She took a deep breath and stepped into the darkness of the box. A small candle on the priest's side of the screen faintly illuminated the profile of Father

Nolan. Agatha, well-used to confessionals, noted the position of the kneeler and the elbow rest before closing the door behind her, shutting out any light from the church windows. She trembled a little as she knelt in the darkness, her elbows awkwardly high on the shelf in front of her, as she put her hands together. She faced the obscuring mesh between her and the priest, wondering if there was any chance at all that he would not recognize her.

In a quaking voice Agatha began the prescribed ritual: "Forgive me father, for I have sinned. It is a week since my last confession and I accuse myself of these sins:"

Nolan detected the quaver in her voice and spoke to her softly, gently; "Take your time, my dear, there is no hurry. When did you say you last confessed?"

"Nearly a week ago Father."

"And have you taken communion since then?"

"No Father."

"But you've been to Mass, surely?"

"Oh, yes, Father. Last Sunday."

"But you didn't take communion then?"

"No Father."

The perspiration was running down her face and neck. She wiped herself with a handkerchief from her sleeve, under cover of darkness. He was going to probe. She knew he would. She dreaded any more questions.

"And why was that?"

"I… I felt I was not in a state of grace then, father."

"But you had just made a confession?"

"Yes Father."

"So did you sin again soon after?"

"Yes Father. I'm sorry Father."

"And what did you do? Unburden yourself now, you'll be better for it, because it will earn you God's forgiveness."

Nolan was confident that the girl's sin must surely be a venial one, and he was entirely sympathetic. In Dublin sometimes serious offences were committed, but here, he was sure, only minor sins occurred.

"I used profane language Father."

"And what prompted that?" asked Nolan, wishing he'd never done worse.

"I tripped in my bedroom Father, and knocked things over, and my chemise fell down and I was exposed and I got confused and I said bad things."

"Who was in your bedroom, might I ask?"

"Oh, no one Father. I was just by myself."

"Well, who did you expose yourself to, then?"

"Only to myself Father, In the mirror."

"Is that such a bad thing?" asked the priest, now somewhat confused himself.

"Well, I thought it might be."

Nolan sensed the girl's problem. He'd experienced the crushing influence of the nuns himself, as a boy. It was almost as if existence itself was a sin; everything you did, it seemed, was condemned as heinous. He'd managed to shrug off some of it early on, and take his chances, living with the thrashings, and with himself.

"I think you're worrying unduly. We all say bad things occasionally. We shouldn't, but we do. But looking at yourself in the mirror, so long as vanity is not involved … and even that, at your age, can be understood and allowances made for it. I'm not condoning it mind, but it not too bad a thing. It's certainly not sinful. And what age are you, by the way?"

"I'm seventeen Father."

"Ah, sure, that's a great age to be. I wish I could turn the clock back."

Agatha sighed with relief. He sounded kindly, concerned. Could she tell him a little more, she wondered, get the rest of it off her chest, as it were.

"And another thing, Father, another reason why I'm sometimes not in a state of grace: I have bad dreams."

"How do you mean, 'bad dreams?' We all have those and we cannot do much about them. What sort of dreams are they?"

"Oh, I cannot tell you Father; they're too shocking. But I cannot stop having them. I've heard that eating cheese before you go to bed causes them. But I've stopped eating cheese in the evening and it's made no difference. The dreams still come upon me."

"And do they terrify you?" asked Nolan. "Are they nightmares?"

"I don't think they are. No, I don't get terrified, I just get hot and sweaty, and toss about in bed, and then I wake up."

"Describe them to me," said Nolan failing, for some unaccountable reason, to intuit the form of Agatha's nocturnal disturbances. "They're obviously a source of great concern to you and we need to understand the nature of them. And then I can give you a penance and offer you God's forgiveness, if indeed that's the situation. There may be no sin to forgive. So, what are they about?"

"Well, they're, they're about ... well, they've got men and women in them."

"So they're not entirely surreal then?"

"I'm sorry Father. I don't know what that means."

"It means, well, actual goings on; realistic activities, if you like."

"Oh, they're realistic all right, Father."

"So, then, you can describe them to me, surely. What are they doing?"

"Well, they're not wearing any clothes. Or at least some of them aren't. And they get hold of one another."

Nolan now knew what she was coming to, and suddenly wondered how he might deal with it. "A Garden of Eden scene, so to speak. Is that what you mean?"

"Yes Father, I think so. I suppose it is, although I've never been exactly clear about the Garden of Eden. I know that Adam and Eve ate apples there and they had to watch out for snakes. And they didn't wear any clothes. But I don't suppose clothes had been invented then. - And it was all a long time ago anyway, so I don't know why I get so hot and bothered about it."

Nolan was now beginning to get a bit hot under the collar himself, and hoped she wasn't going to ask him for a more detailed explanation of the activities in the said garden.

"What do you think I can do about it, Father?"

Nolan found himself at a loss to say. It seemed to be the sort of predicament that had troubled him for much of his young life; these metaphorical allusions to things that were sinful, but you couldn't quite make enough sense of them to know why. You just knew you shouldn't do them anyway. So he'd only painted pictures of them, which had usually earned him a flogging. So now he kept quiet about them. Except for the most public one he'd ever done, which was now on display in the glen. And hadn't he enjoyed doing it? And wasn't he getting a tingle of excitement right now? A pleasurable feeling, as he listened to this young woman admitting to some similar kind of sensuality. Were they not two of a kind he asked himself.

"I hear what you're saying. I can understand your concerns. But perhaps it's not as bad as you think." Nolan was struggling to think of what to say next.

Agatha was relaxing a little now, the pulse not racing quite so rapidly. He seemed to understand. It appeared possible now that he was not going to berate her or speak harshly to her.

Nolan continued "So, they're just sort of milling around are they, the people? Not doing anything too specific." He was hoping she was not going to say they were fornicating. He wasn't sure how he would handle that. Most probably she wouldn't know about that.

"Yes Father, that sounds about right. Just wandering about they are, sometimes bumping into one another, or holding hands."

"Just holding hands - Nothing more?" Nolan felt he needed to be clear about things. He was getting the picture now, and was quite liking what he saw.

"Well, yes, and sometimes putting their arms around one another. I'm not quite sure. It's always a bit hazy. And then I wake up."

Nolan detected a rise in his own pulse rate and his breathing was a little more rapid. He needed to keep a grip on things, keep his voice steady.

"So, this...these dreams... they come upon you quite often, do they? That's how you make it sound."

"They do Father, and I cannot stop them happening."

"I don't suppose you can. When you're asleep you cannot control anything. But you haven't done any actual thing with anyone – with a boy or a man I mean – that might have given cause for these dreams, have you? "

"Oh no, Father. Definitely not. I've been up in these parts only a few weeks. I don't know any men or boys; hardly anyone, yet. And if I did, I wouldn't allow them to be... to be... well, forward with me, if you understand."

"That's good. That's how it should be. We cannot guard against our dreams, but we must keep a check on ourselves when we are awake. That's about all we can do. One day, when you're married, all this will perhaps make sense to you. Don't worry about the dreams. Pray to the Blessed Virgin for guidance. She will help you." Nolan felt himself to be an utter hypocrite as he said this. He knew nothing about marriage, except that his own parents had lived apart for almost as long as he could remember, so it couldn't be that great, although he was supposed to believe that it was. And he knew just as little about a young woman's sexual development.

A closing prayer and Agatha departed the confessional, greatly relieved, leaving Nolan himself in need of some form of relief. My word, he thought, this is a new one to me; I've never heard the like of this before. He was surprised at himself for not admonishing her, and yet pleased that he hadn't. There had been no reason to. She was still pure, simply exploring the mystery of human possibilities in her dreams, in a strange way, an innocent way, almost. And didn't he feel these same impulses himself, and hadn't he yielded to them, and wasn't he deeply worried that the priestly existence he had - with some considerable doubt- pursued, would constrain his natural desires? For how many years could he sustain that level of suppression? Not for many more, he thought. What on earth could he do about it?

The door of the confessional opened with a brief glimpse of light, then closed again. This time, in the gloom, there was a man before him. He had just found out that his wife had been born illegitimately. So had she, and had made the mistake of telling him, for which he had clouted her. He was not so much asking for forgiveness as asking had he done right or wrong. He seemed to feel that his wife was in the wrong for being born a bastard. God help me, thought Nolan, what perverted values these people hold. Am I one of them? Am I cut out for this vocation at all?

The next man in was almost in tears because he knew his young son was doing things to himself in his bed at night. Was he going to go blind? Would he go to hell? How should he correct him? Almighty God, thought Nolan, who am I to tell these people how they should live. They're all at it. Look at the size of the families. Six or eight kids at least. Ten was not uncommon; some had more than a dozen. Copulation, it seemed, was almost the national pastime. How on earth did they find time to cut turf, milk cows, dig potatoes, thatch their hovels, he wondered. And he himself had the same urges, which he'd have to suppress for the rest of his life. But, as a priest, he was supposed to tell others how they ought to behave. He'd have to examine his own position; have to try to plot something out for the future.

The dreary and troubling minutes couldn't pass quickly enough for him. When confessions ended he felt exhausted, and knew that he'd been acting as an utter hypocrite concerning the advice he'd given. His thoughts were already turning to how he might discover more about this young lady with the erotic dreams, and attempt to put her more at ease with herself, although he knew it would not end his own troubles; indeed, it might increase them. He knew who she was, where she was lodging. He needed to get her away from that detestable aunt for a while, maybe take her out for a ride in his car. And he needed to ask himself how much more of this priest's life, this terrible charade in his case, he could take, although he could see no likely end to its tortures.

## CHAPTER SEVEN

Nolan was out and about around the town. There were always things to do. He knew he ought to call in at the school (First Holy Communions, to discuss, Confirmations, that sort of thing) and examine a few of the younger kids on their catechism. That would be easy. He knew that the nuns punctuated their rote- learning by the well-established method of hammer and tongue, emphasizing their instruction with a good pummelling with the knuckles around the head to focus attention on the text. He knew all about that, he'd had plenty of it himself, so the brats would be word perfect, like a flock of well-trained parrots. Whether they understood it or not was a different issue, and one that he was not going to worry himself about right now. And baptisms; there were always those, rakes of them, a never-ending stream. Better check the diary to see who was due in next. He hated baptisms. He was always half-afraid he'd drop one of the squealing little sods into the font and he'd not be able to fish it out quickly enough and then he'd have a funeral on his hands. And, thinking of funerals, he must call in on Jonty McGarigle. There was always a close link between priest and undertaker. Coffins, graves, and the rituals associated with them had established some sort of bond. Even if he hadn't been overtly welcomed into the community, at least Jonty was always pleasant towards him. He supposed that when most of your time is spent talking to corpses you'd be glad of a chat with a live human being. Nolan accepted that he would never be able to fill the shoes of the legendary Father Tom and be everyone's friend so there was no point in trying. Just make the most of the friendship of the few that had accepted you, he always told himself. Do what you have to do and let time and custom ease you into the rhythms of the place. Perhaps. Did that really seem possible? He doubted it, but, for the moment, he must carry on.

At some point he would call in at the post office, and post yet another unnecessary letter. This would provide a chance to smile at young Agatha Nelligan, and to ask the post-mistress how she was settling in. This was just showing a bit of pastoral care, of course, for a newcomer to the community. And thinking of outsiders, there would be no harm in giving a nod to Solly Axelrod the tailor, to see if he'd obtained those clerical- collars he said he could get for less than Nolan was presently paying. Sure, you shouldn't isolate the man, he felt, just because he was Jewish. The bit of superstitious nonsense that was nailed to his door-frame could easily be ignored.

Actually, Nolan quite liked Solly. He liked him a lot. He got on better with him than with anyone else in the town. He appreciated the man's intellect and the dry Dublin wit he showed at times. They'd often have a chat about Dublin. It took both of them back to a busier, more sophisticated lifestyle than their present one. Nolan still missed it greatly. He didn't get much satisfaction from his conversations with these turf diggers, most of whom had never been more than twenty miles outside of the town in their lives, and several had never ventured beyond its boundaries, so they had little to talk about that had any relevance to him. Life in Dublin had been great. There was so much more happening there, more freedom, more opportunities. A pity he'd buried most of them by becoming a priest. How the hell had that happened? he wondered. He'd never had a strongly religious bent. It was all down to his mother's inclinations rather than his own, he thought. He should have stood up to her. But it wasn't just her. She had brothers who were priests; they visited often, and were strongly influential. Nolan liked them, found them amusing, witty, and not overtly pious. They seemed intelligent, well educated, well-travelled. They always seemed to know what they were talking about. And they never seemed to live badly either, considering they'd taken vows of poverty, amongst others. They appeared to have a good life. He was at ease with them when they dropped by. He'd a couple of friends too who'd gone through school with him, at least until he was expelled, but he'd never lost touch, and they'd entered the seminary at the same time as himself and they'd pulled each other along. A bit like being in the army, he supposed, you don't at first consider the wider implications of what effect it might have on you till long after you've signed up. So that was it. He'd more or less drifted into the clerical role. There was no way of drifting out of it, the current was too strong. And now he wasn't just trapped in The Cloth, he was also trapped in this backwater.

Solly, although he liked to talk to Nolan about Dublin and the world in general, and he seemed to know quite a bit about the world, was much more settled into the community. He was at one with most of its inhabitants, rubbed shoulders with them easily. He even attended mass on a fairly regular basis, although he sometimes had to be reminded to take his hat off as he entered the church. Many years of worshipping at a Dublin synagogue had inculcated him into praying with his head covered. Nolan was always slightly dismayed to find a Jew had been better accepted than himself, even allowing for the fact that Solly had lived in Glenowen for years, whereas he was a relative newcomer. Solly knew all the gossip, remembered the names of all of the children and when the next one was about to be born, an almost daily event, it seemed. Nolan was beginning to recognise his own shortcomings here. Perhaps he should try to be a little less lofty with the people, try to understand them more. Just acknowledge the validity of their varied existences, as Solly did.

Despite being well assimilated, Solly had avoided having a large family, which had a lot to do with why his standard of living was above that of many others despite a poor income. But in most other ways he was one of the people, whereas Nolan was not.

After half an hour of good-natured argument and light hearted banter with Solly, and having collected his collars, Nolan was back on the street again, his spirits lifted somewhat. He went into the Post Office on his surreptitious mission with yet another bit of spurious correspondence. He threw his letter on the counter, where it was stamped, and chucked into a sack by the post mistress. Nolan looked over her shoulder and through the open door to the back room to see if Agatha was about. He wanted to give her a smile, show her how friendly he could be. She was not there though, not to be seen. That was a nuisance. It would mean spending on another stamp another day. Too bad. Not to worry, he thought, going back out on to the street. Then he saw her, strolling down the street towards the post office. He noticed the jaunty swing of her hips as she walked, smiling sweetly at every one who spoke to her.

"Hello Agatha, so very nice to see you. I've just been in the Post Office. I thought you might have been in there."

"No Father, I was sent out with a couple of parcels that were needed urgently. You weren't looking for me, were you?"

"No, not for any particular reason anyway. Just thought I'd ask how you're doing. it's not easy settling into a new job when you're in a strange place."

"Oh, It's not so bad Father. I've been here a good few weeks now. I'm getting to know quite a lot of people and they're very nice to me." Nolan's mind immediately went on to the likes of Mullarkey, Murphy and others of a dubious ilk.

"Tell me," he asked, "are you finding it hard to get to and from the post office? It's a long old walk from where you're lodging."

"No Father, It's not too bad at all. It's only two or three miles. I get up early. And in the evening, it can be a pleasant stroll home, so long as it's not raining. I'm going to buy an umbrella when I've saved enough for one." Nolan considered giving Agatha the money, but he wasn't supposed to have any.

"What time do you finish in the afternoon?"

"It depends on what there is to do after the office closes. It varies a bit."

Nolan was hoping for something more specific. "I was just thinking, I drive along that road most afternoons. I'll keep a lookout for you. I don't suppose a lift would go amiss, would it?" He now saw that giving her money for an umbrella would not have been advisable; she'd be all the more likely to accept a lift in his car if it looked likely to rain. Nolan didn't go along that road any afternoon, but he would from now on, so it wasn't exactly a lie.

"That'd be great Father, if you happen to be going in my direction at that time of day. 'Tis a great car you have."

"It's my father's, said Nolan, "but he doesn't want it back, so perhaps it's as good as mine now." Nolan was never one to brag about material possessions. He'd always lived well, the family being quite middle-class. He took this for granted and was pleased with the comfort afforded him; but whilst the abject poverty of others around him scarcely troubled him, equally, he never thought about his own position. As a priest, he was living pretty much like the rest of the clergy, apart from the car, which young priests, and most of the old ones, did not possess. And he always had a few bob in his pocket. His mother sent him a cheque from time to time and he knew that his father kept her account well topped up.

Nolan knew that he would be going in Agatha's homeward direction very soon. He'd make sure he was.

## CHAPTER EIGHT

Anyone in the town who was even remotely involved in any form of trade or commerce, legitimate or otherwise, was asking himself or herself what mercantile gains might be made if this sleepy little settlement became an established place of pilgrimage, the tailor Solly Axelrod being one of them. Solly was as interested in the development of the glen as a place of pilgrimage as were most of the populace. Whilst people passing through were unlikely to place orders for clothes to be made, the odd repair job might come his way from time to time. The particularly devout pilgrim, in an excess of kneeling, might wear the knees out of his trousers and require running repairs. And they'd need them done in a hurry, so they might not argue the price if he inflated it a bit. He could also increase his small income by the sale of a few shirt collars.And studs, of course; studs always got lost when you were travelling. Whilst the armpits of a pilgrim's shirt might reek like a midden, a change of collar every couple of days would prolong its appearance at least. And underwear and hosiery might be required, all extra money. He'd look into that, see who might the best suppliers might be, and who would give him the longest credit terms.Glenowen as a place of pilgrimage could benefit them all. He could even envisage requiring bigger premises in the future.

Solly's innate shrewdness dissuaded him from taking any notice – as a rule- of Mick Mullarkey's nonsensical opinions.

Mick was stupid; Solly knew that for a fact. And as far as he could see, anyone who believed anything that Mick told them had to be a fool also. The whole Mullarkey tribe were the same, he felt, a bunch of feckless scroungers who lived off their wits and by their own rules. They added colour to the place, undoubtedly, along with the trouble they caused, but were well tolerated by one and all. Everyone knew what they were about, so were seldom taken in by them. That was what Solly loved about this community, it was warm, tolerant, all - encompassing, and he remembered how he himself had been quickly welcomed to its bosom when he'd arrived on its door-step, as it were, many years ago. But many of its inhabitants were too superstitious, too naïve, for their own good, he thought. But in this case their gullible natures, and, more importantly, the gullibility of others all over the land, might prove useful, profitable even, to those who were more astute. Solly knew that a few of them were very astute, and thought the way he did, that whatever one group might feel about divine apparitions, another set of them, in which he included himself, could make a shilling or two, reasonably honestly, just by going along with them. Just for once, maybe, the bollocks that Mick Mullarkey was forever spouting might prove useful.

Solomon looked back over his time in the town where he had become a fully integrated, well- regarded member of this close- knit collection of Catholic souls. He was completely at one with this place, where he intended to spend the rest of his life. He was also, like most of its inhabitants, inured to the semi-impoverishment most of them shared, although he was doing a little better now than he ever expected to when he first arrived, and he considered himself better-off than many. However, a little more trade all round would not be a bad thing. Not that people passing through a place would bring much business to a tailor, but if it helped others, they all might have a bit more to spend, and some of it might come his way circuitously.

Solly's trade was almost entirely local and most of these people couldn't afford to part with much money. A customer for his wares placed an order and then expected to wait awhile for it to be fulfilled, by which time he hoped to have the money to pay for it. But even repairs and alterations took a little time to be paid for. Often, when a garment was ready for collection, the man who had ordered it, having given the impression that he needed it in a hurry, sometimes left it for weeks, or even months, whilst he tried to accrue sufficient funds to pay for it. And because you were a friend of his, or an acquaintance at the very least, then he didn't expect to pay much for your skills, and thought nothing of taking a garment away with it only half paid for, and paying the remainder of the debt over the next few weeks.

The only customers who really put butter on Solly's bread were certain outsiders. They were usually avuncular men of early middle-age who came into the shop from time to time, dressed in well-made sports jackets and cavalry-twill trousers, looking for all the world like holiday-makers. They would each bring with them a fresh-faced youth in his late teens, for whom they ordered clothes to be made. They invariably came from distant parts of the country and at first Solly was surprized that they had sought him out from afar. Indeed, he was amazed that they'd even found this lonely cove on a sliver of land jutting out into the wild Atlantic. Their young charges were usually preparing to enter a college, or a seminary, or perhaps about to engage in trade or commerce, or else were about to take a trip abroad, to the States, or some other faraway place. The men always introduced these lads as their nephews and Solly had, at first, been convinced that was indeed the relationship. The 'uncles' were often extraordinarily generous towards these 'nephews', encouraging them to choose good quality worsteds and baratheas for their suits and blazers, and overcoats in the best virgin wool and cashmere, cloths that he could never sell to a local. They always paid him in cash, often in full at the time of ordering, when he'd requested only a deposit. And after bringing the youth back in for a fitting, a postal address for delivery of the garments was given. It was always at least a county away, if not entirely the far side of the country.

Solly had always been mystified as to why these boys came to the shop with their uncles and not their fathers, but after several such transactions the reason was revealed. A young man, upon completion of such a purchase, turned to the older man accompanying him and said "Thank you Father, that's very generous of you." Solly was certain that the youth had been introduced to him as the man's nephew. He saw the older man smile awkwardly and colour rise into his pale cheeks. When this happened a second time, he realized that 'Father' was being used both as a priestly title as well as a familial one. He was mildly amused to find that he, a Jew, was being financially assisted by the funds of the Catholic Church, paid towards the upkeep of offspring sired by its priests. However, Solly was by no means critical of the consequences of voluptuous indulgence. He had been guilty of gratifying the flesh outside of marriage himself, leading to a difficult situation, so he never found fault with others for succumbing to such temptations. In his own case it had brought him to this western outpost, and after initial pain and considerable shame, it had, in the long run, brought him much happiness.

His family's tailoring business was well established in Dublin, the place where he had been born. According to oral history, his forebears had, in their different generations, migrated into Russia, then slowly west through Eastern, then Western Europe into France, with one or two name- changes *en route*, and after a generation spent there, finally moved to Dublin where they all eked out a modest living.

Unfortunately for Solly, he'd got involved with a gentile girl, a devout Catholic, who was equally attracted to him. An intimate encounter had taken place on a bed of hay which cushioned the floor of a brewery dray stationed for the night under an awning in a brewer's yard in Dublin. It was the only sheltered place where he could be alone with the girl. In a short space of time, she found herself pregnant and Solly found himself on the horns of a dilemma. He was facing ostracism by his family if he didn't renounce her. On the other hand, a serious re-arrangement of his bodily parts would be carried out by her family if he didn't marry the girl forthwith. In a blind panic, Solly had decided that flight of a biblical magnitude was called for. A friend had only recently mentioned to him the existence of a remote place in The West, which attracted no visitors, as the next destination from that point of the compass was America, and the tiny town had no seaport to facilitate migration in that direction. It was, so his friend had informed him, a poor but friendly, self-contained sort of community and, best of all, there was not a tailor within forty miles. The friend had thought of starting such a business there himself but had changed his mind when the opportunity to buy an established shop at the right price in Cork had presented itself.

With quiet haste, Solly had packed the basic accoutrements of his trade –shears, needles, threads, buttons smoothing irons, and several swatches and bolts of cloth into a couple of travelling trunks, and a few clothes and personal effects into another. He took every penny he possessed from his bank account and his strongbox, and with the help of a paid carrier deserted the city.

His arrival in Glenowen did not lift his spirits. He had no trouble at all in finding premises for rent.Several shops were empty; the town was on its knees. He found a place up a side street that he felt might lend itself to the needs of a tailor. It had a decent-sized window onto the street and a small upstairs room where he could put a bed. There was a latrine in the yard out the back, and a couple of rain-water barrels. After Dublin prices the rent seemed dirt-cheap.

Solly couldn't help but reflect ruefully on the ancient hand-painted legend on the masonry above the shop door, almost obliterated now by the elements:

JOHN JUDGE

Hay & Oats

It made his recent nocturnal activity in Dublin all the more poignant, a reminder he could well do without. He would paint out that advertisement at the first opportunity, and, he hoped, replace it with his own name and trade. It was obvious that the place had stood empty for a very long time, so there would be no one requesting provender whilst he got around to that small task.

Solly had brought with him a small signboard, stating that he was S. Axelrod, Tailor. It was almost an antique. It had stood in his grandfather's shopfront in Dublin, before they'd had proper signage painted above the door of those premises. This he had placed in the window after he had washed the murky glass, along with his cloth samples and a hand-written list of the clothes he would make to a customer's requirements. He cleaned out the shop and smartened it up as best he could with the meagre savings he had, and waited for business. None came. After a week of waiting, he surmised the problem as he saw it: the shop needed a mezuzah at its entrance to bring him good fortune. He immediately wrote to a close and trusted friend in Dublin asking him to procure one for him from a Jewish firm whose address he'd forgotten, and post it to him forthwith. Ten days passed before he received the vessel, in which time he had still not seen a customer, and had barely eaten. Apart from the pressing need to preserve his money for as long as possible, there was little food to be bought Most of the inhabitants of the place grew their own potatoes and cabbage, produced their own milk, kept their own pigs and chickens… not that pieces of pig were of any use to him, even if he had been able to buy them. He managed as best he could on bread, and on mackerel bought for pennies at the quayside from the men who went out on the currachs, washed down with copious amounts of black tea.

On receiving the mezuzah, he pinned it to his doorframe, angling it in slightly at the top in the prescribed manner. This surely should improve things, he felt.

Then, in the absence of anything better to do, he decided to take in the waist of his trousers. He'd been losing weight for several weeks. Apart from being short of food, he'd little appetite for it anyway. He had been fond of the girl he'd left behind and felt terribly guilty for running away from his responsibilities and leaving her to face whatever wrath her family might inflict upon her. Every day he thought of going back, but his courage failed him. His abrupt severance from his own family and the shame he had brought upon them troubled him considerably, and his feeling that there seemed little chance of earning a living in this hospitable but impoverished community added to his woes. He didn't know what to do. He wished he'd stayed with her in Dublin and tried to make a go of it there. He continued to consider returning to Dublin, going back and chancing the consequences. Anyway, whatever he'd decide to do, he needed to make his trousers fit. A tailor with ill-fitting trousers would never attract trade.

Taking needle and thread, he went upstairs and took off his trousers, chalked a two-inch wide 'v' down from the waistband through the seat, down to the crotch, and picked up a razor blade to cut the stitching. Then he paused as a thought entered his head – if his clothes needed altering, then so might those of others. And repairs too, perhaps. He remembered his father saying that when he and Solly's grandfather first set up in business in Dublin it was repairs and alterations that had augmented the infrequent sales of new garments and had kept them going through hard times. Yes, that just might be a way forward. He ought to draw up a list of alterations and corresponding prices and place it in his window. A good idea, he would carry it out immediately. His own trousers could be altered later.

Dusting the chalk marks off the rear, he prepared to put them on again. At that moment his doorbell rang. His heart leapt at the thought of a customer. The mezuzah had worked its magic, perhaps. "I'll be with you directly," he shouted down the stairs.

Fastening the trouser-buttons and hoisting his braces over his shoulders, Solly hastened downwards. His heart now sank. He was confronted by two burly young men and one, equally large older man, behind whom was cowering a pretty young woman. Their scowling jowels made him feel like a burglar who'd entered a house and inadvertently locked the door behind himself and then been confronted by three mastiffs. Another flight, of even greater rapidity than the last one, was required. The door to the street was still ajar. Nifty footwork was needed now. Solly aimed for the exit but the footwork was not his own. The boot of the older man shot out like a lance and Solly tripped over it and found himself confronting the ancient rustic floorboards with splinters sticking in his chin. In an instant, the foot of one of the others was on the back of his neck, pinning him to the floor.

"Stay there. That's your place. You're a dog!" growled the owner of the foot.

Solly resented the comparison; the dog was one of the few animals he couldn't stand, dirty creatures, all of them. But this was not the time for discussing one's identity. He felt that he would have to let that particular insult pass, at least for the moment. Finding a way of staying alive was higher on his list of priorities.

Calloused hands hoisted him up by the throat and threw him back against a wall, his feet barely touching the floor. His heartbeat rose as rapidly as his breathing diminished. The cries of sweet Maureen, "Don't kill him, please don't," did nothing to lessen his terror.

A hefty cuff to the side of the head dropped him back to the floor. The men stood back and watched him struggling to get up; the brothers waited impatiently, saying nothing, anxious to finish him off. The silence was broken only by the girl's soft sobbing.

The father spoke: "No one here knows you. You'll not be missed. Are you going to listen to reason now, and do the decent thing, or shall we finish the job?" Solly was more than prepared to listen - to anything, let alone reason- and for as long as possible, or at least until his head cleared. Then he found words.

"If you do that, you'll be making a widow of her before she's a chance to be a bride. I know I've done wrong and I want to put things right."Then he spoke directly to Maureen. "I'm sorry I left you Maureen. I've missed you greatly. I just didn't know what to do. I was wrong, utterly wrong to have left you in the lurch like that. Will you have me back? Please say you will. We'll get by somehow. I just need a bit of luck in this place."

"She's no choice," said her father. "I'm giving neither of you any choice. You'll marry her, or you'll be washed out on the tide."

"There's no need to threaten me," said Solly. "I want to marry Maureen. I just lost my head when my family turned against me. I couldn't think straight."

They all knew that he was speaking the truth; crossing religious boundaries was always dangerous, and anyway, his demeanour was convincing. Maureen's face was beaming with happiness despite the tears streaming down her cheeks. She'd always believed he loved her, and now he was confirming that.

"Will you stay here with me Maureen? I think I could make a go of it here. My money'll hold out a little longer and I should soon have some customers. If we can't manage here, we'll go back to Dublin and start again there."

Maureen's father and brothers softened at this. They believed him. It seemed clear that he was genuinely fond of her.

"We can't help you much, but we'll do what we can," said the father. "We can find a few quid between us to give you a start. And if we're going to help, surely you can get a bit out of you own people, even if they do despise you for crossing the line."

A start was what Solly and Maureen made, and life slowly got better. Repairing and altering clothes – most often cutting down father's suits to fit smaller sons who were about to emigrate in search of better things – brought in a meagre existence, and, eventually, the plain-clothes priest trade improved their lot. Maureen did the pressing and sewed on buttons after Solly had cut and stitched the garments, and she learned from him how to make buttonholes, and so helped him there.

Whether they were married or not was never enquired about; it was generally assumed that they were, and that Solly had only left her in Dublin for a short while until he'd found premises for them. The birth of their child endeared them to the community and Father Tom baptized it, sealing their integration within the town. Ah, to be sure, there was no point in drawing attention to your Jewish roots in such a welcoming Catholic community, especially when you might now be less welcome in your own. Weren't they all worshipping the same God –more or less - after all? A surreptitious bahmitzvah could perhaps be arranged over in Dublin sometime in the future, if ever Solly could re-establish connections with his relatives. And if he didn't, he was well accepted here. Even the name 'Axelrod' had never provoked any questions. The few who might have thought about it possibly presumed some erstwhile association with mechanical engineering.

\*

Nolan having departed, Solly wandered across the road to study his shopfront from the other side of the street, with the need to improve trade very much in his mind. He was considering whether or not to spend money on having the frontage painted, and the old 'Hay & Oats' sign obscured and a new, eye-catching sign with his name and trade upon it, made to attract these hoped-for new customers. Might that be too premature, he wondered. His daydreaming was interrupted by the jovial voice of Jonty McGarigle. Jonty was always jovial when he was not at a funeral or talking to the relatives of the recently deceased. Then, he'd have the face of a sick bloodhound on him, looking sadder than the mourners themselves. Ah to be sure, wasn't it incumbent upon an undertaker to look miserable? It was part of the job, surely? People always commented on how involved he was in his work; sure, didn't he always provide a grand funeral? But off the job he could not suppress his buoyant personality.

"Top o' the morning t'ye, Solly!" cried Jonty, from across the street, angling his way over to kill the time he had on his hands. "How's trade?"

"Could be better," replied Solly, non-committal as ever. "How are things with yourself?"

"Not too bad. I'm fetching McCarthy's body into the church this evening. You knew he'd died, of course?"

Solly knew well that McCarthy had died, and was upset about it, but for the wrong reasons. McCarthy had ordered a suit from him a week ago and the cloth – an expensive navy-blue Saxony– had arrived in the post this very morning. And there was a lot of it, three and three-quarter yards. McCarthy had been a big man. Now, Solly had a length of unwanted cloth on his hands, and payment for it was required by the end of the month.

"Yes, I'd heard," he replied sadly, without expressing any form of condolence. "He'd just ordered a suit from me".

"He must have expected to live a good while longer then," said Jonty.

"Well obviously he didn't expect to die yet," said Solly, a note of sour resignation in his voice.

"What type of a suit did he order," asked Jonty.

Solly thought he detected a note of self-interest in the question, so he didn't wish to give too much away. Anyone who knew he'd an unwanted piece of cloth on his hands might try to get it on the cheap. He wished he'd kept his mouth shut.

"It's a thornproof twist" he replied, knowing that would convey nothing to Jonty.

"Yes, but what colour?" persisted Jonty.

"A greenish-brown sort of mixture," said Solly, trying not to tie himself down and knowing that he'd got a couple of lengths of that type of cloth in stock should Jonty ask to see it. That was cheaper and more readily saleable in a rural community than the expensive Saxony. "Why're you asking?"

"Oh, it's just that I'll be needing a suit myself in a couple of months. I've a wedding to go to over in Castlebar."

"I'll be happy to make you one," said Solly. "What sort of thing do you have in mind?"

"I was thinking of either a dark grey, or else a navy-blue serge."

Solly had him now. "You don't want dark grey for a wedding, Jonty. You're wearing dark clothes all the time in your job. A blue suit would be much more appropriate. But not a serge;

that's becoming too commonplace. A nice blue Saxony would be ideal for a man in your position. Mind you, I'd have to order that especially for you; I don't keep that sort of thing in stock. It's too good for the average sort of man around here."

Jonty rose to the implied compliment, as Solly knew he would.

"Perhaps you'd get me a length in to look at."

"I will. I'd be glad to." Another thought then crossed Solly's mind. Jonty was a much smaller man than McCarthy. There would be cloth left over; there would be room here for a little extra profit.

"You'll be needing a waist coat of course."

"I don't think so," replied Jonty. "I hadn't intended a waist coat."

"Ah, sure you need a waist coat for a wedding Jonty. You wouldn't be properly dressed without one. They're very much in vogue."

"You know, I suppose," said Jonty, warily. "I'll leave it to you, Solly; it's your trade after all."

The day was turning out better than Solly had earlier thought it might.

Jonty's mind then went back to a subject that had occupied it for the last few days: Mick Mullarkey's saintly apparition.

"What d'ye make of the saint on the cliff, Solly?"

"I've heard about it," said Solly, not wishing to make a definitive pronouncement on the subject.

"Sure, hasn't everyone heard about it?" replied Jonty. "They're all talking about it."

"I know they are," said Solly, not being in a hurry to open up a conversation before he'd had a chance to see where it might go, his youthful errors having taught him that caution was no bad thing.

"Will it do us any good d'ye think?"

"How do you mean," asked Solly, knowing full well what Jonty had in mind: financial good, trade.

"Well, might it make the town busier, d'ye think?"

"I don't suppose it'll do us any harm; it might bring a few more people into the place, and that mightn't be a bad thing."

"D'ye think the town could become famous, like Lourdes, for instance?"

Solly wasn't too keen on becoming involved in a discussion about the finer nuances of a faith that wasn't his own. The inhabitants of this place had been kind to him. He didn't wish to upset anyone by making an observation that might be deemed blasphemous.But he knew Jonty wasn't easily upset. You had to be made of sterner stuff than most to carry out his sort of work.

"I'd say you're jumping the gun there Jonty. Lourdes is in a league of its own. It's a big hitter; why, they've come close to reincarnation there, from what I hear. But we might get put on the spiritual tourist's path perhaps, and we could all benefit from that. Although I can't see exactly how that might affect you. Your trade seems fairly steady."

Jonty wasn't going to rise to this last comment of Solly's. He knew well enough that his profits were generally derived from someone else's loss. Not always, but mostly. On rare occasions, when someone drew his or her last breath, someone else expressed a sigh of relief, such as a wife who'd struggled for years to make ends meet because her well-off but tight-fisted husband had kept her short of funds. And if any of the Mullarkey tribe were to permanently close their lids the whole place might utter a collective sigh, or even, privately of course, a murmured 'Thanks be to God'. But the demise of any of the Mullarkeys was highly unlikely. They were a tough breed; almost immortal, it seemed.

But Jonty never liked anyone to think that he did well out of the misfortunes of others, so although he'd ideas about how he might improve his lot, he'd no intention of discussing them with Solly Axelrod, or with anyone else.

"We'll just have to wait and see, I suppose," said Jonty, and after a little more small-talk, he went on his way.

Jonty McGarigle felt sure that his line of business could be improved by the influx of pilgrims. Dying, and the dealing with it, was, as Solly had remarked, a fairly steady business. He was never going to be out of a job making coffins. But during the summer months trade always slackened, and he sometimes had to put his carpentry and masonry skills to other uses to pay his way. The very nature of pilgrimage traffic was that much of it consisted of the halt and the lame, the sick and the afflicted, apart from a few lead-swingers here and there of course, but they were in a minority. The genuinely enfeebled were likely to drop off the perch, as it were, rather suddenly. The stress of long-distance travel in search of cures, or even if only for spiritual gratification, might well bring about cessation of all one's ills, and then a box would be called for. A bit more business in that respect might provide the money for a motor van to replace the horse-drawn hearse that Jonty was always repairing. It had been good enough in its day, before the woodworm had infested its boards and the rust got into its springs; stately, even, with its ebony gloss, and gold lining. But it was finished now almost, and anyway, motor-powered hearses were the current modes of transport for the final outing. The trips over mountain roads to outlying settlements had shaken it almost to pieces, and the strain on the horses was considerable. He'd had three of them drop dead on him over the last dozen years or so as they were dragging a corpse over steep mountain passes. And if he had a motor van it would put paid to another problem. It would be too fast for Mullarkey and Dunleavy and a few other ardent wake attenders to follow him when he went out on a job. Mullarkey was the worst. If he'd heard that someone was nearing his end he'd sit around for days at a time outside Jonty's yard, waiting until he'd see the horses being backed into the shafts of the hearse. Then, when Jonty set off, he would soon become aware of Mullarkey pedalling along a hundred yards or so to the rear, keeping clear of the dust if the weather had been dry for a few days. After several miles, when the destination was reached, Jonty would go inside for the body. There would invariably be a group of thoroughly inebriated locals seated around the man or woman stretched out on the kitchen table, some of them too far gone to remember why or how they had got there. Jonty would join them for a glass or two; there was never any hurry. The horses needed a good rest anyway. A few minutes later Mullarkey would turn up and prop his old bike against the wall of the hovel, sometimes accompanied by Dunleavy or Murphy or various other misbegottens, if they'd also got wind of the death. They'd all profess to be old friends of the deceased and hang about until they were given a drink, and then another, until they were asleep on the floor with the rest of them. The next day, or even the day after, if the poitin held out, they'd slowly make their crooked way home and wait for the next such event.

Another problem with the horse-drawn hearse was that of bringing in a corpse at night. It could be done only if the sky was clear and with at least a bit of a moon to outline the way. Then, there was the nuisance of pedestrians hitching a lift. The horses would suddenly falter, as out of the dark someone would spring up onto the running- board and expect a ride to the next village, or wherever else they were going. It made the horses struggle. No wonder they dropped dead from time to time. Yes, a motor van would be a great improvement, a great asset to the business.

Jonty knew that Matt 'The Knife' Laffey, the local butcher, had a decent van, which he was looking to replace, so he said, although he'd been saying it for a long time. He too never wanted to give the impression that he'd any cash to spare. Everyone reckoned that he charged too much; he was in no hurry to confirm their beliefs. If Jonty could buy it from him cheaply enough and paint out Laffey's name, and, just as importantly, the word 'Butcher', then it might make a good enough hearse. He'd have to paint it black though; its present burgundy colour was hardly sombre enough. It was fine, no doubt, for carting a dead cow around, or a pig or two, but not a respectful shade for transporting dead humans. But that would not be a problem. Sure, Eamon McCann was a useful brush-hand, he'd do a job like that for a few shillings, he was seldom doing much else. To be sure, if this pilgrim business took off, it could put a few bob in everyone's pocket. Fair play to Mick Mullarkey; his perceptive vision might yet make the oafish lump the hero of the town.

\*

## *Two of a Kind*

Theo McNally, the schoolmaster, was another who had a strong interest in seeing Glenowen develop along commercial lines. He was not too good at the teaching game and detested it anyway. He detested too the stupid little bastards that he so badly taught, and was looking for some other way to make a living.

Maths had become his main subject, and he was at least better at that than anything else. It was widely acknowledged that he could work out the odds on a six-horse accumulator, down to the last farthing, with astonishing alacrity. But it was his love of horse racing that had led to a physical disaster in the first place, and a downturn in his fortunes generally. Which was why he was no longer in the Dublin that he loved, and had ended up in Glenowen, which he hated.

As a young man he had been tipped for a promising cricketing career and was filling in time, whilst making progress in that direction, as a sports master at a decent Dublin school. But his equine interests, and the gambling associated with them, led, quite literally, to his downfall. Whilst making his way towards Leopardstown racecourse via a string of Dublin pubs, his nose buried in a sporting chronicle, he had failed to notice an uplifted trapdoor in the pavement, which led down to a public-house cellar, and consequently he vanished instantly from view. His scream of pain, followed by muffled cursing, had startled the dray-horses, which shied and pulled forwards suddenly, causing the unsecured barrels to fall off the dray, crash to the pavement and spill beer in every direction as they rolled around, causing pandemonium the length and breadth of the street. The curses of the draymen, directed at McNally for his lack of observation, and his reciprocal oaths to them for leaving the cellar-door open, added a little local colour to the melee, especially to the cheeks of prim, middle-class young ladies who were browsing the nearby shop windows. When he was eventually hauled ignominiously from the cellar and deposited heavily on the pavement, covered in dust and cobwebs and reeking of spilled beer, still cursing loudly, it was discovered that his ankle was broken. That had terminated any aspirations of a sporting career, and eventually cost him his temporary job at the school. After applying for several teaching posts that did not require sporting ability, but asked for more intellectual acumen than he'd been blessed with, he had eventually fetched up on this God-forsaken peninsula professing to be able to teach mathematics and geography. He did at least know the difference between lines of latitude and longitude, and was good at mental arithmetic, but maths in general was another issue altogether. And he could still drive a bunch of uncouth gossoons up and down a football field by bellowing at them from the side-lines like a deranged minotaur. So he got the job. The fact that he was the only applicant might have played some part in the committee's decision

McNally's interest in promoting the area as a place of pilgrimage was two-fold. Being of a pronounced superstitious nature and a firm believer in divine intervention – he had a distant relative who claimed to have been cured of some mysterious malady at Lourdes – he was very much taken with Mick Mullarkey's assertion that the work of God in the form of Saint Patrick on the rock-face ought to lead to the Church declaring the place a holy shrine. And maybe, just maybe, miracles might continue to happen there, just as they did at Lourdes. Therefore, perhaps his shattered ankle, which the medics had given up on a long time ago, could be restored to its original condition. Although too old now to return to a sporting career should such a miracle occur, a restoration of his former mobility might open other possibilities. In short, almost anything that got him out of this place would be an improvement.

His second reason for wishing the place would become attractive to pilgrims had a more mercantile basis. He needed to make some money by means other than trying to instil knowledge, of which he didn't have any to spare, into the heads of these unkempt miscreants and hoydens who sat in front of him every day and made his life a misery.

He was hard pressed to think how a lame teacher could earn money from pilgrims visiting a religious shrine in the middle of nowhere – if, indeed, it ever became a shrine – but the germ of an idea was forming in his mind. It stemmed from his racing interests. Although the place was scores of miles from a proper racetrack, there was often horseracing of an amateur sort down on the strand, a relatively straight stretch of firm beach that ran for over a mile between two headlands. Here people, mainly tinkers, would bring their best nags from a few miles around and compete- in a somewhat unsportsmanlike way – for small prizes. Hitting one another with their whips, or leading a mare in season under the nose of a heavily-backed stallion was considered to be fair game. All that sort of entertainment made it a good family day out, especially if a bit of fisticuffs with a quid or two at stake, winner-take-all, occurred on the side-lines. The erstwhile Father Tom McGrath had usually acted as starter for the races; he was a great racing man. And his massive presence ensured that in the hurly burly of betting and boxing outright mayhem did not occur.

A favourite admonition of his was "Ye didn't ought to be doing that now," be it to an errant schoolboy or a troublesome tinker, and always said in a voice that suggested physical retribution if the offender ignored it. A book would be made and quite a bit of money would change hands. Some of it always went into McNally's pocket. He wasn't a bad judge of horseflesh, probably as good as Father Tom himself. And an even better judge of the nefarious characters that trained and bestrode the beasts. He could smell a fix from a mile away. He was often asked why he had not put money on a red- hot favourite that was bound to win. When it trailed in well down the field he would go and collect his dues from the bookmaker.

McNally knew that pilgrims were not likely to be punters, but if a shrine put the place on the map, then the settlement might thrive, a few hostelries would go up and a proper racecourse might be developed. Then he might even earn himself a few bob as a tipster, or even, if he could acquire a bit of capital, he might become a bookie himself. Whatever, surely there must be a better way of turning a shilling than standing in front of these rustic clowns, day in, day out, casting pearls before swine. He despised the lot of them.

The previous day in the classroom had been a typical one. "The square of the hypotenuse," he was explaining in Maths, "is equal to the sum of the squares of the other two sides." Donal McCormack, on the back row, daydreaming as usual, was dangerously teetering his chair at an angle of forty- five degrees on its back legs. He was adept at this. So good, in fact, that he could, momentarily, take his feet off the floor and his hands off his desk and hold the position for several seconds, without toppling over. He was so well accomplished at this lark that he had earned himself the nickname 'Simeon,' after Simeon Stylites, the ascetic of ancient times, who allegedly teetered around the top of a stone pillar for thirty- seven years. (The names of several such masochists who had achieved preposterous feats, if history could be believed, were well known to the pupils. Such painful self-denial was highly recommended by the school, and exemplars were named on a regular basis to encourage emulation.)

McCormack's skinny frame was totally obscured by the massive bulk of Paddy O'Reilly who always sat in the row in front of him. This was just as well, as McCormack was about to perform his next party trick, still leaning back in his chair, which was to extricate his semi-tumescent member from his trousers and wave it around like a wand. McCormack was inordinately proud of this organ, and justifiably so. It was hugely out of proportion to its rather frail looking owner. McCormack often whittled away the long hours of a tedious day by this diversion, and several others, such as imitating McNally's pronounced limp, with great exaggeration, whenever his back was turned. He was well-liked by the other kids for all the gratuitous entertainment he provided.

If McNally had been watching the faces of the four teen-age girls on the back row, across the aisle to the left of McCormack, he'd have seen that they were all turned a tight ninety degrees to the right in McCormack's direction, the one nearest to him sitting upright, so as not to obscure the scene for the other three, the others leaning forward by varying degrees, to gain the best possible view.

All of them had witnessed this spectacle many times before, but McCormack's member still held a magical fascination for them. They never tired of studying it in all its glory. At least it was more entertaining than anything else they had to study, and took their minds off McNally's monotonous drone.

But right now, McNally's gaze was concentrated on Paddy O'Reilly, who was conducting a transaction of his own which involved the surreptitious exchange with the boy seated next to him of a penknife for a packet of woodbines. McNally continued with what he was saying about the hypotenuse, at the same time slowly reaching out for the blackboard eraser resting on his desk. This was his favourite missile, although almost anything else, if he could lift it, might be hurled in anger. But he was a crack shot with the blackboard rubber. This derived from his cricketing days; he'd been a renowned fast bowler before he'd fallen into the pub cellar. His intent was always to land the rubber smack in the centre of the forehead, and he usually found his mark. One day it would surely take an eye out, but it hadn't happened yet. The frequency of this occurrence – it happened on a daily basis – had caused most of the lads to develop lightning reflexes. They could duck or twist with the speed of a striking snake, then the lad in the next row got it, unless he was just as fast. As the missile left McNally's hand, O'Reilly spotted the movement, and flattened his chin to his desk, thereby exposing McCormack, who took it full in the mouth, looking, momentarily, like a dog with a bone in its jaws. He immediately overbalanced and fell flat on his back, still in his chair, spitting out bits of broken teeth, and struggling urgently to return the rapidly subsiding member to its former confinement before McNally realized what he'd been up to. The four girls were doubled up in a paroxysm of hysterical laughter, almost choking in their attempts to stifle their mirth.

## Two of a Kind

McNally, still unaware of McCormack's amazing feat of entertainment and totally unconcerned that his missile had found the wrong target – he didn't believe that any boy could be an innocent victim – set off down the aisle to flog O'Reilly and his desk-mate. With all the graceful agility of a three-legged rhinoceros, he lumbered down the classroom and swiped O'Reilly and the boy next to him over their heads. All the lads had developed a strategy for dealing with this sort of warfare and therefore were not unduly troubled by it. In any case, they got as many clouts at home as at school, and dished out as many amongst themselves, so were well inured to gratuitous violence. They fell on the floor, stifling guffaws and feigning terror as they rolled around dodging McNally's ineffectual assault. "Aagh, no sir, please sir, ye'll mortalize me sir. Don't hit me again sir, I'll reform m'self, sir". Long experience had taught them that McNally couldn't kick them effectively, as his damaged ankle could not support his considerable weight if he lifted his other foot to kick. And if he bent over to swipe them his sizeable midriff got in the way, so such forays ended quickly. Soon order was restored and lessons resumed. Such boisterous melees lightened an otherwise oppressive day. Having pocketed both the penknife and the fags, McNally considered he'd done well out of it, but days such as these, and there were many of them, were grinding him down. Surely the development of the town as a place of pilgrimage would open up new possibilities. Almost anything would be better than this. And if a miracle cure could be found for his lameness, then he would be out of the place immediately.

*

Few of the glen's inhabitants had given thought as to why the appearance of a face on a rock should be that of Saint Patrick, nor as to why the copious waters flowing down the mountain, around the rock and across the road into a pool that was older than Methusulah might suddenly become charged with miraculous powers. And who was it who'd identified Saint Patrick? None other than the idioticMick Mullarkey. Whilst the community was tolerant of most of its inhabitants, glossing over their many faults and misdemeanours and trying to look the other way to avoid noticing unusual, even nefarious practises, it was generally felt that the Mullarkeys were a dubious bunch, and social interaction with them was best kept to perfunctory transactions. And yet, Mick's dogmatic assertion that the face on the rock was that of the great exterminator of serpents was starting to carry weight and, as rumours will, was beginning to run under its own steam. The ownership of the rumour was slowly slipping from the collective memory, as the possibility of monetary benefits began to assume greater importance.

Most of the glen's small population quickly developed a keen interest in the suggestion of the place becoming a shrine, and not always from an entirely mercantile perspective. The initial thoughts of the curative potential of the holy waters, overlooked by the purported face of Saint Patrick, were not exclusive to Theo McNally, who held high hopes for repairs to his ankle. But several others in the community soon developed hopes and fantasies of personal enhancement of a more cosmetic nature. Whilst they all believed that the whole world and everything in it, themselves included, was the work of the Good Lord, sure, hadn't he been a little slipshod at times?

## *Two of a Kind*

Mary Flannagan was keenly aware that she had breasts of slightly differing sizes. Not, perhaps, noticeable to the casual observer – although, as she was generously, if not equally endowed, not all observation was casual – so whenever a gaze lingered, she was never entirely sure of the reason why. The discrepancy had once been of little concern to her, until her husband had cruelly pointed the fact out to her on one of the rare occasions when he had shown interest in them. He was not considered to be what anyone might call a red-blooded sort of a man; she often wondered why she had married him. But if bathing them in the pool might rectify the imbalance, then so much the better. Better still if she had a bigger pair altogether; that would shut his big gob, when all the men were admiring them. But you couldn't ask the Good Lord for that, that would amount to vanity. But a bit of general improvement would do no harm. No difference, really, between that and having a broken ankle restored, or a hunched back straightened out. Although how she would get herself into the curative waters without the priest knowing her reason for being there was another matter. She'd have to think about that one. Perhaps she could pretend to have a bad leg and hobble for a couple of weeks on a walking stick, or walk with a stoop, whilst holding her back and feigning chronic pain. Then, in taking the waters, she could immerse her bosom at the same time, say a prayer to Saint Patrick, and emerge in a greatly enhanced condition.

The hermit, Peter Keighley, who lived in a tumble-down old cottage with his donkey and an elderly lame cow, both of which he kept in the house during winter – sure didn't they help to keep the place warm, and they were almost pets anyway – expressed an interest in the site after someone had explained its possibilities to him. Peter was a bit slow on the uptake and rarely spoke with anyone, so he'd missed out on much of the discussion that had already ensued. But when he grasped the potential that a saintly shrine might hold, his thoughts turned to the well-being of his cow. She'd been born with a deformed leg, but she was one of God's creatures, wasn't she, and would surely be entitled to benefit if miracles were to be had. She was more deserving than several people he knew, in particular, that brazen tart who was staying with Bridget Nelligan and who'd flashed her drawers at him and his donkey, frightening them both half to death. Peter knew that no priest would stand for miracles being performed on animals, nor perhaps, would half the population of the place. Whilst most of them kept animals for eating or working, they were hardly animal lovers. God had created different orders of creatures, and miracles were not to be wasted on the lower echelons, but Peter thought, nevertheless, that he'd give it a go. Perhaps he could walk her through the waters of the pool late at night, under cover of darkness, and she might drink a few mouthfuls, and he could say a prayer for her before the face on the rock. You never knew, a miracle just might occur. It would be nice for the old thing to have a bit of ease in her declining years.

All in all, most of the glen's inhabitants, for a variety of reason, were uplifted in the belief, or at least the faint hope, that in one way or another some changes were about to occur; and mostly they felt, they would be for the better.

## CHAPTER NINE

The vision in the glen, with the help of newspaper exposure, soon brought in visitors, although at first, not many of them were pilgrims. It was not so much Saint Patrick that they came to gawp at, but rather the sensual scene that surrounded him, or whichever saint it might be. Tales, mostly heavily exaggerated, had quickly spread throughout the land. Nolan's faith in the powers of permanganate of potash was not misplaced. The scene he had created with it looked convincingly like the dark stains of naturally occurring minerals that ran through the sand-coloured rock, but the form they took could not have occurred by chance. That was undeniably a scene all about the prelude to nature's most essential activity, which was always, it seemed, on everyone's mind, even the minds of those who claimed to be horrified by the very thought of it. Everyone who saw Nolan's artistic embellishments wondered how they had got there. Surely no human could have done it. They were not painted on; they were shadowy, almost as if they had oozed out of the rock and assumed their form unaided. They were like the marks left by pre-historic fauna in rocks that occasionally split open to reveal them. Although most disputed such 'evidence' from the ancient past, believing *those* to be the work of the Lord Himself, without, of course, having an explanation for why He might have done it. But would he have done this? Surely not; no, it was beyond all comprehension. The only person in the whole of the locality who had suspicions, although he couldn't quite give them form, was long John Donohoe. He didn't know why he thought Nolan might have something to do with it, but he remembered the dark brown hand that the priest had been rather furtive about, claiming that he'd slammed a door on it.

It wasn't long before someone on the other side of the country had suspicions also. Newspaper coverage, describing the figures on the rock in as much prurient detail as censorship would allow, caught the attention of Monsignor O'Flaherty, still based in Dublin, but now about to occupy the Bishopric of Erris. The name Nolan touched some faint memory deep in his brain. It was associated with the door of a latrine in a Dublin school he'd once visited. Although the parish priest he was accompanying at the time had almost taken a fit at the sight of it, and the headmaster was practically in tears at his sudden disgrace caused by such well-executed pornography, O'Flaherty, having a keen interest in art and some considerable knowledge of the subject - he even had a substantial collection of his own, about which he was somewhat secretive – had recognized an outstanding talent behind its creation, despite the obvious lewdness of the scene. He'd witnessed the flogging of the schoolboy artist and deemed it appropriate; sure, pain and suffering were good for the soul, were they not? The boy might benefit from it. But O'Flaherty was wise enough to know that it wouldn't change him. His instincts would out, and his wonderful talent, being a natural outlet for these instincts, would be exercised accordingly. Ah, sure it would be a sin almost, to suppress such creativity; it only needed to be channelled into something a little less controversial.

But still O'Flaherty groaned inwardly. If it was the same

## Two of a Kind

Padraig Nolan, and he was now a priest in Glenowen, then he was going to be a thorn in his flesh when he became bishop over in that direction. O'Flaherty made a mental calculation of roughly what age that amazingly gifted but filthy- minded young miscreant would have reached by now. It would be possible, he sadly concluded, that he would be just about old enough to have become a priest, but he couldn't have been long out of the seminary. He would not have had time to become established anywhere, would not have had many opportunities to do any serious damage. And he would not be missed if he were to be smartly moved on.

A little research soon established in O'Flaherty's mind, to his great dismay, that it probably was the same Nolan. Therefore, swift and forceful action would be necessary if future embarrassment at the very least, and outright scandal at worst, were to be avoided.

*

The inhabitants of Glenowen were glad to notice strangers visiting their little community, the pace of life seemed to be picking up a bit. Although mostly hale and hearty, in rude health, they all made enquiries about the likelihood of the place being a shrine with miraculous curative powers. The answers they received were varied as there was no endorsement of Mick Mullarkey's vision of divine adornment of a local rock face by anyone associated with the Church. O'Flaherty had quickly sent a missive to Nolan, telling him, in fairly plain language, to keep his mouth shut. However, noting the increase in trade for whatever small amounts of goods and services the township could produce, those with any kind of business interest told the visitors that they thought something miraculous had occurred and directed them to the part of the glen where the statue – as they now described it – of a holy figure could be found. (It was, since Nolan's handiwork had been applied to it, no longer referred to as Saint Patrick.) Although the weather had been mostly good since he had wielded his brush, the Garden of Eden was looking a little faded now, but still erotic enough to stimulate the imaginations of many, especially those who had little 'hands-on' experience of such matters and would be glad of any sort of stimulation. And when it would finally be obliterated by the elements, the vaguely anthropomorphic shape of that lump of rock would remain. It was hoped by most that the reputation of Glenowen as a place of pilgrimage would endure, flourish even, as not only was there money to be made out of it, but the mingling of newcomers with the established inhabitants might make life more interesting. Those seeking a wife or husband felt they might now have greater choice than before, and in that respect Glenowen might even give Lisdoonvarna some competition as a marriage centre. Marriage and miracles together in the one town would definitely be a money- spinner. The place might eventually outdistance even Knock and Croagh Patrick as a focus of pilgrimage. In any case, the conversations alone they had with these strangers were interesting. It took them out of their habitual discourse, the same old saws, the hackneyed discussions about trivial issues. The visitors often dressed differently, expressed slightly unusual points of view. Some came from as far afield as Cork or even Dublin and seemed more worldly wise, a little more sophisticated perhaps, less reserved, more outgoing. A tiny flutter of excitement was sometimes felt when a stranger engaged a local of the opposite sex in conversation, especially if that visitor were a city-dweller and had a somewhat prosperous look about them. It was as if they might offer a conduit to another place, to a different way of life.

Many people suddenly acquired proficiencies of which they'd previously been unaware. The blacksmith found he could do certain kinds of emergency work on motor vehicles, providing it wasn't the engines themselves giving trouble, but the occasional job of bolting together bits and pieces that were at risk of parting company, having been badly rattled over the rough roads, was well within his grasp. And of course, there were more horses requiring shoes. He was also asked to replace springs on pony-traps. Others snatched at the chance to mend punctures in bicycle tyres. Walking-sticks were made by the less skilled of the population and sold cheaply, and crutches repaired. Boots and shoes, holed by walking miles on the stony roads, were roughly repaired by the local self-taught cobbler, who now had a rudimentary sign placed outside his house which suggested that he was part of a long-established family business.

*

As a slight increase in prosperity began to make itself felt throughout the settlement a sense of pride amongst its inhabitants started to evolve. People held their heads higher. They were more ready to converse, to answer questions, to give directions or offer advice. They felt slightly more important than they ever did before. Even the meekest had more to say for themselves, having been, if only for a moment, put in a superior position by a visitor asking his way to 'the shrine' or if there was a better class of hotel where he might rest, or somewhere where he might at least get his clothes washed. Slowly but perceptibly, the whole place began to thrive. The better-off in the community even talked about getting electricity put into their houses if trade continued to improve. Unfortunately for Nolan, none of this was attributed to him, even though the local economy was doing even better now than when the legendary Tom McGrath had been the priest in charge. And what was worse, as far as Nolan was concerned, was that if anyone was to get the credit for any of this, it seemed likely to be the loud-mouthed fantasist Mick Mullarkey.

# CHAPTER TEN

Not everyone was pleased with the burgeoning growth of the town. Garda Dan Doyle for one, who now had his work cut out because of the problems often thrown up by some of the anonymous travellers. Not all of the pilgrims ostensibly seeking restoration were as lame as they purported to be. An overdose of whiskey could have amazing restorative effects on some of them, causing them to stand firmly on two good legs and crack a skull or two with their now superfluous crutches before he could get in and crack theirs with his baton. And Nolan himself was finding drawbacks to the town's increasing prosperity. He was now getting far more confessions than he cared to listen to, as more sins were being committed than before. People who were a long way from home often took advantage of their anonymity, and got up to tricks they might not have dared in their own communities. And weren't some of the women glad of it, he'd noticed, although they always tried to play down any encouragement they might have given to a would-be seducer when they were trying to explain to him, euphemistically of course, what had brought them into the confessional. Sure, you didn't come there to say you'd been sinned against. Nolan wasn't going to fall for that one. So, he made them squirm a bit before he forgave their indiscretions. He liked to finish confessions early on a Saturday evening, as Sunday was a long day for him, what with two Masses in the morning and then the evening service, and mostly a baptism or two in between, so he could have done without this increase in the sin rate.

Peter Keighley the hermit was greatly troubled by this influx of foreigners, as he called them, even if they'd travelled from only twenty miles away. They had low morals, he declared, having found one of them relieving himself behind the stone wall enclosing his paddock, and then having the audacity to wipe his arse with a couple of handfuls of Peter's newly scythed hay, drying in the sunshine. All the while telling Keighley to piss off and stop looking at him like a pervert whilst he was about his ablutions. His opinion of outsiders with loose living standards had begun with his view of Agatha Nelligan's nether regions as she'd careered past him on her aunt's bike, and he knew she wasn't a local. So all visitors he viewed with suspicion, especially if they were the female sex. In any case, he felt that the extra footfall past his crumbling cottage was unsettling for his cow and his ass.

But all in all, things were looking up for most of the locals. Solly Axelrod sold a few pairs of socks and underpants each week that he wouldn't have sold otherwise, as well as a few starched collars and collar-studs, as the pilgrims felt they had at least to look clean, and he made a bob or two now and then patching up trousers whose occupants had been a mite too enthusiastic in their crawling around the holy rock on their knees whilst praying for some miracle or other to be worked upon them. He'd even been given an order for a suit to be made and it paid for in full, with the instruction that it be posted to an address in Kerry.

The need of an undertaker increased significantly, so Jonty McGarrigle did quite well out of the pilgrim business. Although some of the visitors were simply better-off people with time on their hands, tourists really, with a prurient interest in what the newspapers said about the so-called shrine and its rapidly fading embellishments, there were many people who genuinely sought divine intervention for conditions the medical profession had long given up on. What with their overall frailty and the strain of travelling it was hardly surprising that some of them passed on to the graveyard instead of receiving a cure. They might have lasted longer if they'd stayed at home. Or they could perhaps have done better if they'd gone to one of the more established shrines. Or, if they could have afforded it, travelled to Lourdes, the creme de la crème of miracle-working, where a cure could almost be taken for granted. Glenowen was new to the restoration game, and not yet too good at it. The miraculous power of the saint-shaped monolith seemed a bit feeble just now. Peter Keighly had led his pet cow on a halter past the pool in the middle of the night and had managed to get her to dip the hoof of the lame leg into the water, whilst he uttered a prayer to Saint Patrick. But then she panicked, no doubt thinking he might be trying to drown her. She purged violently and made off down the road, dragging Peter behind her, desperately hanging onto the rope, and trying to avert his face from her rear end, but certain that she must be cured as he'd never known her move so fast. It was only when daylight came that he saw that her leg was as crooked as ever. He resolved to give it another try, when he might get her to stand in the pool for a while and then lead her across the road to gaze upon the holy figure. He'd need a well- moonlit night for that though; he wasn't too sure just how well she could see in the dark.

The following night Mary Flanagan left her bed, her husband Patsy lying there in a drunken stupor, having had too much of the hard stuff taken on top of a gallon of stout at Darcy O'Neill's place. She made her way tentatively towards the pool, stopping every few yards to listen in case anyone else was making surreptitious progress in the same direction, in search of some kind of cosmetic enhancement similar to that for which she was hoping. On reaching the pool, which she could discern only faintly by the glimmer of moonlight on the water, she listened again. Hearing nothing out of the ordinary, she stripped to the waist, and, lying face down at the pool's edge, like Narcissus worshipping his own reflection, she trailed her un-matching breasts in the water. After the first few breathtakingly cold moments she found she quite liked the experience and soon found that her nipples were protuberant, a sensation she had not experienced for a long while. Very pleasant, she thought, giving her breasts a rub and resolving to visit the pool again when her man came home drunk, which was more often than not.

She then noticed that her knees were very damp; from the dew on the grass, she thought at first. Then an unpleasant smell assailed her nostrils. She had knelt in a substantial cow-pat deposited by Keighley's fearful cow the night before. Whilst overhanging the pool in order to bathe her bosom, and dwelling on the pleasure it brought, she hadn't thought about where she was placing her knees. She washed her legs as best she could with as much of the sacred water as her hands could cup, made her way home, and quickly re-entered the marital bed, Patsy still being comatose.

She had not been long in bed and was just dozing off to sleep when Patsy started to come round, the soporific effects of the stout and whiskey he had consumed being unequal to the rousing stench of dung; Mary had not, in the dark, made a success of cleaning herself. The holy water was not yet up to removing cow-dung effectively.

Propping himself up on one elbow, Patsy sniffed the air like a foxhound finding a scent. Becoming increasingly concerned for his well-being, he threw back the sheets, climbed unsteadily out of bed and searched the bedside table for candle and matches. After burning his fingers a couple of times, and very nearly setting fire to the tattered curtains, he finally got a match to the candle and created a flame, enough to reveal that the bed was badly stained. This was an awkwardly embarrassing situation, one for which he took himself to be the cause. "By Christ, I'll have no more o' that feckin' stout of O'Neill's; it's upset me stomach. I'll have to stick to whiskey in future."

And with that, he took himself outside in the darkness to the water-butt and began sluicing himself down with cold water, gasping and shivering the while, and cursing O'Neill.

Mary, upon realizing that she had not cleaned her legs sufficiently at the pool, quickly rolled up the sheets and wiped her legs with them, before throwing them out of the window on the opposite side of the house to where Patsy was conducting his ablutions, to be dealt with later, in daylight. Patsy had often called her a dirty cow and she'd no intentions of lending substance to his cruel claims, the drunken good for nothing. In any case, she had quickly grasped the potential benefit in letting him think he'd befouled himself, as it might give her the whip hand in any future debates they might have concerning his drinking habits. She had clean sheets on the bed by the time Patsy returned, for which, to her amazement, he offered her his thanks and apologies.

*

Whilst McGarrigle the undertaker was doing well out of the increase in corpses and was secretly hoping that the place might continue to thrive as a shrine, but without being too successful in any curative way of course, long John Donohoe was hoping for exactly the opposite. The extra dying was causing a great deal of extra digging for him and he was starting to wonder if the strain of it all might hasten his own end. He'd now little time for the much easier caretaking duties he had previously carried out in and around the church; he was mostly digging graves. He now had a constantly aching back and blistered hands, felt utterly exhausted and was fed-up with women all over the place asking him where his erstwhile energy had gone. If things continued at this rate, he'd soon be in need of divine assistance himself.

He was somewhat aggrieved to find that Mcgarrigle was doing so well out of it whilst he was nearly killing himself, and resolved to take him to task about finding a fairer way of distributing financial gains, although he knew that McGarrigle, having made a down payment to Matt Laffey for his van, which he'd had re-painted (although the word 'BUTCHER' could still be faintly discerned on its sides by the more observant) would plead poverty on account of this debt, which he'd agreed with Laffey to pay off in the next six months. And whilst McGarrigle had let Joe Murphy have his hearse on the promise of eventual payment for it when Joe had converted it into a jaunting car, in which he supposed he was going to take visitors around the area to look at 'places of interest', it would be a long time before that payment would be collected. Joe had never driven a horse-drawn carriage in his life and would probably terrify his passengers rather than entrance them with scenic outings. He had committed himself to buying the hearse only because Colm Mullarkey had encouraged him to set himself up in business as a jarvey. And that encouragement had come about because McGarrigle had offered Mullarkey a couple of quid if he could find him a gullible buyer for his worthless vehicle. Until then, Joe had contented himself with the idea of renting towels to pilgrims emerging from the holy waters of the pool, an enterprise that might just have been within his capabilities. At least it would have been safer for all concerned than following Mullarkey's advice to become a carriage driver.

Life had become easier for Jonty McGarrigle once he'd learned how to drive Laffey's van. This skill had taken him only a couple of weeks to acquire, at the cost of a dead sheep (and a punch on the nose from its disgruntled owner, who'd had to sell the carcass to Laffey at a much -reduced price, even though he'd argued that Laffey had been saved the trouble of killing it), a demolished wall, and a replacement rear fender when he'd failed to set the hand-brake whilst parking on a slope. Jonty now got his corpses into his parlour without fear of his horses dropping dead on a long slog over the mountains, and it was taking him nowhere near so long to bring them in from outlying places. And, best of all, Mullarkey, Dunleavy and the rest of the wake crashers couldn't follow him out on their bikes when he'd a collection to make.

Darcy O'Neill was also pleased with the increase in trade. His public house was the busiest it had ever been. With the erstwhile Father Tom now established in Cork, he was selling a lot more whiskey, Father Tom's potent poitin now laying out the inhabitants of Cork. The one downside though was that Colm Mullarkey almost lived in the pub now, as there were so many visitors who were naïve enough to be taken in by his tales of various miracles whilst he talked a drink out of them. That meant that he usually finished up dead drunk on the floor each night and Darcy had to haul him across to the door and drop him down the steps into the darkness, where he snored loudly, until he was sober enough to get back up onto his feet and stagger home.

## CHAPTER ELEVEN

One mid-week afternoon Nolan was behind the wheel, cruising along, watching out for stray sheep on the road. He didn't want any dents in his car. He was also keeping his eyes open for Agatha Nelligan. He spotted two people up ahead, male and female. As he drew nearer, he could see that it was Agatha and Mick Mullarkey. He didn't want to have to offer that cocky young bastard a lift, but he supposed he'd have to pick up both of them and drop her outside her aunt's cottage, just to get her away from Mick's sphere of influence. As he pulled up, he realized that they were not walking, but merely engaged in conversation. He wondered what sort of rubbish Mick would be pouring into her head and what untoward suggestions he might be making to her.

"Hello Father," said Mick, cheerfully, opening the passenger door so that he could converse with the priest.

"Hello Agatha; can I give you a lift? How're you doing Mick?"

"No thanks, Father," said Mick, certain that he was included in the offer. "I'm going the other way. I was just talking with Agatha. She can go wit' you."

Nolan seethed. The cheeky sod had taken over the situation again. Didn't he despise the lout!

"Jump in Agatha," said Mick. Nolan could hardly believe his luck. He'd expected Mullarkey to get in just for the ride, regardless of which way he was intending to go.

Agatha settled herself into the seat. The car was small and

Nolan accidentally nudged her knee as he searched for the awkward gears. She moved her legs away and apologized for getting them in his way. Nolan didn't need an apology; he loved the brief, titillating touch.

"I'm not used to travelling in cars, Father. Its lovely, isn't it?" She took in the smell of the leather seats, the faint whiff of oil and petrol coming in from Nolan's half- opened window. She studied the gauges on the dashboard, thinking how clever a driver must have to be to make sense of them. Nolan's mind, meanwhile, was otherwise occupied, trying to come up with a vaguely acceptable reason to detain her for a while.

Just as they were approaching the entrance to the lane leading to Aunt Bridget's house, Nolan asked "Have you seen the new shrine they've set up outside the next village, Agatha?"

"No Father. I've not been to that place yet; I've had no reason to go there."

"I'll take you to have a look, if you like. You've a few minutes to spare, haven't you?" He knew she must have; he'd saved her quite a bit of time by picking her up.

"I'd love to Father. Is it far? I don't want to be putting you out of your way."

"No, less than a couple of miles."

They soon pulled up onto the grass and heather adjacent to the little shrine. It was no more than a small hollow excavated in the ground, where a natural spring bubbled through. A sizeable statue that was supposed to represent the Virgin Mary had been situated alongside it, as well as a sign in Gaelic which read 'Mary Immaculate.' It had been there a couple of years, certainly longer than Nolan had been in the parish. It had been described to him as 'the new shrine' because some other had occupied the spot previously. What had happened to that one he had not the faintest idea, nor did he care, but if this one was considered an improvement the last one must have been less than mediocre. His artist's eye told him that the virgin was crudely carved and the proportions were not right. But the villagers were pleased with it, it seemed. Sure, what did it matter?

"It's lovely Father," said Agatha, not at all sure that it was. There was something unappealing about it, she felt. There was nothing more to say. There was an awkward silence for a moment, the road empty, the village, which she wouldn't have minded seeing, stood a good half mile further on. She could just make out the first houses on its edge.

"Will we be going now Father? Aunt Bridget might be getting the tea ready and wondering where I am." She felt uneasy saying this, as she knew he'd done her a kindness by picking her up. They got back into the car. Nolan did not start the engine immediately.

"Agatha," he said, there's no need to always address me as 'Father,' unless we're in church, of course. You can call me Padraig, if you like."

"Oh, I couldn't do that, Father. I'd be embarrassed to speak to you like that."

"Why not? I've not yet got used to the title myself. After all, I'm only recently ordained. And I'm only a few years older than you are. Quite a few of the older people, the one's I've come to know quite well, they always call me Padraig. Try it. Call me Padraig."

Agatha blushed. She could feel the blood rush to her cheeks. And she also needed to use a lavatory. She'd been about to disappear behind a rock when she'd been accosted by Mullarkey. It was those cups of tea she had drunk before leaving the office. It was a long walk home when you'd been drinking tea. "All right Father... I mean Padraig." She said shyly. "There, I've said it. Padraig. 'Tis a lovely name." She glowed with a strange warmth. She felt it suffusing her whole body. They had somehow established a different relationship now. She felt that they could be friends. That would be wonderful. The thought boosted her, put her on a higher plane somehow. She glowed even more, the blush suffusing her cheeks and making her even more attractive to Nolan.

"We'll go now, "said Nolan, sensing Agatha's unease. He'd soon see her again.

*

Nolan was greatly troubled by the fact that although the local economy was picking up a bit, and this might, in part be attributable to his embellishment of Mick Mullarkey's apparition, he could claim no hand in it. In fact, he had to do his best to conceal his part in it. It seemed, somehow, unfair. He was no better thought of now than when he had first arrived at the place. True, many of the women still got on well with him- some of them very well indeed- and would lie to others about how close they'd been with him. But that didn't endear him to the menfolk, who were now more than a little suspicious of him. He wished that he was out of the place. He knew he would never fit in. Even the woman who were pleasant to him didn't really help. All their kindly attention only increased his sexual frustration, and therefore his feeling of being trapped. If he wasn't garbed as a priest, he could be having a much better time of it all round. And he would then have been able to openly pursue this absolute darling of a girl, the lovely flame- haired Agatha. God Almighty; what a situation he was in. Why had he let this happen to him, he wondered? More to the point, how could he ever get out of it? He could not, it seemed. A tortured existence lay ahead of him.

## CHAPTER TWELVE

Nolan was by now absolutely certain that he was in the wrong vocation. The rubbish he spouted from the pulpit each Sunday was no more convincing to his own ears than those of his congregation. And he was not entirely sure that the sermons of any other priests were any more worthwhile than his own, although, as far as he could tell, they at least were sincere about what they preached. No, he was not the man for the job he was doing. He had to admit it. And, more than just facing that fact, he had to find a way of dealing with it. This hopeless charade could not go on much longer. He'd have to abandon his vows and somehow disappear. But his connections with Agatha made that seem impossible. He'd no intentions of abandoning the seemingly insurmountable idea of forming a relationship with her. He would have to find a way of housing and supporting at least himself, and preferably both of them, if he was ever to realize that wild dream. And it was just a dream, he knew it was. Agatha had never given him the slightest suggestion that she wanted him as a close friend; not even a hint of it. His hopes had no foundations, not yet anyway. And if he pursued her openly, expressed his longings for her, what might she do? She'd probably say that he was a bad priest with whom she wanted nothing more to do. That would be an awful blow. But if he was to leave the priesthood anyway, and he knew he must, then perhaps she'd come with him. He needed to get to know her better. The thought then struck him: wasn't

Agatha one of these poor people, these struggling people, who, up to now he'd looked down on? And yet to him she was flawless. Her naïve simplicity, her natural, unsophisticated charm attracted him just as much as her physical presence. There was something about her that was far deeper, more sincere than the upper-class hubris of the well- heeled, well-dressed, expensively perfumed Dublin women he had known. Perhaps he needed to adjust his perspective.

If he could leave, and hopefully leave with Agatha, how would he support them both? She would ask for little. She been used to living almost off nothing, like many of them here, that much was obvious. He supposed he could rough it a bit, for a while, anyway. Not that he ever had. He asked himself what it was that he most liked doing. What was he able to do that might earn him a meagre living? And preferably something which would interest him. At first nothing came to mind. He was not suited to heavy physical exertion; he was not the strongest of men. Intellectually, whilst he was no dunce, he'd never been an outstanding academic, so a career in that direction was out of the question. In any case, time had slipped by, re-training wouldn't be easy. What was he good at? The answer, he knew, in fact the only answer, was art. He could draw and paint almost anything. He'd always been able to do that, effortlessly it seemed. He was a natural. He'd been able to draw an instantly recognizable picture of another human being since he was a young schoolboy. And hadn't the school – at first anyway – encouraged him, told him that he had real talent and an original style. It was just that he found the landscapes and buildings and ships they took him out to sketch far too easy, not stimulating. He wanted to capture Life, to put vivacity on the canvas, not inanimate things. So he'd drifted off sometimes – too many times - into a reverie and then found he'd embellished his canvas with bits of scenes he held in his head: scenes which were always more exciting than those he'd been instructed to reproduce, and that always gave him a stirring in the loins; and if he didn't over-paint them quickly enough, usually earned him a flogging. And yes, that was the other thing he loved, the sensation in the loins. And that was brought about by looking at women, talking to women, and then drawing pictures of them. Yes, he liked women, liked their coquettish ways, their perfume, their bodily scents. When safely alone, he liked to draw pictures of them in beguiling poses he envisaged, and some of the poses could stretch the imagination quite a bit, and they were frequently without clothes. That was not what a priest ought to do, it was totally contrary to the Church's teachings. But he liked doing it, and probably always would. He'd have to leave the Church. But the life of an artist was a precarious one; few of them made a proper living out of it. You'd need a very understanding woman behind you, if you were lucky enough to have one at all.

He'd never had any sexual congress with a woman, never laid hands on one. That was what he would have liked. That's what he was starved of. But it would have to be the right woman; not any woman would do. The thought haunted him: that the thing he wanted most, to lie in a clean bed with a warm-hearted, free-spirited woman would most likely be an experience always denied to him. He'd made a monumental blunder in thinking that he could ever be a priest. Both the flesh and the spirit were too week for that.Yet priest, in appearance and title at least, was what he was. He had been ordained a priest. That awful inescapable truth bore down on him. The improvidence of youth and the thrashings he'd had for the lewd content of some of his early pictures had somehow driven him into this cul-de-sac from which there seemed no escape. He considered how he could gratify his carnal desires and still remain a priest. Was it possible? He knew that in the Dublin he'd so recently left behind there were women who gave men pleasure in exchange for money. He'd seen them, even been approached by one once, with a smile and a twinkle in her eye, until she had seen the cleric's collar beneath his scarf and altered her greeting. She had been attractive too. Yes, he could go there, allow himself to be thus accosted, and afterwards make a confession, anonymously, of course, at a city church, and take the invective the priest would heap upon him. And that little dalliance might suffice, until the next time, and then the next. What a life; what an awful existence that would be. He reflected on this for days and knew that was not what he wanted. He wanted to share himself with someone, not buy a part of her for a few brief moments and then fade away into the night with the same detachment you'd have for a pint of stout; pay for it, knock it back and say good-night to the barman. No, he wanted-needed even- a true relationship, a warm, sexual union, but, more importantly, a loving relationship, if that were possible. It seemed impossible, yet not unreasonable. But somehow, he would have to leave the Church. And that, apparently, was completely out of the question. The vows he'd taken could not be broken. He'd never heard of any priest leaving, or being told to leave the church. It just did not happen. Although he knew he was a failure as a priest and had thoughts and desires a priest shouldn't have, there was one thing he could not do; he could not break his vow. He wished that the Church would throw him out, get rid of him, but he'd never heard of such a thing. The Church looked after its own. Even its disreputable own.

It had become obvious from what he had seen and heard around him, especially from the confessions that were made to him, that most people were like him, had the same needs. Love and sex, it seemed were the drivers of human activity. But they were all too often separate entities. If you could combine both in a single relationship it would be wonderful. And if you could also do something by way of earning an honest living – and his present position was far from being an honest one – something that did not involve telling others how they should live, or hearing them confess to things they didn't ought to feel bad about – wouldn't that be better? He had started to hate listening to penitents telling him about what should remain known only to themselves, and then make a pronouncement on their 'sins', as if he were better than them. But that was his job. That's what they came to him for, however reluctantly. No, he needed some way of life where you just mixed with the crowd and stopped deceiving yourself that you had a reason for being apart from it, stopped thinking you were better than the rest, or even that you ought to be better. For too long he had looked down upon them, when he saw now it was himself who required scrutiny. How much better it would be if you could live and love and paint, for instance, and be the way your god had made you, without feeling guilty about it, wouldn't that be superb?

## CHAPTER THIRTEEN

"Agatha, I think Father Nolan is looking for you," said Miss Cronin, with more than a hint of irritation in her voice. The priest had just drawn up outside the post office in his car. It was still quite a few minutes before closing time, but far too late for him to have any chance of catching the day's mail. Everything was bagged up and ready to go. Nolan had nothing to post; he'd been in three hours earlier and attended to that. As well as throwing a smile in Agatha's direction. The post mistress, Miss Cronin, knew what his errand this time was likely to be. It was the third time in less than a fortnight that he'd called in towards the end of the day to offer Agatha a lift home. It was becoming something of a nuisance to Miss Cronin as Agatha usually worked on for longer than she was officially required to. She double checked the day's entries in the ledgers, re-stocked the shelves with various items of stationary, cashed up the till, tidied things away. She ensured that everything was in its place for the following day. It all made life easier for Miss Cronin.

Nolan always made it clear that he was prepared to wait for Agatha to finish her duties, but he distracted her whilst he was waiting. Miss Cronin wouldn't stand for that; she didn't want any mistakes to be made. So she let her leave early, it was safer that way. But it did not suit her style of management. She believed in getting every ounce of labour out of anyone who worked for her. And Miss Cronin was one of the few women who did not care for Nolan's form of *bon homme*. He seemed to her to be too forward – with women anyway, not so with men. She'd noticed that. He tended to be more cautious with men, less likely to become involved with them. With women he would chat easily, never being short of a word and always trying to elicit an opinion or point of view from them, as if trying to find out where they stood on any topic of interest. Perhaps that was why several of them were attracted to him. He talked at length with most women, especially with those of his own age or just a little older, and with obvious sincerity. He was not so good with the old ones, and Miss Cronin seemed as if she'd been born old. She was hatchet faced, set in her ways, and distrusted men. They were best left alone. So Nolan only politely paid her the time of day, there was never any meaningful discourse. But she couldn't deny a priest his opportunity to carry out a charitable duty, even if she did think that there was something other than charity connected with these end of day visits. In any case, Agatha was a good worker, always in before time in a morning, always thoroughly efficient in whatever she did, and quick to learn. Always polite to everyone on the occasions when she had to stand behind the counter, methodical and industrious. Miss Cronin couldn't fault her. She would have to put up with the minor irritation of Nolan, and that, she felt, was not Agatha's fault.

Agatha herself was embarrassed by Nolan's calling for her, despite the delight of riding in his car and chatting with him amicably. They were becoming friends now: she loved his company. She knew that Miss Cronin did not like her early departures, so she tried not to leave any task unfinished when she left for home. When he didn't call, she'd work maybe half an hour longer than she needed to, but she didn't mind that. Even at the end of the afternoon there was more happening in the sleepy little township of Glenowen than around Aunt Bridget's house, a good two miles at least outside of the town and in the middle of nowhere it seemed. Even now, in summer, where her aunt lived was an almost silent place. Agatha was not looking forward to the long walk home in winter. It would be total darkness all the way. That would be when she'd really be glad of a lift from someone, anyone really. But it would be nice if the someone was Padraig Nolan. She was getting to like him a lot. He had absolutely no similarity to any other priest she had met, nor indeed, to any other man. He'd make a great walking-out-friend; sure, it was a pity he was a priest.

Agatha collected her coat. She'd already changed her office shoes for stouter footwear. She thanked Miss Cronin for letting her go early, and thanked Nolan for his offer of a ride home as she brushed closely past him, he holding open the door of the post office, but not too widely. He then opened the car door for her to get inside. At that moment old Mrs Leahy came panting by, carrying two heavy-looking bags. "Good evening, Father," she gasped, "how are ye? Oh, hello, Agatha."

"Excellent, thank you, and how's yourself Mrs Leahy?" Nolan knew from boring experience the Mrs Leahy was a great talker – although what she had to say was never worth listening to – and was hard to escape from if you let her get started. He didn't want to waste any time. It was bad luck that she'd turned up just now. Before she could open up one of her interminable conversations, full of empty digressions, Nolan forestalled her. "I was just taking Agatha home," he said quickly. "She has an awful long way to walk otherwise."

Mrs Leahy wasn't too concerned about Agatha's difficulties, or for that matter, anyone else's. "Oh, that's a shame," she said. "I was just about to ask her if she'd mind giving me a bit of a carry with one of these bags. They're fierce heavy. The rheumatics is getting into me shoulders now and I'm finding it terrible hard to lift things."

Nolan knew that she hadn't even noticed Agatha until after she'd spoken to him, so it was himself and the car that she was after. That was no doubt why she was out of breath; she'd hurried to catch up with him when she'd spotted the car and before he had time to get back into it. Agatha wanted to offer assistance but equally she didn't want to keep the priest waiting. Nolan didn't want to wait either; sure, he was a priest wasn't he, not a cabman, and he'd other things on his mind, although they were not of a priestly nature. Leahy should have thought of her transport problems before she'd bought whatever it was she'd got in the bags; ,potatoes, most likely, and you didn't have to buy two big bags of them, surely, on the same day.

This was where Nolan differed from the erstwhile Father Tom, and was one of the reasons why he'd not a hope of ever filling 'Big Tom' McGrath's shoes. Father McGrath would have thrown anyone's bags into his car before they'd had time to ask for help and would have delivered them home, talking to them the whole way and not letting them get a word in edgeways; then put them out promptly, as he'd always something else to attend to, some deal or other. Nolan found himself being coerced into lending reluctant assistance.

"I'm going in your direction Mrs Leahy. Put your stuff in the car and get in. I'll drop you at your house." As she lived just beyond the edge of town it would take only a couple of minutes to get her out of the way, but he'd have to stop her from talking or they'd be there for an hour.

Mrs Leahy was effusive in her thanks as she disembarked, a prelude only to a pointless conversation. Nolan pre-empted her: "Agatha, would you take Mrs Leahy's bags and run them up to her door?" Agatha did so with alacrity, even though the manner in which Mrs Leahy had hoisted them out of the car – the two of them in one hand – suggested that her rheumatism had miraculously diminished significantly in the last couple of minutes. She'd set them on the ground in preparation for her intended discourse but her anchorage had been whisked swiftly away and now stood on her doorstep, much to her chagrin. Nolan's gratuitous revving of the car engine unnerved her somewhat, and he heightened the sense of urgency by shouting through the open car door, "Be as quick as you can Agatha or you'll be late home."

With bad grace and a sour look on her face, Mrs Leahy shuffled up her path to join her bags, asking herself why Nolan should be wasting his time with that trollop; surely *her* young legs didn't require four-wheeled assistance. Agatha returned to her seat at Nolan's side with a renewed sense of anticipation. A slight shiver of excitement quivered through her young body.

They were away now, clear of the town. "Watch out!" shouted Agatha. "There's Keighley with his ass." He was wandering all over the road. It was impossible to guess his intended direction, if indeed he knew himself. Nolan made a mental note to slow down a bit, he was becoming a little agitated. There was no real need to hurry. Although Mrs. Leahy had wasted a couple of Nolan's precious minutes, Agatha was still a long way ahead of her usual time of arrival at Aunt Bridget's. There was still time enough for a short stop. But he would have to think of a reason. His mind searched for one.

"Have you seen the trout in this stream?" he asked suddenly. "They're wondrous."

"Which stream?" she asked, surprised by his out-of-the-blue question which seemed to have no relevance to either of them.

"This little stream that is running alongside of us now; just off the road there."

"Sure, that's hardly a stream at all; I could jump right over it. I'm sure there are no trout in that. It's barely a foot deep." She blushed, suddenly embarrassed by the familiar way she had spoken to him.

"I know, but there are trout in it. Wait until I show you."

A small rocky prominence covered in grass and heather was coming up ahead, a hillock little more than the size of a large barn. Agatha was familiar with it; she often nipped in behind it on her way home for a moment's privacy when she'd a drop too much tea taken at the office late in the afternoon. She'd never bothered looking into the water. The stream at that point ran away from the road and disappeared out of sight around the hill, before emerging again, then diving deeply into a gully beneath the road and losing itself in the bog on the lower side, where it drained eventually into the sea. Nolan stopped the car against the eminence, easing it off the road by a couple of yards. He switched off the engine.

"Walk with me around to the other side of the mound," he said. They walked together, the sound of the runnel now becoming distinctly louder than it was nearer the road. There was clearly more depth at this point, and it was also a little wider. He stopped there, but encouraged her to go on.

"Walk forward slowly, to where the sound is the loudest," he said, "that's where the deepest holes are, where the water's splashing. Stay in the shadow of the hill, then they won't see you. Tread lightly – fish can feel vibrations. Bend down low and move forward to that big rock at the water's edge."

Agatha followed his directions. "Now ease yourself over the rock – just your head – slowly, and look down into the water." She lay face down on the upward sloping rock and pulled herself upon it until her long russet hair was cascading down over the little stream.

"Fix your eyes on that deep hole until they adjust to the sun's reflection," said Nolan, "eventually you'll see through to the bottom. It's a couple of feet deep just there."

Agatha held her gaze, and then she saw them, saw their shimmering shapes holding almost motionless against the current before barrelling away, the speckled brown of their backs shading to amber and beautifully spotted hues of pink and silver as they turned, before resuming their upstream- facing positions in another place. She was mesmerized. "I never thought there could be fish in here," she said without turning her head. "It's little more than a rill."

She continued to gaze into the deepest pool, looking through her own face reflected in the water. quite entranced by the swirling weed-beds in and out of which the fish swam. The quiet beauty of the place with only the sound of the burbling water captivated her for several moments. Nolan remained behind her. Whilst there wasn't space enough for both of them against the rock at the waters' edge - it was altogether too narrow - that was not the only reason for his immobility. Agatha's stretched out position had drawn her dress up high on her hips and the breeze had lifted its hem above the tops of her stockings. Nolan was as mesmerized by this delightful view as she was by the fish. But oh dear – a problem was arising quite literally, an inexorable tightening of the trousers, a not infrequent occurrence whenever he was in the company of an attractive woman. And wasn't this one delectably attractive? Then, as if jerked out of a reverie, he responded to her words:

"I know; it isn't much more than a trickle for most of its length, except for this deeper bit, but there they are, and aren't they beautiful? Little brown and gold bars of glittering jewels, resting on the golden gravel of the stream bed. People take them by lying patiently on the bank as you are doing, with their hands immersed, until the fish swim over them and then they catch them. It's known as tickling, tickling the trout."

There was a pause in the conversation. Agatha hung over the rock, now studying her reflection in the water, watching her long red- gold hair wisping across her face as the breeze tangled it. She felt utterly relaxed, quite at ease with the situation, enjoying the moment immensely. The breeze rippled her dress, making her suddenly aware just how high it had ridden up. It must have been like that for a couple of minutes. She resisted the impulse to pull it down, she just hoped she wasn't revealing too much. She was at one with the heather and the wind, the musical sound of the shimmering brook, and the almost magical fish. And with Padraig. He also sounded at ease. Behind her, he was on his haunches now, his back against the rise of the hillock, gazing longingly up her dress, along the lovely white thighs above her stockings, right up to where the line of her drawers began. She must be aware of her disposition, he felt. She might like him perhaps. She was obviously becoming quite relaxed in his company.

"Have you ever done that Padraig?"

"What?" he said, startled, lost in his dreams as he studied her divine rear, her beautiful curvaceousness.

"Caught trout?"

"Oh. No, no, I haven't. I couldn't do that. They're so beautiful; I couldn't think of destroying them."

"Don't you eat fish then, Padraig?"

"I do. Perhaps I shouldn't. I suppose I'm a hypocrite." An awful shudder passed through him as he said it. He knew he had massively understated the truth.

"Aren't we all? she replied, as she pushed her chest off the rock and stood upright, turning to face him. She felt her dress drop back into place, and realised how high it must have risen, knowing he couldn't have missed the obvious exposure. He was looking straight at her. The bulge in his trousers was inescapable; she blushed, but did not avert her eyes. It was too wonderful. So, it really was like that, just like the adumbration on the rock face that had made her blush and quiver with excitement. She was trembling now, such a wonderful, all - encompassing feeling. He smiled. There was high colour in his cheeks. She returned his smile. Nothing seemed to matter now; something had been established between them.

He beckoned her to sit beside him on the grass, with their backs against the mound. She dropped down easily, not bothering to pull her dress down over her knees as it rode up over them, but leaving it as it had fallen. Why shouldn't she, she felt, there were only the two of them. He obviously didn't mind. She wondered what might happen. Then he asked, "What's that upon your hand?" taking her small hand into his own larger one to examine it. As he took it, she realized that both their hands were trembling. "Oh, I see; it's only ink. I guess that's an inevitable problem with your job."

"It is," she said, "but it's about the only one. I don't worry about it. I didn't have time to wash my hands when you called for me. I usually do." Nolan sighed regretfully, wishing that his problems were as insignificant. But now was not the time to dwell on them.

"What happened to your hand Padraig?"

"Ah, sure it's only wood stain; it'll wear off." She realized that he had not released her hand, at the same time as he knew he must, and let it go. At least for now. He placed his hands on his lap. They both needed something to say. The situation had been getting more than a little out of their control. They were both a little tremulous, breathing faster than usual, their quavering voices betraying their feelings as they conversed.

"How's your day been Agatha?"

"Fine, Padraig, I've enjoyed it. I've been kept busy, but that's how I like it. How's yours been?"

Nolan hadn't expected a reciprocal question, and could have done without it. He had to focus on an answer, and that wasn't easy. Whatever pleasurable moments occurred in any of his days were either offset or severely undermined by reflections – whenever he permitted himself to reflect – on just what it was he was doing. He was acting – that was it - just acting – as a priest. He wasn't being a priest. He couldn't be. It wasn't in his nature. He was a fraud. But he couldn't say that to Agatha. Not now anyway. But at some time, he might have to, sometime soon, perhaps, if the opportunity arose. He needed to tell her. It might help him to think his way through the situation he was in. But as a priest he shouldn't do that; he should keep his problems to himself.

"It was all right I suppose. Most of my days are just about all right. Could be better, if you know what I mean."

Agatha did not really know what he meant. She thought that a priest had so many important things to do – and of course everybody looked up to a priest, respected him, so that surely meant that it must be a wonderful vocation, although she wished it wasn't *his* vocation.

"I suppose most of us would like our days to be better," she said, feeling that some sort of acknowledgment of his hazy statement was required.

"What are your plans for the future Agatha?" asked Nolan, his voice steadier now.

"I don't know Padraig. It's nice to have a job. It's the first time I've had a bit of money of my own. And it's not too bad living here. Near Glenowen, I mean; the people are very nice, but I'm not sure my aunt likes having me around. She was used to living on her own. But eventually I'd like to do something better, but I don't know what. Something more exciting, if that's possible. Does that seem wrong? Perhaps I should be grateful for what I've got, do you think?"

"No, I don't think like that. There's nothing wrong with wanting to improve yourself. I think any girl your age would like a bit more than there is to be had around here. But where do you think you might find it?"

"I've heard a lot about Dublin; that's where I'd really like to go. I'd do anything to get over there, but I don't know how I'd do it. It's just a dream I have."

How like himself, he thought; they both had dreams.

"Sure, Dublin's a great place; it's the best place I've ever been in."

"That's where you come from isn't it?"

"That's where I was born. I lived there right up until the time I came here. There's no place like it, and I've been to a few places."

"So, you've travelled around Ireland then?"

"No. No, I haven't, not much anyway. This side of the country is foreign to me, and to be honest, I don't much care for it. But I've been to France and Italy. I much prefer Dublin though, it's a wonderful place."

"You're a lucky man Padraig, to have seen so much of the world. I'd love to travel like that. What made you go abroad?"

This was starting to become awkward. Nolan did not want Agatha to know that his parents had separated when he was a child; he'd have to be careful with his answer.

"My father often works abroad. He's an architect with a big company, and travels a lot. Once or twice, I've spent my school holidays with him when he's been working away. He was starting to teach me some Italian when I was with him in Italy."

"That's wonderful; now that's what I call exciting. I'd love to travel like that."

"You'd like Dublin."

Nolan knew that he'd like to be back in Dublin too, but not

## Two of a Kind

as a priest. Were they really two of a kind, he wondered? He felt that was perhaps as near as he wanted to get to introspection right now. It was becoming uncomfortable.

"Let's be going," he said abruptly, standing up and grasping her hand to pull Agatha to her feet.

The suddenness of his movement surprised her. She hadn't time to set her feet, and when only partially upright, they slipped from under her, and she fell back to the ground again, and in a most revealing way. He made no attempt to avert his gaze. They both felt the blood rush to their cheeks, but it didn't seem to matter anymore. It was exhilarating. Nolan did not seem like a priest anymore to Agatha. He was just a very attractive man. Nolan felt much like a prisoner in the garb of a priest. Here he was, in the company of a very attractive young women whom he would have liked to seduce, and one he was fairly sure would have welcomed his advances. They were in a situation they would both like to escape from, yet, for himself at least, the leap for freedom might have a painful landing. But would it be any less painful trying to continue with things as they were?

For Agatha, Padraig's priestly vows ruled out any future, as far as she could see, of having any kind of open relationship with this man, and any other kind of relationship could be disastrous.

They returned to the car. Their brief glimpse of a different future had gone. Suddenly they were sad. They somehow knew that each shared the other's sadness. For a few magical moments it seemed, a door had opened, offering a sublime vision of another world. It had immediately closed again, walling them in. Another world didn't exist. Not for them. They travelled in silence, until they reached the lane where they knew they must part. Both of them glanced cautiously around, like fugitives, as Nolan slowed the car to a halt. Was this how it must be from now on? Agatha got out quickly, still looking all around, and after giving Padraig a wan smile with quivering lips, made her slow way along the lane. He waited a few moments, then realized that the road would not remain deserted. He turned the car around and drove away.

## CHAPTER FOURTEEN

Another day, another chance to see Agatha. But Nolan was late today, having been held up by one person after another. The post office was closed now, as he knew it would be, Agatha was already out on the road, making her way home. He found her, a lone figure ahead of him, walking briskly a mile outside of the town. She smiled as he pulled up alongside her, delighted that he'd come looking for her, yet immediately afraid of the next parting. It had happened several times now, and each time their friendship grew deeper. But the partings were increasingly painful. Whilst feelings had been left unspoken, they were both beginning to read the silent, wistful messages, always tinged with sadness, with hopelessness. She opened the car door and sat in without asking him if she should. "Lovely to see you Padraig; I guess you must be going my way." She knew full well that whichever way she'd be going, he would be going her way.

"I thought a lift home might be helpful; it looked like rain, although it's cleared away now." They were already in sight of the little hill, behind which the speckled trout swam in the shallow stream. She knew he'd stop there. It was such a lovely quiet spot; no houses or people anywhere near. This time he pulled of the road completely, and eased the car carefully behind the hill. He had not done this before. There had been several consecutive days without rain, so the ground ought to stand the weight, he thought; bogging down was unlikely. They both knew that looking at fish was not the objective this time; the intrusion of the noisy car would have made that impossible. But still Agatha got out of the car and leaned over the rock at the side of the rill, unconsciously feigning innocence, not wanting to appear too eager. A moment later Nolan's hands were at either side of her, planted on the rock, almost touching hers. His torso was nearly covering her back, his head close to hers, only just a little higher, both of them pretending to be looking into the water. The rock was just about wide enough to accommodate both of them in this position. His chest was not quite touching her shoulders but his lower body made light contact with her hips. She could not have moved away from him; she was already tight to the rock. She had no wish to, she was loving the nearness of him; nearer still would be better. She could feel his breath on her neck. He seemed to be breathing quickly. What would he do, she wondered.

"I feel I'd like to kiss you Agatha"

"I'd like you to, but we shouldn't."

"I know we shouldn't, but can I?"

"I don't know…"

"I'd like to."

"If you really want to…"

He nuzzled her neck softly with his lips, wondering how this should come so naturally to him when he'd never done such a thing before. She remained motionless for long seconds, trembling with an exquisite pleasure quite unlike any other pleasurable moment she'd ever had. Then she turned to face him, placing her lips softly to his own. They pressed themselves together and she felt his hardness. His hand went to her breast but she pushed it away. "No Padraig; it's what I want, but I'm not letting you. We need to think this out. It would be the ruination of you as a priest. And it would be the ruination of me if anything went wrong."

"You're right, I know you're right. I'm sorry. Please forgive me."

"I'm forgiving nothing. We both want to, it's not just you. But it's just not possible. We'll go back now, but we'll have to try to think things out. If that's possible. I don't see how it can be. Do you think I should move away? Go back home to Geesala, or something?"

"No. No, don't do that. Please don't do that. It's my fault. But I don't know what to do. You're right. There's no thinking to be done. I'm bound by vows I should never have taken, but they cannot be broken. They're indissoluble."

"You were about to break one of them just now, and I'd have been glad to help you to. But if you're going to break that one then the rest will have to go too. At least if you're going to do it with me. C'mon; let's be going."

\*

Agatha was in turmoil. Although she knew Padraig wanted her in a sexual way, she strongly felt -and hoped- that he wanted more than that; that he, like herself, desired an enduring relationship. Nothing in his manner had ever suggested that he wanted to exploit her or take her for granted. He'd always been kind and considerate to her. But how a loving relationship could ever be established was beyond her comprehension. She was wishing for the impossible. She knew that she could – all too easily - fall in love with the man. Perhaps she already had. She couldn't tell exactly how he felt; he'd said nothing about his deeper feelings, other than to state the obvious fact that he was physically attracted to her. And she'd said nothing to him about her feelings. How could she? It wasn't in her place to, was it? And anyway, did she know herself? They were in no position to discuss this sort of thing. What they were contemplating was totally wrong. She was mixed up inside, confused. She knew only that she was immensely attracted to him, like iron to a magnet, and it was obvious that he was just as keen on her. But then, if it was only for sex, he might be equally attracted to other women. And, if he was capable of loving all of her, what pressure would she be putting him under if she encouraged him? He was a priest after all. This was wrong. They were both doing wrong. They would be pilloried for this if ever the community found out. She would, certainly, for leading a priest astray. It ought to be halted before it went any further; but had it gone too far already? She felt that something beautiful was starting to form, but something which they would both have to destroy, no matter how wonderful it might have become.

She'd asked him again should she go away, go back home to Geesala. He'd said that would not be an answer. And anyway, she knew that was impossible. She'd have no job. Penniless, she wouldn't be welcomed back. She'd be just an encumbrance. She'd soon be shoeless and scrawny, like the rest of them, dressed in rags as she had been before. But she knew she would have to leave. She couldn't stay here, even though he'd said she should. Here, she would see him almost every day, and have to pass him by with only a courteous "Good morning, how are you, Padraig?" or, even worse, "Good morning, Father," if anyone else was within hearing. That would be an agony, brutal, too harrowing to think about. And it would still, in the end, ruin his life. No, she would have to go, disappear, without telling him where she had gone. There were jobs to be had in Dublin, she had heard, although how you went about getting them and accommodation at the same time, when you had no money, was beyond her. She didn't have even the bus fare to get all that way, to travel the whole breadth of the country. But maybe, if she could find a way of getting there, then, in the dangerous mayhem of a big city she could lose herself, and, in time, a very long time, she might lose her feelings for him.

\*

Padraig too was being pulled apart. He examined his feelings for Agatha. He'd all too often found a woman attractive. Not so much in this place, where they were mostly a drab, down-beaten lot, kindly enough, in their way, and mostly well-meaning, but nevertheless, careworn, depleted and physically unattractive. But in Dublin he'd known many a well-heeled woman. He'd loved conversing with them, when he took the opportunity to soak up their expensively scented ambience, admiring their well- tailored clothes, their classy jewellery, their opulent confidence. Being of upper- middle-class like himself, they were at ease with him, and he with them. No-one was deferential, not even after he had acquired the priestly garb, shortly before leaving the city to go west. He had loved their chattering company.He remembered the times he had sat with them in a Bewley's coffee house. He'd watch lasciviously as the hem of a dress slipped up a little too high as a long nyloned leg was crossed over a knee, sometimes giving the glimpse of a stocking-top that the wearer was in no great hurry to conceal, or when a thrilling décolletage occurred as a women bent a little too far, perhaps unnecessarily so, over a table, to reach for the sugar tongs which he'd left on his side. Then, he'd happily yielded to his fetishes in the days before ordination interfered with his desires.

Whilst he'd never made a single improper suggestion to any of these women, nor succumbed to what at times he felt sure were thinly veiled hints of a desire for closer interaction, he'd revelled in the thoughts of various possibilities. Was this what he was doing now with Agatha, just lusting over the possibility of a purely physical relationship? He appraised himself honestly, asking himself was there a difference, and, if so, what was it. He was sure that now it was different. The difference was the authenticity of their friendship. A few of the well-off women he had known had been warm and were possibly sincere, but several had chinked hollowly like the china they had held in their hands. They had gushing, insistent voices, but seemed devoid of real feeling. He remembered that he'd sensed it at the time, young and naïve though he was. It hadn't mattered then; he had been the same himself. And he would soon not be available for any relationship anyway, if such transactions could be called relationships. So, he'd feasted his eyes, and fed his libido on their more obvious delights, without compunction, and he'd guessed these women were doing the same with him. And the occasional one of them with the nerve to make a more overt suggestion -before he wore the collar- were only seeking to provide themselves with the opportunity to boast in the future to their closest confidants that they'd once seduced that priest.

Padraig knew that his feelings towards Agatha were fundamentally different. He ruefully accepted that he'd been blatantly class conscious and had not tried to allow for the cultural differences in his parishioners, who were mostly beaten down by their material deprivation, by an environment they had no way of changing. Therefore, he'd avoided close communion with many of them simply because of their shabby, often filthy appearance, and their coarse ill-mannered ways. And he knew they had seen him as the sophisticated city man, an image that he himself had knowingly perpetuated. He'd never tried to understand their lives. No wonder they had not taken to him. So, what was so entrancing about Agatha? If she'd come to this place to better herself, what did she leave behind, he wondered.

He recognized in her an innate intelligence. She was capable of rapidly grasping any scrap of information and formulating it into whatever might be called an education. Things he'd heard about her at the post office confirmed that, and suggested intellectual potential. She was warm and good-natured and kindly disposed, tolerant of everyone. He was beginning to wish he'd more of that about himself. Recognizing that deficiency, he started to wonder how long she would put up with him if he didn't develop a more altruistic attitude to others, a more mature understanding of other people's existence, an existence which had been forced upon them, not one they would have wished for.

As well as acknowledging that Agatha most certainly had a brain that could be educated, and was quickly developing an interesting personality to match, he was acutely aware of her wild untrammelled beauty and, he was almost certain of it, a powerfully sexual nature. He sensed that even when later years drew her nearer to the grave, people would still perceive her as a striking woman. She was a force of nature that he wanted to be a part of, without subduing her or impeding her in any way. He would have liked to have been able to add something to her, although he felt he had nothing to give; it was simply a desire to be a part of her. At the very least, he wanted not to detract from her, not to hinder her development, she was still so young, had so much before her. He realized that he must not allow his older years, his priestly status - admittedly now tenuous - to influence her adversely. Yes, he had wanted - still wanted - to possess her body, to possess all of her, but in a way that would complete both of them, make them one solid unit, as strong and as natural as the surrounding mountains, and yet all was he doing was possibly ruining both their lives.

CHAPTER FIFTEEN

Nolan's dilemma was soon to be resolved for him. The resolution manifested itself in the form of Monsignor O'Flaherty, about to become bishop of Erris, and currently making his way across County Roscommon. He was behind the wheel of a car that was far too big for someone with his limited driving skills. It was only recently that he had come to grips with the management of a motor vehicle, and he was still not too good at it, especially in the hurly burly of Dublin. But out here in the western wilderness it was much easier and he was doing well. In fact, he was coming close to enjoying the experience.

He had been making his annual pilgrimage to visit relatives of whom he was not overly enamoured. It was an onerous duty rather than a pleasure. Duty done, he would have liked to have returned home forthwith; he'd much to do. But uppermost in his mind, scratching away like a burr under one's collar, was the constantly recurring thought of a wanton wastrel of a priest, now only a county away. And very soon O'Flaherty himself would be living in that county, where he would be bishop. And then Nolan would be much more than an irritation. He would be a downright disaster.

O'Flaherty was a straightforward sort of a man who liked an uncomplicated life and aimed to ensure that it would remain that way. He'd no intention of inheriting problems, and he knew that Nolan could be nothing but a problem, so he'd decided to pay an unannounced visit to Glenowen to put paid, once and for all, to Nolan's potential for causing mayhem. The monsignor was somewhat aggrieved that his necessitous mission should take him into the next county west, and right over to the far side of it at that, when he'd rather have been returning eastwards. But perhaps it was a good thing that the young reprobate was lodged in the thinly populated western extremity where, hopefully, he could do the least damage. It would be even better if he should take a dip in the sea there, and fetch up somewhere in the vicinity of the Statue of Liberty sometime in the distant future, but that, unfortunately, was highly improbable.

Nolan was looking out of a window of the presbytery, vaguely wandering what the weather was going to do. He had some home visits to make, but rather fancied a walk instead. He put on his jacket and was reaching for his hat, when, much to his amazement, a large black sedan pulled in off the road and parked across his view. He wondered who on earth could be visiting in a car like that. A black- garbed figure, tall, and of a commanding aspect, got out, and stood scrutinising every detail of the priest's abode, even throwing his head back to study the upstairs windows. Nolan had ample opportunity to study the countenance, the piecing, omnipotent gaze. He'd seen it before somewhere, but a long time ago. Then it registered, hitting him like an electric shock. Holy Christ! he thought, it's O'Flaherty. He remained where he stood, rooted to the spot. His only recollection of O'Flaherty was one of severe pain and humiliation, even though the Monsignor himself had not been directly responsible for either of those conditions. What on earth, he thought, can have brought him out here. Then he remembered that all the talk was of O'Flaherty perhaps becoming the next bishop when the present incumbent retired, which was rumoured to be imminent. The thought of O'Flaherty moving westward had troubled Nolan when he'd first heard of the possibility, but, amongst his other troubling concerns, it had faded to become only an intermittent worry. Now, when it had seemed that things could hardly get worse, the evidence that they could stood squarely before his eyes.

Ignoring the front door, O'Flaherty strode assuredly around to the rear of the presbytery. He was in no hurry, just checking to see who might be around. He then banged heavily on the rear door and immediately entered. By this time Nolan had recovered himself enough to be making a move in that direction, and they met in the hallway.

"Good morning – sorry - afternoon, Monsignor," stammered Nolan. "It's a pleasure to see you. And an honour to have you drop in on us," he added hastily.

"So, you remember me then" said O'Flaherty, absolutely certain that Nolan would never have forgotten their earlier encounter.

"I thought you might."

O'Flaherty surveyed his quaking quarry, silently taking in the slight physical changes the few intervening years had wrought on the reprobate, and letting the passing seconds inflict their own ferocity. He wanted to get down to business immediately, but knew that time can have its uses.

Finally, he broke the silence: "Are we alone?" he demanded to know. The threat in his booming voice terrified Nolan.

"Yes Monsignor," said Nolan, trying in vain to keep his voice steady.

"Are you expecting anyone?"

"No Monsignor."

"Right, I'll come straight to the point then. And by the way, in a few months' time, you'll be addressing me as 'Bishop.'

"I shan't ask what part you've played in the development of all this baloney about Saint Patrick in the grotto, Nolan. It'll save you from having to tell me lies. But I've heard there were lewd drawings accompanying this supposed apparition, and, according to the more discerning observers, no doubt exonerating their own prurient scrutiny of them, they were of a highly artistic nature, extremely well executed, or so I've been told. So, you did them. And don't say otherwise."

Nolan uttered not a word, no point in prolonging the agony. He was wondering what might come next. O'Flaherty's tone softened: "You're still a very young man, Nolan," he continued. "Often, when young men are ordained, they have not yet found themselves. They have doubts, insecurities. Usually, they get through them. But not all do. And they are the ones that seldom make good priests. Would you say you're a good priest?"

Nolan began to stammer.

"Stop: think before you answer me. Remember, we can all make mistakes. Sometimes it's better to take a step or two backwards and reconsider a situation, rather than to blunder onwards, compounding your errors for the rest of your life. Now tell me – are you a good priest?"

"No, I'm not Monsignor."

"Can you ever be, do you think?"

There was a long silence, whilst Nolan thought. This was painful. He was being forced into introspection, a situation he'd suffered enough of in the last few weeks.

"No Monsignor. I know I can't be"

"Not even if the Church gave you support?"

"No. It's not in me. I've made wrong choices, bad decisions, blundered along, as you say. I've only recently started to realise this, to think about the future, and it doesn't look too good."

"That's what I thought," said O'Flaherty. "It's not looking good. But at least you're being honest. How do you fit in with the parishioners? Have they taken to you in the short while you've been here?"

"Not too well.Not well at all, actually. They don't take me seriously as a priest. No one does, not even the kids. They have little respect for me, and I can't say that I blame them. I'm only going through the motions, if you understand me. My mind is elsewhere. I feel that many of them seem to sense that."

O' Flaherty felt a sense of relief. He was not going to meet with much resistance, either from Nolan or anyone else, if he encouraged him to leave the priesthood, although how he was going to get rid of him was a significant problem. But he knew he'd have to do it somehow, whatever means it might take. The vows a priest took were as binding on his superiors in the Church as upon the priest himself, and they were obliged to help him through his difficulties. But with this man, well, he seemed a hopeless case. No good would ever come of keeping him in the clergy. It might prove a calamity if he was not 'helped' out of it. And in any case, wasn't the man himself admitting he'd had enough of it?

"You're an artist, aren't you," he asked.

Nolan wandered what was the relevance of this question, and

where was it leading to.

"I like drawing and painting," he answered.

"But you're good at it, aren't you? Really good, I mean."

"Well, it's hard for me to say. I like doing it, and I've always found it very easy to do. Before I was ordained, I was always looking for challenges in terms of subjects to draw and different ways of presenting a picture, although, when I think about it, I've never found any subject too difficult."

"You're only confirming what I already thought," said O'Flaherty. "I'm remembering a picture that I'm sure you're always trying to forget. One that covered the whole of the inside of a lavatory door. It was lewd, and you deserved the flogging you were given for doing it. But it was clever. And, given where it was, you must have done it in minutes."

There was a long silence, O'Flaherty wondering if Nolan would present him with a way forward, or would he have to take the initiative, Nolan waiting for O'Flaherty to castigate him. It was Nolan who spoke first: "Where do I go from here?" he asked. "What am I to do?"

"Well, there's no doubt that you've got an outstanding talent – as an artist, that is – it's a pity you've not used it more wisely. As a priest…well, you haven't got a prayer, if you'll excuse the unintended pun. You've got a dirty mind, in my opinion, although many would disagree with me. A lot of art is controversial. Many renowned artists have painted what some would regard as lewd pictures. If you remain a priest, and I hope you don't, you'll get yourself into a lot of trouble, I'm sure. And that would mean trouble for me too. But artistically I feel you could do well. Some artists, a tiny few, I admit, do make a living at it. Perhaps you could. You'd have to almost starve for a while, maybe for a long while, but there's a market for what you seem to like to do, the more erotic stuff, for want of a better description. You wouldn't sell it here – in Ireland, I mean – but of course, you would know that yourself. But it would sell in London or Paris, in my opinion."

"Do you think so? I'd love to be able to earn a living- even a very poor one – by producing some half- decent artwork. And I do actually like doing landscapes, and, particularly, seascapes."

"So, you're not entirely obsessed with - for want of a better description - life drawing, then?" Nolan didn't answer immediately, but he was relaxing now. O'Flaherty appeared to understand him, and, more importantly, seemed prepared to help him out.

"No, Monsignor, I'm not. I love all kinds of art." There was another silence, O'Flaherty giving Nolan time to think his way through their mutual problem.

"I think the priesthood would be better-off without me," he volunteered, wondering if that could be made possible. Could some sort of sickness be invented he wondered, before immediately dismissing the thought. He knew the Church supported many frail priests, even some with his kind of frailty.

"I'm certain of that," replied O'Flaherty. "I know I'd be better off without you."

"Is it possible that I could somehow leave the priesthood, do you think?"

"It'll have to be made possible. Look, I'll be straight with you: I want you out. I've nothing against you; there's nothing personal in this. But I want you out, and I'm going to have you out, don't you doubt that. You're in no way suited to the priesthood.

You've admitted it yourself. You made a big mistake if you ever thought you were. But others must have made mistakes too, by encouraging you in that direction. If I don't get you out, you'll become a thorn in my flesh, and I'm not having that. The duties of a bishop are onerous; I'm not going to add to them. I'll give you what little help I can to drift away quietly. The Church has an unoccupied cottage over near Foxford. I'm sure I can arrange for you to live there for a while, rent free, providing you keep quiet about ever having been a priest. The second piece of assistance I can give you is this: I have a friend in Dublin who is an art dealer. I have a small collection of art myself, much of it bought from him."

The priestly vows of poverty flashed through Nolan's mind, but he wasn't about to bring *that* subject into play. He knew they were broken regularly.In fact, he constantly broke them himself, by owning a car, and having regular cheques from his mother. O'Flaherty continued: "I could get him to look at your work. He pushes a lot of… the 'racier' stuff, especially, into England, where he has lots of contacts, and the even more risqué work across to France. He might be able to do you some favours. But whatever else happens, I would like you to fade away as quickly as possible. What do you say? Can we do this amicably or not?"

A massive sense of relief ebbed over Nolan. He could have cried with happiness. The priestly existence he'd experienced since his ordination had not been all bad, nor was his time at the seminary. He was gregarious up to a point, and had got on well enough with his fellow seminarians, and he'd enjoyed the brief company of a small few of his parishioners since taking up office, his relationship with the Jew Solly Axelrod being one of the most rewarding, as their mutual knowledge of Dublin life gave them a connection. But he knew that he had not a scrap of piety in him and would be hugely relieved if his priestly duties were taken from him.

He missed the art that he knew he was good at. He should have gone to art school – and could have – but he'd been edged away from art by those who thought it to be bohemia, where his erotic inclinations would be forever fuelled, until he'd end up raking the devil's coals.

He'd been celibate – well, almost – up until now, but he knew that couldn't last; nor did he want it to. It now seemed totally unnatural to him. Although he'd considered visiting the professional ladies of pleasure, he knew that was not what he wanted. He needed a meaningful relationship, marriage, in the long run maybe, so long as it was with someone with the same fleshly instincts as his own. And a love of art; that would be essential, even if the person was not an artist herself. A conventional, homely sort of wife was not what he was thinking of. He needed a bohemian way of life but with just one person, an oxymoron surely, but perhaps, he hoped, something like that could be possible. Anyway, change itself was a move in the right direction, and this was being offered to him by, of all people, Monsignor O'Flaherty, the man he'd been most afraid of. He was going to snatch the opportunity with both hands.

"You're awfully kind Monsignor. You can obviously look deeply into a man and see him for what he is, and not for what he's trying to appear to be. I wish I'd looked into myself as much a few years ago. I might now be much happier and I wouldn't be putting you to all this trouble."

O'Flaherty didn't need compliments from anyone, least of all

Nolan. "I'm not kind, and I'm not intending to be. And the trouble I'm putting myself to now is only to avoid a mountain of it in the future. So, what do you say about the cottage near Foxford? It's running with damp at the moment; It's been unoccupied for over a year. It needs a fire in its grate. The priest over there hasn't needed it; he lives with his elderly parents nearby, to keep an eye on them. It's yours for a while if you want it, so long as you keep a low profile and don't let it be known that you were in the priesthood. I'll put the present man in the picture. I know he'll keep his mouth shut."

"Can I think about it for a couple of days Monsignor?"

"No, you damn well can't! What's the matter with you Nolan? You admit you're no good as a priest, and I'd tell you that for nothing, whether you admitted it or not. Can't you see that I'm doing you a favour, as well as myself? It's not easy for me; I'll have to enter into lengthy correspondence with the Vatican to try to get some kind of annulment. Why would you want to think about it? I want you gone, out of my sight altogether. You need to go. You've no friends here, so few people will ask where you've gone. And for the benefit of those who might ask, you can put it about that you're going on a retreat for a while."

"I've one close friend, Monsignor."

A long pause as O'Flaherty stared at Nolan. Then the penny dropped.

"What sort of a friend is it you've got? Is it a woman?"

"Yes"

"Oh, for Heaven's sake Nolan; you're incorrigible. Now I definitely want you out. Forthwith, whatever it takes to do it. She's not pregnant, is she?"

"No Monsignor. We've not done anything like that. But we do have a close friendship."

"She's a local girl I suppose?"

"She's not actually; she's been living here only for a short while. She moved in to lodge with her aunt so that she could take a job at the post office. She's no other friends or relatives around here."

"Well, that at least is useful. She probably wouldn't be greatly missed either. She sounds somewhat like yourself, a bit of a misfit. I hope she's kept quiet about her relationship with you?"

"Oh yes, she has, most certainly"

"Well, I'll tell you now. You're not taking her with you, not to the place I'm offering you. It's known to belong to the church, even though it's out in the wilderness and the present incumbent isn't using it. Look, Nolan, I'm trying to avoid a scandal, not just move one around to a different place. Let's get down to some detail: I want you away from here as soon as possible. I'll put it more bluntly, seeing as you seem to have difficulty in understanding my position. I will have you out, come what may. You need to be out of the priesthood, for your own good. Those two things are possible, even if I fail to get the Vatican to release you from your vows. A small number of priests do leave the Church unofficially. They just drift off into obscurity, go abroad, whatever. They make another life for themselves and after a while they're forgotten about. Why can't you do that? Tell me, although I'm not greatly concerned about it, how could you support yourself until such times as you might begin to sell your artwork? If you ever do of course; there's no guarantee of that. Although, for the sort of thing at which you seem to excel, there probably is."

Nolan took his time in replying; O'Flaherty gave him time to think. He wanted this to work, to have Nolan well out of the way without any scandal, without friction; almost without anyone noticing he'd gone. And, if possible, he'd prefer it if Nolan did do what he was good at; he'd nothing against the man personally. Whilst at the last resort he knew he'd win the day, he also knew that it would be better if Nolan was helped into making a decision that suited them both, rather than be forced into one he might resent later. He knew that Nolan had almost ruined himself, and he had little sympathy for him. But O'Flaherty wasn't a vindictive person; he'd no wish to kick a man when he was down already.

Nolan was thinking to himself that he'd have to take this opportunity to extricate himself from the disastrous situation he was in. He desperately wanted to be out of the priesthood. He could hardly believe that a way out was not only being offered to him, indeed, it was being insisted upon by his superior. But he needed to take Agatha with him. If he could do that, and find an occupation that suited his nature and utilized his abilities, he would be deliriously happy. He would take O'Flaherty's offer of the cottage - on his own for the moment- it would be a quick way of resolving the main part of the problem; It would give him freedom, but still with a roof over his head, and he would return for Agatha. He was particularly mindful of O'Flaherty's connection with the art dealer. This could be the break he needed to enable him to make a living from the talent he knew he had in abundance. He needed to keep on the right side of the man. And, he needed an income, however meagre.

"Monsignor," he said. I'm massively indebted to you. I'd love to move into the cottage. As for my ability to support myself, well, I cannot do that unless I sell my paintings. Therefore, I'd be grateful for your assistance in putting me in touch with the art dealer you know. In the meantime, I'm sure that my father would help me out."

"Tell me about him," said O'Flaherty, who was now becoming more relaxed about the whole situation; it looked as if things were going his way. To have Nolan out of the picture quickly would save him a great deal of trouble in the future. "Could you not, for a while at least, go back to living with your parents? After all, a lot of young men of your age still live with their families. And you say your father might support you – so you wouldn't need the place at Foxford."

"My parents have not lived together for years, for many years. I've lived only with my mother since I was about six or seven, but I wouldn't want to go back to living with her, much as I love her. She wanted me to become a priest, she's going to see me as an abject failure. She'll get over it in time, but I wouldn't want to be putting myself right under her nose just now. And her own accommodation isn't spacious. I'd be in her way."

O'Flaherty roared with laughter. "You seem to be good at that don't you, getting in people's way." Nolan managed a rueful grin, but said nothing.

"What about your father then? Where is he?"

"Oh, he's all over the place. He's an architect, you see. He heads a large company of architects. He's worked all around the world. He's in France now, I believe, at least he was when he last wrote to me. He stays in touch, but I very rarely see him. He'll always help me out financially, though. And, of course, he supports my mother. She has a flat in Dublin."

"He earns a lot of money then?"

"Yes, he does, he always has. He's had many big commissions."

"So that's why you have a car. I had wondered."

"Yes, it's his old car. He gave it to me when I left the seminary. It's still registered in his name though."

"I'm surprised he let you enter the seminary. He must have had some idea of your proclivities, and your talent. You seem to have been wasting that, whilst trying to be what you could not possibly be."

"He didn't want me to become a priest, but my mother did, and he probably assumed that I did. So, he didn't say much about it. He was never there to say much about anything."

"What sort of man is he?" asked O'Flaherty.

"Generous to a fault, big hearted, a bit of a womanizer… a heavy drinker too, but a good, kind sort of a man. He's hugely talented as an architect."

"But not a great parent, eh? Despite the more laudable qualities amongst those you've just mentioned."

"No, I don't suppose so," agreed Nolan.

"I'm beginning to see why you've turned out the way you have; the influence of your father's talent for drawing, for creativity, and for the good life, whatever that is. And your mother's lack of foresight: you'd have to admit she sadly misjudged you when she influenced your choice of vocation, wouldn't you?"

"I suppose so," said Nolan, somewhat miserably. But it wasn't just her. There were others in the family too. She has brothers who are priests; they had some influence on me."

O'Flaherty raised his eyebrows at the latter part of that statement, but withheld comment.

"Take the cottage, and for as short a time as possible. Take your father's financial support. He can obviously afford it, and I'd say he owes you that, and more. I'll provide you with some connections in the art world."

"That's great, thanks, Monsignor."

"And you might do me a small favour in return for my getting rid of you."

"I'll do whatever I can," said Nolan. "What is it you think I can do for you?"

"I'd like one or two of your paintings when you get back on your feet. Nothing too extreme, mind, but let's say, something… something on the racy side of erotic. I collect paintings. I'll give you a fair price, but I don't want to be swindled."

"I'd be glad to, Monsignor."

"And one other thing Nolan. I've been looking at your hands Why does one of them look as if it should be attached to the arm of an Arab?" Taken by surprise, Nolan dropped straight back into the lie he'd told John Donohoe.

"I trapped it in a door, Monsignor."

"That's not bruising" replied O'Flaherty, knowing that he'd got less than a half-truth. "That's a stain of some sort."

"It is. It's something I treated it with; something I use on my feet from time to time."

"Don't tell me you get your feet trapped in doors, as well as your hands," said O'Flaherty. They both laughed at the absurdity of the situation, and both were glad to let it go at that.

"I'll be greatly relieved when you're gone," said O'Flaherty. "You'd give me nightmares if you stayed around. But I cannot help liking you all the same."

"It's remarkably kind of you to say that Monsignor, given all the trouble I've caused. But it makes me feel a little bit better about myself. I'm most grateful to you. Thank you."

"Right. Now that's all settled, I could do with a pot of tea. I've a long journey ahead of me. Do you have a housekeeper lurking about in an outhouse or a cellar or somewhere?"

"No, but I'll be glad to make us a pot."

"Good heavens, how you people live. What is it I'm coming to, I wonder?"

## CHAPTER SIXTEEN

The next morning Padraig was out early, intending to catch Agatha before she reached the town. He'd stopped calling for her at the post office. It had become all too obvious to several people that he'd been doing that possibly for reasons not necessarily of a spiritual nature.

He saw her coming out of the lane onto the metalled road; she'd obviously only just left her aunt's house.

Agatha heard him coming as he pulled alongside. She kept her head down and walked on. He wondered what was the matter with her, and drew forward, stopping the car a few yards in front of her. He leant across to push open the passenger door.

"Padraig, what are you doing stopping here? If Aunt Bridget's looking out of her bedroom window, she could see us."

"Jump in the car, Agatha."

"I don't want to Padraig."

"Why ever not? What's wrong Aggie?"

"We can't go on like this." She was starting to cry. "It won't work, Padraig. It'll be the ruination of us. I'll move away. I'll find somewhere to go to." She walked on.

Nolan moved the car forward again.

"Agatha, I need to talk to you. I've something important to discuss with you. I need your help," he said, trying to add urgency to his request, being slightly alarmed by her apparent petulance.

"How can I help you Padraig? We could both do with some

help, we're in a right mess."

"We might soon be out of it. Get in the car."

Agatha sat in and slammed the door. "Drive off quickly, Padraig, she mightn't have seen us yet. And don't talk to me about impossible things."

Nolan accelerated away, then slowed. The road was empty. Agatha choked back her tears and forced out her words. "We can't go on Padraig. I won't let it go on. I love you, and I don't want to see you hurt. And that's the end of it. I don't want you to see me again."

"Things have changed, Agatha. if you'll only listen to me for a minute, I'll give you some good news."

"How can you say that? Nothing has changed. There is no way out of the situation we're in. I'm trying to face up to it, and so must you. We cannot go on."

Nolan had stopped the car. There was still a lot of time before Agatha was due to start work.

"There is a way out of it, it seems. I've had a shock today, but not altogether a bad one. Monsignor O'Flaherty, who'll be the next bishop over here, has visited. He's told me he wants me out of here, out of the priesthood altogether.And as quickly as possible. He sees me as a bit of a nuisance. Well, worse than that, more like a blot on the Church's landscape."

This insult to her man, for which she presumed herself to be the sole cause, led to more tears. She'd always known she'd be the ruination of him. She began to sob bitterly, not seeing the vista that Padraig was trying to put before her.

"That's cruel of him. And you can't leave the priesthood. You know you can't. You're in it for life. Unfortunately! And that makes any future for us impossible. We've both known that all along. So, what are you talking about? How can he be telling you to leave when he knows you can't? He knows the rules better than you do."

"That's what I thought, Agatha, but O'Flaherty has thrown me a lifeline."

"What are you talking about Padraig? You're not making any sense" She was angry now, bitterly angry. Angry with the world, angry with life itself.

"What sort of a lifeline? Is it the sort of lifeline that would have saved the *Titanic*? Because that's what we need. I feel as if we're drowning."

Although Agatha was seeing only obstacles, having, until now, believed that everything was utterly hopeless, Padraig's words were slowly sinking in, and they were suggestive of hope. Could there be other possibilities? She was confused, but she let him continue.

"Monsignor O'Flaherty has told me bluntly that I am no good as a priest, and that he wants me to disappear as soon as possible. I think he'd like me to vanish off the face of the earth, if that could be arranged."

"How can he say that? Sure, he's a cruel man."

"No, he's not, Agatha, he's just being realistic. And honest, which is more than I have been with myself. I have to admit that he's right. You know that he's right."

"So, what's the lifeline then?"

"Isn't it obvious? I'm a useless priest; I know that. And I'm in love with you, and you are with me – you've just said so. And O'Flaherty wants me go. That's the lifeline, a new start in life.

Freedom, freedom to start all over again."

"He can do that? He can absolve you of your vows? said Agatha, with some amazement in her voice, wondering how The Church could bend its own rules.

"It seems he can. And he's going to, whether I want to or not. And of course, I want to."

"Padraig, I can't believe what you're telling me." She felt as if she could breathe again, as if she had been under water for a long time, and had finally broken the surface.

"This could be wonderful. It is wonderful. We could be together openly. But we'd have to get out of this place. People would make life unbearable for us here, whether you were in the Church or not."

"He's more or less set that up for me as well, but there's a slight drawback to it, but only a temporary one. That's what I want to talk to you about."

"What's is it - The drawback?" She was becoming confused again. "Tell me."

"Well, it would involve us being apart for just a little while."

"Why would that be Padraig?" His words were like a slap in her face, "I don't understand. If you get out of the priesthood, why couldn't we be together somehow? Openly, I mean.It's been bad enough, never knowing when I'm going to see you, and then only for minutes at a time, and us looking over our shoulders all the while. And people are talking about us all the time. I know I've just said I didn't want to see you anymore, but that was because I thought there was no future for us. And I don't want to ruin your life any more than I have already. Now it seems there could be a future, but you're saying we've got to part. I don't understand you; you're being cruel." She was beginning to realize that the man she loved might soon be free of everything, and she knew other women found him desirable.

"Let's drive on a bit. Then I'll tell you the rest of it."

Nolan started the car again. He'd lingered longer on the road than he normally would have done, and needed to get off it. A feeling of some kind of relief – a way forward - was slowly enveloping both of them, despite Agatha's confusion, but it was still a bit risky to attract more notice than they had done already. He drove them to their favourite meeting place at the trout brook. There they'd be safe. Again, he pulled behind the hillock, out of sight, and switched off the engine. There was more than enough time to drive Agatha to the post office, and this might be the last time they'd set tongues wagging. He put his arms around Agatha and hugged her closely.

For a minute or so they were silent, contemplating possibilities. Padraig had had more time to think about the change that had so fortuitously been forced upon him, whereas Agatha was still coming to terms with it. They looked around at their idyl, this tiny secluded Eden which had concealed some wondrous moments. Even the clouds seemed higher than ever before, the horizon more distant, as if nature shared their new-found expansiveness. Then they heard the sound of trotting hooves, rapidly coming closer. Agatha froze, then slid down in her seat, pushing her head into his chest and trying to be invisible.

"There's someone coming Padraig. He might pull in here. This'll ruin you. Hide me somehow."

"I'll get out of the car, Aggie, and lead him away. Keep your head down."

Nolan got out quickly, closing the door behind him quietly and making for the road, trying to come up with an excuse for being there. He needn't have bothered. The horse and cart had already passed their hideaway. The driver had no intention of stopping, he was making for the town, no doubt.

Nolan checked that there was no one else on the lonely road and walked back to the car. He got in and put his arm around Agatha, who was visibly shaking. "It's all right. He's gone."

"That's the sort of thing that I can't stand. That we have to act like criminals."

"Not for much longer Aggie. Padraig continued with his news, and tried to soothe her jaded nerves.

"This is the deal: O'Flaherty has offered me the use of a cottage over Foxford way, providing I keep my head down and move on again as soon as I can. It would be like a retreat, where people go for a while to contemplate, to reflect on their lives. At least I could claim that if anyone over there asked me what I was doing. In fact, O'Flaherty has suggested that I do that."

"Can't I come with you?"

"O'Flaherty says no. It's a Church-owned dwelling, and it wouldn't do for a woman to be seen visiting. He won't go back on that. I've asked him. He'd throw me out immediately if a woman was seen there."

"So, he knows about us then?"

"He does, up to a point. He doesn't know about you exactly, but I told him I have a close friend I wouldn't want to leave, and he guessed the rest."

"I'm pleased you said that Padraig. For a moment I thought you were running out on me. But how would we see each other? And how would you support yourself, for heaven's sake? You'd starve."

"That's something else he's offered to help me with, although it might turn out to be no help. He's seen something I painted once, a long time ago. He knows I'm good at art, and has offered to put me in touch with a dealer he's friendly with. But that would take ages before he made me any money. And it might never happen. But I'm not too bothered about that. For a while, at least, maybe for a good while, I think my father would lend me some support. He's always kept my mother in comfort, and me too, of course, before I left home to go into the seminary. I think he's been generous with his money as a way of making up for never having been there when we needed him. So, I'm sure he'll keep me going for a while."

"Then why bother with O' Flaherty's offer. Why not go straight to your father for help?"

"Because O'Flaherty wants me out now. Straight away. He says I'll bring scandal on the Church and he doesn't want me around for even another day if he can help it. I'd rather approach my father after I've got clear of the Church and made one or two contacts in the art world, so that I can tell him I've got some kind of a career plan. And anyway, he's out of the country at the moment. But when he comes back, I'll tell him about you. About us. But also, I don't want to spring this on my mother too suddenly. She persuaded me to go into the Church. I need to break it too her gently. So, I'll have to go to Foxford for a short while, then we'll be together again, I promise you. I swear I won't let you down. And I'd love to introduce you to my father."

"That'd be great, Padraig. Would he like me, d'ye think?"

Agatha's mind was already moving forward, hope was beginning to blossom.

"I'm sure he would."

Agatha relaxed a little. Things were beginning to make some sort of sense. Her mind went back over a brief conversation she'd had only the other day with Miss Cronin.

"Padraig, how far away is Foxford, and where is it exactly?"

"It's in the direction of Castlebar, but a bit further on. Castlebar and Ballina are the nearest large towns."

"All these names of places mean nothing to me, Padraig. I don't know where any of them are. It's not anywhere near Swinford, is it?"

"It's not too far from there. Quite a few miles, but not far by car. You could do it on a bike in an hour or so. And it's not on a bad road. Why? Do you know someone there?"

Padraig was slightly annoyed, Agatha seemed to be pursuing a different line of thought, as if she were not grasping the importance of what he was saying to her. Right now, he didn't want to hear about Swinford. The place was of no interest to him.

"No, Padraig, I had no idea where it was.It's just that Miss Cronin pointed out to me that they have a position for an assistant at the post office there. She thought it might be a promotion for me as it's a higher grade than mine. She's not wanting to be rid of me, she's only trying to help me better myself. It's kind of her really. She suggested I should apply. She even said she'd write me a good reference for it."

"When was this?"

"A couple of days ago"

"What did you say to her?"

"I said I'd consider it. She was a bit put out that I didn't jump at the chance."

"Why didn't you?"

"How could I Padraig? I didn't know where Swinford was, I just presumed it was a long way off. And I didn't want to be far away from you."

"Do you think it would be too late to apply now, Aggie?"

"Why? Do you want me to?"

"Well, if you were at Swinford and I was at Foxford, we wouldn't be far apart. And it wouldn't be for long. I've got to get out quickly, and O'Flaherty's offering me a way of doing that. And I know people are talking, talking about us, so I can see why he's in such a hurry to get rid of me. The locals have realized that when I visit it's not your aunt Bridget that I come to see. And you've been seen in my car a lot. People have even asked me what I find to write about, as I'm always in and out of the post office with letters in my hand. I write to anyone I can think of just so that I can see you. My mother says she has never had so much correspondence from me."

"Padraig, I'm excited by what you're saying. I know Aunt Bridget wouldn't be sorry to see the back of me. In fact, she'd be glad. I'm too much of a worry to her. I don't get on well with her at all; we hardly got on from the start, and things have got a lot worse lately. So, we'd both be glad if I left. I don't know if it's too late to apply now, but I could try. If I got the job in Swinford I'd earn a bit more than the pittance I'm getting presently, and then I'd be able to pay for lodgings. But I don't think we could go on like that for very long, you in one place and me in another, even if you did drive over frequently."

"I wouldn't want us to, Aggie. We need to be together. If I could just begin to establish myself in the art world, as O'Flaherty is suggesting, we could find a house of some sort near to your work, but a bit out of the way, where I could paint. You could bring in a few shillings, we'd manage well enough. I'm certain that my father would help out with the finances for a while. And you could be my Dora Marr, and I could paint you," he said, laughingly.

"Who's Dora's ma?"

"No Dora Maar – that's what she's called – Picasso's woman."

"Was she the one with the funny nostrils?"

"Well, yes and no. She didn't have funny nostrils, that's just the way he pictured her. He drew her in all sorts of poses, even in the nude."

"You wouldn't want to draw me in my skin, would you, Padraig?"

"I…I'd like to. If you'd let me, that is."

"Oh, I'd love that. Just think of it. It would be shocking, but I'd love you to. I'd like to shock people, but here I have to avoid drawing attention to myself, to us. It would be nice if we could be ourselves. You might make me famous, like her - what's her name – Dora Maar. But you wouldn't draw me with funny nostrils, would you?

"But what if you couldn't make money as an artist? I don't think many of them do make much."

"Then I'd have to think of something else. We'd have to move to Dublin; there are opportunities there. We could both find something to do there. Whether or not I ever establish myself as an artist, we'd still probably be better off there in the long run. It's a freer way of life in Dublin, more cosmopolitan. I used to love living there. You'd enjoy it, I know you would."

"I've always wanted to go to Dublin. I've heard so much about it. It must be wonderful. Oh Padraig, this is exciting; this is wild." She threw her arms around him, her head on his shoulder, momentarily contemplating this huge change of fortune. "And to be with you all of the time; that would be wonderful, the two of us together, and you always painting. It would be great."

"It would be a dream come true. I should be the happiest man in the world. Hold me Aggie, hold me. I need your love." They were laughing and almost crying at the same time, marvelling at this sudden twist to their lives, as they hugged each other fiercely.

"I'd better be getting you off to work, Aggie, said Nolan as he started the car. Keep the right side of Miss Cronin; you'll need a good report from her. He eased the car out from behind the hillock and up to the road. He glanced around before joining it, but a little less furtively than usual; he would soon be out of this place. Its inhabitants could say and think what they liked then. Ah, sure they'd soon forget about him, he felt.

\*

Nolan received a letter from O'Flaherty three days after their meeting. 'Everything is in place now,' it said. 'I'm presuming you will go to the cottage, so please do so immediately.' The letter provided him with an address of the parish priest over in Foxford, who would take him to the place.

The following morning Nolan intercepted Agatha on the road to Glenowen as she walked in to work. She heard a car coming up behind her and knew it must be his, but she still looked at him with slight surprise as he drew alongside and stopped on the empty road. Now, with widening horizons before them, the fear of their friendship being criticized had diminished just a little, so she was delighted to see him.

"Hello Padraig. This is nice. I didn't expect to see you so early in the day. Are you going into Glenowen?"

"Get in," he said, without answering her question. She sensed that he was on edge. She was immediately afraid.

"What's happening Padraig? Why are you out so early? And you're hardly speaking to me. Have I done something wrong?"

"No. No, of course not." He was driving more quickly than usual, erratically, almost, and they quickly reached their trysting place. He swung the car off the road and in behind the hillock. Agatha knew that romance was not on his mind, there was a different urgency in his manner. She wondered what was troubling him. Had O'Flaherty changed his mind, and decided to keep him in the Church somehow?

"I'm away to Foxford today, Aggie, to the cottage I told you about. O'Flaherty wants me gone. Now." Agatha was taken aback by the suddenness of it all and by his terse, uncommunicative manner. She felt as if he were abandoning her.

"You're not leaving me, are you Padraig?" She was immediately embarrassed by what she had said, and slightly ashamed that she was suspicious of him. Until now she'd felt sure of him, and wildly hopeful of the possibilities opened up by O'Flaherty's insistence that he leave the Church. But now she could see that Padraig would soon be his own man again, living alone, without any ties, and a long way away from her, in a place where he would be unknown. He would soon be free to go anywhere, do anything he wanted to do. She was frightened. She felt inadequate, a gauche young girl again, who knew next to nothing of the world, or even of this little bit of her own country. And him a middle-class, sophisticated Dublin man, good looking, educated. Why would he stay with her?

"Please don't leave me Padraig, You won't, will you? I couldn't bear it. I know I wasn't saying that a couple of days ago, and that was cruel of me, but things were different then."

"I won't leave you Aggie. I couldn't. Look, we've been through this already. You know I've got to go away. This is only for a few weeks. Then we'll see each other every day when you move to your new job in Swinford." They were out of the car now, and in each other's arms. She was sobbing. "I haven't yet got the job in Swinford. I might not get it. And you'll be gone, and I'll be left here on my own. Then how will we see each other?"

"If you don't get the job, we'll have to think of something else. We'll move to Dublin or somewhere...I'll have to hope my father can find me somewhere to live. And fund me for a while..."

All certainty suddenly seemed to have vanished. Agatha sensed that Padraig was guessing at a future, if he was contemplating a future at all, for both of them. Alone, he could almost certainly get by, at least, probably even do quite well for himself. She might be only an encumbrance to him if she had no job and he had to beg money from his father to keep the pair of them in poverty. Even that she could cope with. But if he left her forever in Glenowen, and she didn't know where he was, what he was doing, she doubted if she could cope with that. She'd kill herself, she thought. She'd have to.

"How do I know you'll wait for me?" What's to stop you finding someone else. You've got everything going for you; I've got nothing."

"I will, I will. I promise. Trust me Aggie."

"I'm sorry Padraig. I just feel so frightened. And I couldn't blame you if you left me. I got you thrown out of the priesthood. I should never have let you become involved with me. But I couldn't help myself. I love you.I always felt you could have found someone better than me, like an educated city girl, who might know something about life."

"City girls don't appeal to me, I've seen enough of them, believe me. And as for the priesthood, well, I was a fraud. My heart and my mind were never in it. I knew I was doing the wrong thing from the start. I've told you that before. Anyway, stop blaming yourself. I can't tell you the sense of relief that has come over me since that meeting with O'Flaherty. I could have hugged the man when he told me I was useless. He was right, but I don't feel so useless now. I'm an entirely different man.Just stick it out for a little while longer, then we'll be together again, openly. And we can talk about getting married."

At that her mood lifted. He'd never mentioned marriage before. She'd never thought about it. Just seeing each other whenever they could had seemed to be the limits of their friendship.

"I'd love that Padraig. Do you really mean it?"

"I do. Eventually, when things are sorted out."

"Then take me with you now." Desperation was making her unrealistic again.

"I can't. You know I can't. O'Flaherty has made it clear. In any case, I don't how I'm going to support myself for the next few months, let alone both of us. In Swinford, if you get the job, you'll have a wage. Little as that may be, it'll keep you afloat until I can come up with something better. If you don't, then stay here until I get myself set up, and then I'll send for you. Don't worry Aggie. I promise you it will work out. Just keep your head up and try to look cheerful for the next few weeks. I'm leaving under a cloud, but you don't have to. When I'm gone the gossip that has surrounded us both will die down and people will stop associating you with me, and they'll all wish you well when you move on. In the meantime, I'll be writing to my father for some financial assistance, and I'll see what else I can come up with. O'Flaherty suggested that I paint some pictures for him for a price. That might help us. Get off to work now, and try to keep smiling. I'll write to you tonight and tell you how Foxford is."

Agatha watched him turn the car around and drive away. There would be no way now that she could find him if he were to desert her. And she'd be stuck here with her miserable aunt. Oh, how she detested that woman! But if he did make contact, it would prove he loved her and wanted to stay with her. And then something wonderful would happen, as he had said. She walked on towards Glenowen, her mind a tumult of conflicting emotions, of doubts and fears, along with desperate hope.

## CHAPTER SEVENTEEN

Nolan drove to Foxford, to the address given to him by the Monsignor. He found the place easily in the small settlement, a modest house, well kept, and with a productive garden. He knocked tremulously, expecting a brusque reception at best. The door was opened by an ancient stooped woman, who greeted him uncertainly. An old man stood behind her asking: "Who is it? Mary."

Before Nolan could introduce himself a middle-aged priest pushed his way between them. "You must be Padraig," he said, shaking Nolan's hand warmly. "I'm Michael Toibin. Welcome. Come inside and sit yourself down. You've had a long drive; you must have a great thirst on you. We've a fresh pot of tea on the go, will you take a drop with us?"

There was friendship in the man's voice. Nolan had not expected this, and was greatly relieved. The priest introduced his parents, both of whom seemed lost in a mental fog. Nolan could see why Father Toibin needed to keep an eye on them as Monsignor O'Flaherty had said.

After the tea had been drunk, Toibin said, "Would you drive us round to the cottage? It's a bit out of the way and I don't have a car myself. I've been round there once today already and it's a long walk." He picked up a cardboard box from behind the door as they left the house. Nolan wondered what it might contain. The old woman followed them out with a large sack stuffed softly with something bulky. These parcels were placed on the rear seat of the car.

The priest chatted amiably enough as Nolan drove. "I lit a fire in the place yesterday, and another this morning. They've taken out the worst of the damp but you'll have to keep them going for a bit. It hasn't been occupied for a while. I've swept it out today too. The windows could do with a wash, you can hardly see out of them. But I doubt you'll be staying long enough to worry about that."

Toibin continued with what Nolan recognized as deliberately inconsequential chatter: "It's grand soft weather we've been having isn't it?" and, "The salmon have been running well, there's been some great catches taken." He could tell that the easy small-talk was intended to avoid any taboo subjects being brought to the fore, and he was grateful for that. And he was not being made to feel a pariah, an outcast, even though that was the case. Clearly O'Flaherty had put Father Toibin 'in the picture,' but without denigrating his character entirely, it seemed. It confirmed his initial impression of the Monsignor, that he was blunt, forceful, but fair. That might bode well for the future, suggesting that he would keep his word about trying to help Nolan break into the art world.

As they drove up a narrow lane with grass sprouting in the middle of it, Nolan was amazed to see only the chimneys of a sizeable house showing through a veritable wilderness of vegetation. The term 'cottage' was clearly used ironically. This once imposing dwelling, the better part of a century old, was long neglected and now dilapidated, but not entirely ruinous. It was almost impossible to see it from the lane because of the trees and hedges all around it. Nolan immediately realized that this could prove useful when Agatha moved in this direction.

Father Toibin led him to the rear of the place by a route that had only recently been hacked out of the vegetation. Near the back door was a circular stonewalled well with a rusty winding-chain and a rotten wooden cover intended to prevent the ingress of debris, but now adding to it. A dominant life-sized statue of the Virgin, mounted high on a stone plinth, overlooked the scene. Father Toibin noticed Nolan's surprise as he gazed at the effigy. He explained that the place had once housed a small cohort of nuns who had chosen a particularly austere mode of existence. "They planted the trees," he said, "but the rest of this jungle has taken over since they've been gone. The place has hardly been used in years, except, very occasionally, by the odd person making a retreat."

The priest indicated a small outhouse with a good stock of well- dried turf and some kindling. Then, the adjacent latrine. Nolan observed wryly the shovel just inside its half-open door, a necessity for burying its contents. This was going to be different from what he had been used to. It was little wonder that Toibin chose to live with his parents; It wasn't only so that he could keep an eye on them. Nolan then made the mental observation that so many of the people in the parish he had just left lived in much poorer conditions than these. His own education was about to be further enhanced, he felt.

Father Toibin asked Nolan to bring in the sack from the car. "These are some sheets and blankets I had our housekeeper air yesterday for you. You'll have to do your best to keep them dry.

There's a drying rack somewhere in there for putting against the fire."

Toibin himself carried in the box and set it down on a scrubbed deal table. From it he produced a few eggs and a loaf of bread. "I had the housekeeper bake this for you this morning." Then out came a canister of milk, which had somehow remained upright during the short journey, a packet of tea, and a pat of butter wrapped up in paper. "That'll keep you going until you get into the shops tomorrow. Oh, by the way, there's a good stock of candles in that cupboard over there, and I've left you a few matches. But don't buy too many of those at a time, the damp perishes them quickly.

"Perhaps now you'll drive me back home. You can then come back and settle yourself in."

When Father Toibin got out of the car he said to Nolan, "If you need me, you know where I am. I won't come troubling you. When you leave, drop the key into the church poor box just inside the porch. I'll find it, and know that you're gone. Best of luck for the future."

Nolan shook his hand and thanked him for his hospitality. As he turned the car around, he heaved a huge sigh of relief. He could tell that his brief presence here was not going to be noticed. His sense of freedom was immense. The next thing to do was to write a letter to Agatha. His instinct was to drive back to Glenowen the next day, but he resisted it. Even if he picked her up on the road, well clear of the town, someone was bound to see them, and that would make things awkward for her. No point in doing that just for the sake of waiting a couple of weeks more. No, he would write to her, tell her where he was, how he was feeling. And most of all, how much he loved her and wanted her and needed her.

And how bright the future now looked for the two of them.

*

Returning to the 'cottage' Nolan repaired the dying embers of the turf fire, made a pot of tea, and sat down to write a letter to Agatha.

'My dearest,' he wrote, 'I'm sorry I was abrupt with you this morning. I was struggling to hold myself together, I was so sorry to be leaving you.

'Let me tell you about this place. (The house, not Foxford; I've not seen that place properly yet.) It is unbelievably primitive, but nevertheless habitable, at least for a few months if necessary. That is, providing O' Flaherty lets me stay there that long. But, and very much in its favour, it's quite isolated. I've not yet seen a soul pass by, and if they did, they'd hardly see it from the road, it's so overgrown with vegetation. It's well outside Foxford and on the Swinford road, so when you get over there, I'll be able to bring you here to sit with me in the dark around a turf fire. Won't that be wonderful? Just the two of us. With no prying eyes or wagging tongues. And another thing: Not being a fisherman, I'd not given a thought to the fact that the river Moy, the best salmon river in the country, runs through Foxford and Swinford, and out through Ballina. So, there will be plenty of anglers around, many of them visitors, strangers like ourselves, and we'll be able to mingle with them, openly. I'll have to get used to the fact that I'm no longer a priest; I keep forgetting. Oh Agatha, I never thought this day would come.'

*

## *Two of a Kind*

The next day, on awakening, Nolan realized that he had nothing in particular to do. He was out of a job. Whilst it might be a long while before O'Flaherty obtained a Papal dissolution of his vows, he was in every practical sense, a free man. At first, he didn't want to go into Foxford, being afraid to get into conversations about where he was staying, what he was doing there, how did he make his living. He felt like a newly released prisoner trying to avoid recognition in an attempt to start a new life. The need for food drove him into the shops, but first he sought a men's outfitter, where he bought a tweed cap. He thought that without the clerical garb, and with his head covered, he might look different in the unlikely event that someone from Glenowen should be visiting Foxford. Despite his burgeoning sense of freedom, he had frequent moments when he felt he was being watched, as if he was doing something wrong. In the shops, although he was always greeted cordially, he was cautious in his replies to any questions.

He saw a shop selling an incongruous collection of goods, including some sketch books gathering dust and dead flies in a corner of a window. They were reduced to half- price. He knew that he ought to get started on some pictures for O'Flaherty. He purchased the remaining three, along with some pencils. As he was paying, he noticed other artist paraphernalia. "Do you think you could obtain some artists canvases for me?" he asked

"We can Sir, be glad to. We have a supplier in Dublin. Can get them in a week, Sir. Would that be any use to you?"

Nolan confirmed that it would.

"Give me the address you're staying at Sir, and we'll deliver them to you." That was a problem; he did not wish to draw attention to his present address.

"Ah, I'm looking for new quarters. I'm not too sure where I'll be next week. Let me pay you for them now, and I'll come in again and collect them."

"Right you are, Sir."

"Are you doing any fishing Sir?" the man asked, keen to prolong a conversation if it might delay his customer long enough to find something else to sell him.

"Well, not exactly," he replied prudently. "I'm just taking a bit of a rest. But I like to do a bit of drawing now and again, and the river makes a lovely subject."

"We've seen quite a few amateur artists lately," continued the shopkeeper. "We had a barrister from Dublin down here last week who was doing a bit of painting. A fella by the name of Yeats - Jack Yeats, I think it was. He bought some turpentine from us. Somebody said he was fairly good, but I couldn't see it m'self. Anyway, I wouldn't want him defending me in court." Nolan couldn't help smiling to himself.

On leaving the shop he reflected that the balance of the last cheque his mother had sent him must be getting somewhat eroded. He'd no wish to write to her asking for further financial assistance as it would mean telling her all about the situation in which he now found himself. No, he'd have to try to manage a bit longer, or write to his father and explain things. And ask *him* for a cheque.

If it were not for the drawing of voluptuous scenes that might satisfy O'Flaherty, and several others of the river, for himself, which at least got him out of the lonely house and gave him exercise, he would have gone mad in his isolated setting. However, he was feeling more confident now, less concerned about his past. He did not see himself as a fraud or as a failure anymore, but as someone

*Two of a Kind*

who had made a few mistakes – admittedly serious ones, which he now intended to put behind him. He now walked into Foxford openly, and out along the river for miles, occasionally talking to anglers and other walkers. Every day he posted a letter to Agatha. Their frequent correspondence strengthened their bond. She was soon able to inform him that she had got the job at Swinford post office and would soon be moving. There was almost palpable excitement between the lines as the day for Agatha to move to Swinford drew near.

## CHAPTER EIGHTEEN

"I'm sorry to see you go Agatha, but I'm glad for you. I'm sure you're doing the right thing." It was Miss Cronin speaking, on Agatha's last day at Glenowen's post office. "You've done more than I ever expected of you. You'll be hard to replace." She was now wishing she had never suggested that Agatha should apply for the job at Swinford. She was much too good to let go, but it was too late now to stop her.

Miss Cronin knew that none of the locals would have put so much of their own time into the job, they'd other things to be getting on with. But as Agatha had been an outsider, and, with little else to occupy her time – at least as far as Miss Cronin knew – she'd been free to work more hours than she was paid for. Free of the many distractions a local would have had, apart from the distraction of Nolan's unnecessary visits of course. They had been a nuisance to Miss Cronin and she was glad that he'd gone off somewhere - on a retreat, it was said. If he didn't return, then she'd lost a good worker for nothing, all through that wretched priest.

But she found some solace in the fact that she had done something worthwhile for Agatha. "You'll be better off in Swinford," she told her. "There'll be more chance of further promotion for you. I'm pleased you were able to get lodgings with that woman whose address I gave you."

"Yes, thanks for that Miss Cronin. I'll be fine there, I'm sure.

She's written a nice letter to me. It's been a pleasure working here though, I've met some nice people. They've been kind to me."

When Agatha told Bridget of her impending departure, she knew that her aunt would by no means be distressed by the news. In fact, Bridget could not contain her sense of relief; it was almost palpable. She'd always preferred her own company, and she didn't like young people anyway. They just did not know their place. Her niece's stay had attracted too many visits from Nolan for all of them to be entirely innocuous. In fact, Bridget had doubted his motives almost from the start. And various lads from around the glen – Mick Mullarkey being chief amongst them – were always asking after her. Bridget felt that she was being saved – thanks be to God – from some kind of catastrophe, when she finally and thankfully said goodbye to Agatha. She did however write to her brother, Agatha's father, to make it quite clear that she was in no way the cause of her departure, that she had not shirked any responsibility she might have owed to her niece.

Bridget was not one to use deceit lightly or frequently, of course not, she had once been a nun. But in some situations, the truth can sometimes be less than adequate, so when truth wasn't good enough, she could lie like a gypsy-woman reading a palm.

'My Dear Michael,' she wrote,

'By now you will have heard from Agatha that she is moving to Swinford, where she has great job prospects. I am terribly sorry she is going; I will miss her greatly, and I am certain she is sorry to be leaving me. We've been a source of great comfort to one another. However, it is in her best interest and I'm sure she'll do well. I suppose I'll find ways of managing without her.

'I'd like to think that I have enhanced her education whilst she's been with me, and that such improvement may have helped her to get the job.'

After further statements about the woeful state of the country and its mostly dubious, indeed sinful, inhabitants, she concluded:

'Kind Regards from your devoted sister,

Bridget.'

\*

Agatha waited for the bus to Ballina. It departed from outside the post office, where a sizeable group of passengers, and the relatives of some of them who'd come along to see them depart, was gathered. Shopkeepers on either side of the post office building, and the rest of the townspeople who knew her, were among the group. Padraig had been right when he'd told her that she would not have to leave under a cloud of suspicion once he had disappeared. He'd been instantly forgotten, and everyone was talking to her again. A number of people wished her well.

This weekly journey was always something of an event. Some travellers were taking the three-hour journey all the way to Ballina. A good few would get down at various isolated outposts along the way, often with no sign of habitation in sight, and tramp a mile or three to visit a relative at some lonely abode hidden amongst the hills. For others, this was only the first stage of a much longer journey, onwards to Dublin, or, for some, from there to the boat, and on to England. Dermot O'Leary, the regular driver, was leaning against the wall of the post office, smoking a woodbine, whilst taking the money for seats, and chatting amiably to half the town. He had been driving the route for years, and was known to all of them, and he knew half the people in every other town to which he drove a bus. He was the carrier of messages and gossip between all these places, and kept everyone informed of faraway happenings. Dermot was considered to be a great driver. Whilst anyone who could drive a motor vehicle was something of a marvel, a man who could drive a bus, and sometimes bring it in more or less on time, was a hero. He'd never once gone off the road, despite some appalling weather and various other hazards. Even with a drop taken at several hostelries along the way, Dermot was the man who always got you home. He knew all the unusual stopping places, and his wise brown eyes constantly scanned the road ahead for problems, watching out for places where the edge of it might have broken away, or a rock-fall from above seemed imminent. He had the patience of a saint, and would wait calmly for a couple of cows or a flock of sheep to be driven out of his way, chatting and joking all the while with his passengers. If he spotted a tribe of kids in the distance, running like goats down a mountainside, and waving frantically, he'd pull in and switch the engine off, and wait whilst an old granny on a stick hobbled her slow way down to the road and the kids would push her on board, along with her baggage, and wave her good-bye. And then she'd be greeted warmly by the other passengers, despite the fact she'd delayed them by several minutes

"Hello Agatha, where are ye travelling to?" he asked.

"Ballina," she answered, proffering money for a ticket.

"Have ye been there before?" asked Dermot.

"No. I've never been anywhere but here and Geesala, where I was born."

"Sure, it's a great town, you'll enjoy yourself there. But I'd heard you were leaving us for Swinford."

"I will be going there," she said, hoping that he would not pursue his question.

"Well, it's a long old journey we've got ahead of us. Find yourself a seat somewhere in the middle of the bus, it's less bumpy there. A lot of these are only going some of the way, so they can put up with being bounced about a bit."

"Thanks, Dermot." She climbed on, and Mick Mullarkey detached himself from the group, where he'd been waiting for some opportunity or other to show itself, and passed up her case and wished her well. He'd given up on making advances to her. He'd accepted she wasn't overly fond of him and was completely untroubled by that fact.

It was the first time Agatha had been inside a bus. When she'd come up to her aunt's cottage from Geesala she'd covered the first few miles on the cart of a farmer whom she knew, who happened to be going roughly in that direction. She'd walked the rest of the way, putting down her small cardboard suitcase tied with string every mile or so, whilst she rested briefly. Today's mode of travel would be a new experience. She was quite excited, and just a little nervous.

O'Leary knew that he was well on time. He could afford to wait a few more minutes. He was enjoying the banter. Agatha looked out of the window. She could hear everything through the open door, all of it confirming what she knew: that she was leaving a warm and friendly community, despite it not accepting her man. But the city lights, which so far had existed only in her imagination, had for long beckoned, and to go there with her city man would be like going to another world.

She watched through the window as a middle-aged woman accompanied by a young man rattled down the street, the pair of them pushing a small chest of drawers on castors. "Can we get this on board, Dermot?" asked the woman.

"Jesus! Is it a bus I'm driving, or a feckin' furniture lorry?" fumed Dermot.

"Ah, go on Dermot. I'll give ye a couple of bob to cover it," she said. "Me mother left it to me in her will and they're clearing the house out now. I had to take it. And sure, I'm only going a couple of miles."

"Ten, more like," he said "Ah, keep your money Madge, and get it on. Take that seat right at the back. I don't want you blocking the gangway. And hang on to the joinery, or it'll take off when I brake." He watched through the window as the furniture was trundled sideways to the appointed place.

The woman took her seat, but the lad, having settled her, walked to the front and climbed down from the bus, shouting "Goodbye Auntie Madge, God bless ye."

"Cormac, are ye not travelling with her?" Shouted Dermot.

"No. Could ye give her a lift down with it when she gets to the other end? Me uncle is meeting her with the pony and trap."

"'Tis a great pity he didn't come here with the pony and trap," said Dermot, wishing he'd accepted the bribe she had offered in the first place.

This was what had endeared the township to Agatha almost as soon as she arrived, the warm, easy-going tolerance of the place, the friendly chaos. Everybody rubbing along with each other, despite their differences. The painful, humiliating fact that they had taken exception to her beloved was, she supposed, to be expected. It was impossible for them to tolerate what they had suspected was going on. And that was her fault as much as his. Once again, she blamed herself.

One or two more got aboard and Dermot was about to take his own seat at the wheel, when another elderly woman appeared, carrying two hens in a sack tied at the neck. Their heads were sticking out through slits she must have cut in the hessian for them. "How much will you charge me for these passengers? Dermot," she asked.

"Poultry is not on my passenger price list Kath, unless they're parcelled up in a box," he replied, "so there's no charge. But I hope they're not going to squawk all the way, are they?"

"They might, but it'll keep you from dropping off to sleep. But no, Dermot, I've another bag I can put over their heads. They'll think it's night-time and shut up."

"I might want a bit of a nap whilst I'm driving," he said. "But why didn't you cover their heads earlier? They could be sleeping now."

"I wanted them to have their last bit of freedom. It's such a nice day, it'll do them good. They'll be in the pot tomorrow."

"You wouldn't want me to neck them now, would you? It would save you having to cover their heads."

"Sure, you're a terrible man, Dermot."

"Sit in that single seat there Kath, behind the bulkhead, and make sure they don't get out. If they escape, I'll neck the three of ye. It's a good thing you're not going far."

"Thanks Dermot, you're a good man."

The woman settled in the seat and the hens squatted quietly

in their sack between her feet, clucking softly to themselves. She then twisted round in her seat and began a conversation with the passenger behind her, then with Agatha, and eventually, with the whole bus. Agatha was glad of that, she needed friendly distraction to help take her mind, to some degree at least, off her doubts and fears.

She was filled with bursting excitement, and at the same time, with considerable trepidation. She was wildly excited at the thought of seeing Padraig again, and being held in his arms. Also, at the thought of a whole new way of life opening up for her. The limited beginnings of her life looked as if they soon might bother her no more. But things could still go wrong. For one thing, she was uneasy about the new position she was going to. The job she had taken at Glenowen had not been a real choice, except that of being shod or shoeless, of being fed or staying half starved, of having hope of something, instead of the promise of nothing. But she had done it well, and had found approval and friendship. She was giving that up, putting her faith in the continuation of a new and beautiful love, a wonderous experience which was transporting her to heights she had hitherto only dreamed about. But now she was doubting her ability to manage the greater responsibilities that she would have to assume. And if she failed – what then? It would be up to Padraig to support them both, and he was in no position to do so right now. And there was the greater fear, much greater – what if he'd reconsidered his position? In every one of his letters, he'd declared his love for her, yet still she worried. He'd had time to think, to consider other possibilities. Would he be there? And if he were, would he still feel the same way about her? After all, he must have spoken with other women whilst they were apart.

If he were not, she didn't know what she might do. This journey, the longest she had ever taken, was making her aware just how little she knew of her country. She'd never been so far away from home.She was lost. She hadn't realised the distances one might have to travel in life. When she left the bus, she would be all alone if he wasn't there for her. She didn't even know if there would be a bus today to take her onward to Swinford should Padraig fail to meet her, and she couldn't afford to stay overnight in Ballina.

With everyone on board, Dermot eased the bus down the narrow street, squeezing it between a couple of donkey carts, then stopping when a larger cart blocked his way. He waited patiently whilst its owner was shouted out of O'Neil's to move it. When the inebriated man arrived, barely able to stand, Dermot, greatly amused, shouted through the window, "It's a good thing your nag knows the way home Martin."Eventually, with a bit of shouting and swearing and some coaxing with a stick, the cart was moved, and enough space to pass was created. Dermot headed towards the glen, and out on to the open road.

The green rolling countryside and the road, fringed here and there with masses of head-high fuchsias, seemed empty. From time to time a distant man making hay or stacking turf, or repairing the thatch of a lonely dwelling, or a woman boiling washing in an old drum over a turf fire, would put up their hand on sighting the bus, and Dermot would sound his horn in friendly response. The vehicle was as much a symbolic link between communities as it was actual transportation. Even to those who had never left their village it served as a reminder that other places existed and that people moved between them. There was something exotic almost about a bus. Every hand uplifted to its passing signalled good wishes to the travellers within it, but Agatha was too lost in her own thoughts to feel any connection. She sat in exquisite anticipation, mounting excitement changing places with pangs of anxiety with every diminishing mile. She watched her world slip by, desperate for the journey to end.

Eventually they arrived in Ballina. As the bus drew in, she scanned the street for Padraig, and her heart sank. She almost fell down the steps as her eyes searched for him, instead of watching where she was going, and stumbled over her tattered case, as it collided with her legs.

"All the best," shouted the passenger who had sat next to her.

"Thanks, and to you too" she shouted back, feeling embarrassed at her own thoughtlessness. "And thanks Dermot, I've enjoyed the trip."

Then she saw him, waiting across the road in the mouth of an alleyway. He'd had the foresight to know that there would be several on the bus who would recognize him, so he'd concealed himself for Agatha's sake. She crossed the road and fell into his arms, sobbing with relief. They hugged with a powerful ferocity, too overcome with emotion to find words. They were free now. Normal, free people.

"The car is behind this hotel Aggie," he said, putting an arm around her shoulder and pointing her in that direction. They walked to it. She was in a dream. In the car they hugged again. She had tears in her eyes, but they were tears of joy. Their world was changing. There was now a chance of dreams being realized.

"How are ye doing Padraig?" she asked. It was all she could think of saying, her mind was in such a whirl.

"I'm going mad, completely off my head. I'm living in the

back of beyond, out in a forlorn wilderness, and all the time worrying about you and wishing the days would fly for me to be able to see you again."

So his letters had been true. He did love her. He was now her man, for ever, she hoped. And she was his woman. They were truly two of a kind.

\*

Before taking her to Swinford, Nolan took her to his dwelling at Foxford. He didn't expect to impress her with his insalubrious premises, but he felt that she would feel more secure if she knew where he was situated and she could see for herself that they were not going to be far apart. He also wanted to make love to her.

Agatha was hugely impressed by the large spacious dwelling, unlike her man, who was still appalled by its condition. "This is grand, Padraig. What a wonderful place to be."

"Do you think it's all right then?" he asked, surprised at her calm acceptance of the state of the house."It's cold and damp and dirty. There are no facilities for keeping yourself clean. And, as you can see, it's in the middle of nowhere."

"You've never seen the place where I used to live. You should be thankful you've got this."

After a pot of tea had been drunk, along with some bread and jam he'd purchased earlier, Nolan took her to her new lodgings. They both got on well with the woman who owned the house, a friendly woman, very welcoming, and not inclined to ask personal questions. After another pot of tea, Nolan left, and returned like an exile to his place in the wilderness, leaving Aggie to settle herself in. Her landlady was a widow, who was grateful for the small subsistence allowance she'd agreed with Agatha. She was very easy to get along with, an entirely different breed from Aunt Bridget. She even liked to take a drop of stout of an evening, and sometimes shared a bottle with Agatha. She had accepted Agatha's introduction of Padraig as an old friend from over Foxford way, and did not seem inclined to probe any further.

The new job proved no more difficult to master to than the previous one had done. Within days she was feeling sure of her ability to cope. The Postmaster was kindly, and generous with his time as he trained her in her new responsibilities. She started getting to know the regular customers, and was soon at ease with the place.

Nolan's stay so far at Foxford had convinced him that the house where he now dwelt was so out-of-the-way that it was safe to take Agatha there from time to time. So, as he'd said they would, she and Padraig often sat in the darkness around a turf fire. They also spent some time in his bed, but no activity there went too far. Despite her raging sexual attraction towards him, Agatha held him off in that respect, and although he lacked her strength of will, he accepted the form of celibacy she insisted upon for both of them. And it was only just celibacy, by the very smallest margin. Whilst the main fruit of the tree remained forbidden for now, he had been permitted, encouraged even, to rustle the leaves and push aside the branches; had been given a clear view of the ripeness that lay in store. Agatha's powers of seduction were equalled by her resolve to retain the last vestige of her chastity until they could see for certain a route to secure freedom, and she was sure they would always be together. O'Flaherty had opened up that avenue, and she felt an immense sense of gratitude towards the man, whom she had never met, even though she was aware that he had not acted altruistically. She knew, despite Padraig's errant ways, her darling man had been completely in thrall to vows that had become strained to their limits on an almost daily basis, and she too had felt that they should not be broken, even if they were both blatantly disrespecting those vows. So, if he could - more or less - keep those, then he would surely keep any promise he might make to her.

For the moment she would let him explore her body, and sinful though it still seemed, it was much less so now. She loved that. It was so delicious, so wonderful. He was so gentle yet so provocative, so sensual. And when he was about to explode with tormented desire, she could quench his creaming excitement with her beautiful lips or her slender skilful fingers and he would similarly untie the knot in her and they would lie in trembling exhaustion, wrapped in blissful hopefulness. Then, one day, he could make vows to her, which she could be sure he would keep. He was becoming a serious man now, a little melancholy at times, perhaps, but no longer dejected. He just needed to find a new setting for his talents, a new way of living for both of them. Their natural proclivities were the same. But one other thing troubled her: even if they were married, she did not want children for a while. She needed to talk with some mature English women; they seemed to know something about these things. She hoped she might meet some in Dublin, eventually.

\*

*Two of a Kind*

Nolan's departure from the glen was scarcely noticed. The new man –Father Tim Ruddy - who took his place was from the south west. He was a village man, not a city sophisticate like Nolan. His farming family background fitted him well for the Glenowen community, he'd slot in well with most of them. He was middle-aged, conservative, and quiet in his disposition; unassuming, but not bland. He was liked immediately.Monsignor O'Flaherty had moved him in on the day he moved Nolan out. He told the new incumbent to tell the congregation at the first opportunity that Father Nolan had gone to a retreat for a while, and that they should pray for his health and general well-being. Nobody prayed for him. It was just stated in a jocular way, and not for very long, that "the Quare Fellow" had retreated. He was soon forgotten.

Nolan's lewd handiwork soon faded from the rock leaving only indistinct shadows of its former glory and so the new priest was able to have the palisade around it removed. The glen was no longer in the news, no more a topic of national interest. The flood of tourists and pilgrims lessened, but not significantly; trade remained reliably good. The place benefitted from a steady stream of visitors who all spent money there. Almost everyone felt that they were at least a little better off than ever before, and many developed a very comfortable standard of living.

Mick Mullarkey absorbed most of the credit for the town's upturn. His feckless father, Colm, made sure that everyone who visited heard how his son had been the first to witness the miracle in the glen. He reiterated the fact ad nauseum to every trader in the place, never letting them forget that it was Mick who had put money in their pockets, and hoping that a little of it might come his way in the form of a pint of stout. Nolan's part in the transformation was never talked about, although 'Long' John Donohoe often wondered about it.

## CHAPTER NINETEEN

Nolan was making his lively way through the shimmering flowerbeds and sweet grassy acreage of Saint Stephen's Green, having gained that delightful situation *en route* from Merrion Square and heading towards Grafton Street. He was a different man entirely, his shoulders back, his head held high, his step jaunty. Hopelessness had been entirely replaced by faith: faith in the future, a future for himself and the woman on his arm. His face creased into one smile after another, his head turning in every direction, looking up into the trees and the dappled sky above, where shades of blue were showing signs of supremacy over the weakening clouds. And every few moments looking to engage with the beaming countenance of the woman gazing up at him lovingly. They inhaled the myriad scents of the park, laughing at the antics of the screaming gulls as they disputed between themselves and the pigeons the ownership of every morsel thrown to them by the morning loafers. The peaceful and generous environs of the park were encompassed only by the distant cries and mingled sounds of Dublin traffic, and rather than intruding, these enhanced their burgeoning sense of freedom.

Nolan was very much at his ease now. Agatha was somewhat less so, but still wonderfully glad to be there with him, their passion openly displayed now, no secrets to hide. "Sure, isn't this the most amazing place, Padraig," she said. "I'd heard so much about it but I still could not have imagined that it would be as grand as this. It's so busy. I cannot believe the amount of people that I'm seeing, there's thousands of them."

"So, you're glad I brought you here Aggie?"

"Of course I am, I'm loving every minute of it. I'm not frightened now."

"When were you frightened, and of what?"

"I don't know, just the sheer size of the place I suppose. I immediately thought we'd get lost. I'd forgotten that you know it so well, that you were born here. And the traffic at first frightened me too. I thought we'd be crushed the first time we crossed the road. I'm getting over it now. And the people are so friendly; I didn't expect that in a big city. The woman selling flowers that you spoke to, she knew you of course, but she was nice to me too."

"Sure, it is a great place, truly it is. There are some bad parts to it of course, but we won't go looking into those. No need to look for trouble. I'm pleased you're enjoying yourself."

"I am, Padraig. The only thing I'm afraid of now is meeting your father. I hope he likes me and that he doesn't blame me for leading you away from the priesthood."

"He won't, he's not one for blaming people. And you didn't. I've told you that already. In any case I don't know if he ever wanted me to be a priest, we never really talked about it. He didn't have much time for the clergy. Anyway, wait till you meet him. You'll like him."

They were out of the green now and soon onto Grafton Street, throbbing with city life, the sound of the clattering hooves of the horse-drawn delivery wagons and the jaunting cars mingling with the fuming engines of the motor vehicles, the trams, with their ringing bells, and the raucous, vulgar language of their drivers; the teeming hordes of cyclists; a constant battleground of noise. There were people everywhere, picking their precarious way in and out of the melee in a surprisingly relaxed fashion.

"This is Grafton Street now," said Padraig. "Bewley's coffee house is not so far along it. We'll soon be there. He said in his letter he'd meet us there at eleven. He'll be there all right."

Agatha couldn't believe how far things had moved on in only a couple of months. Herself established in a new job in Swinford post office, Padraig in the cottage that Monsignor O'Flaherty had afforded him in Foxford. The clergy seemed to have forgotten about that. He'd not had a visit from anyone. Although they were living apart for now, they were seeing each other regularly, thanks to Padraig's possession of a car. And now here in Dublin for a couple of days, they were together openly, not caring who knew about them. It seemed so utterly normal.

They entered Bewley's, and Padraig immediately made his way over to a table where a large bearded man with thick wavy hair was seated. The man's handsome craggy features broke into a huge grin as he stood up from the table and hugged his son. For a brief moment Agatha felt excluded. Then the man turned to her, still wearing the big smile, laughter in his eyes. She knew instantly that he was a kind man.

"And you must be Agatha, he mentioned you in his letter." With that he swept her up into his arms as easily as the wind lifts a leaf, hugging her so hard she couldn't breathe. Setting her down again, he said, "Well, aren't you the gorgeous girl, but I knew you would have to be. For all his faults he has good taste. He takes after his father for both. Sit down, the pair of you, whilst I get something ordered for us all."

That accomplished, Connor Nolan rested his elbows on the table, clasped his hands together and stared earnestly into his son's face. "Now, let's get some serious talking done. First, let me be sure about this: you're finished with the priestly business. Is that right?"

"It is Da, it wasn't for me. I wasn't the man for it."

"I could have told you that, and I should have done. I think a lot of them aren't. And some of them, well, I don't know what they're fit for. But once you're in it, you're in for life. I don't know how the devil you got yourself out of it, but I'm glad you did."

"That's a story for another time Da."

Connor Nolan's words cheered Agatha considerably. She'd been afraid he would castigate her for leading his son astray.

"Anyway," continued Connor, speaking directly now to Agatha, "it's to my enduring shame that I ever let him get into it, but I did, and I'm sorry." Then, turning back to his son, he continued, "I've got a lot to apologise for. I've neglected you. I've been forever in and out of the country, I'm almost a nomad. I've communicated with you only by writing letters. That's no way to relate to a son. I should have done better, but I didn't."

"It wasn't your fault Da, Mam wanted me to go into the clergy. I don't blame her for that of course. And my uncles too had an influence. And also, a couple of school pals were doing the same thing, and as far as I know they made good priests. I just went along with them, but it was the wrong vocation for me."

"I ought to have opposed your mother, but I'd caused her enough grief by leaving her, so I didn't want to do any more harm.

And I was never at home before we split up. That was the nature of my work I suppose. But I must admit it, it was mostly down to me, to the way I was, the way I am, perhaps. Anyway, I wasn't a good father, and I need to make it up to you. Let's have some more coffee." Connor beckoned a waiter.

"Agatha, I'm sorry if I appear to be leaving you out. I don't intend to," he said suddenly. Agatha had not felt excluded. She'd been totally absorbed by this frank and heartfelt confession. She was amazed at the warmth that so obviously existed between father and son, who had lived apart for so long. She had never found this affection in her own family. "But let me get my son set up first and we'll see if that helps you."

"Tell me Padraig, surely you're not intending to stay in some out-of-the-way place like Foxford for much longer. It must be deadly. You cannot make a living there surely. How are you surviving?"

"I'm barely surviving. Monsignor O'Flaherty gave me a few quid for I couple of pictures I painted for him and he's lodged another one with an art dealer he knows, but no money has come in from that one yet - although it might, and, if it does, it could be quite a bit. He's established some contacts for me. But I'm struggling, although that's pretty much what I expected. Mother still sends me the odd cheque. But these days I'm full of hope. I'm more optimistic now. I'd no hope before."

"I could get you work at our office here in Dublin. That's why I asked you to come up here today"

"If you're thinking of technical drawing Da, I wouldn't be up to it. I know I was good at it at school but I couldn't do it now. I have absolutely no interest in it. It's in no way creative enough for me. I'm sorry da, I don't mean to be ungrateful when you're trying to help me, but I don't want to make another mistake. It just wouldn't be my thing at all."

"I know it wouldn't. No, I wouldn't want you to do that. I wasn't even thinking about it. Wait till I tell you what I have in mind, then turn it down if you want.

"The firm employs several artists on an *ad hoc* basis, not for technical drawing, obviously, but to do what we call artist's impressions of how an intended development might look if it were completed. For instance, if we were planning a big hotel abroad somewhere, with maybe a cocktail bar at the side of it and a water feature in front of it, all joining on to a piazza or an arcade of sorts, then they'd draw and paint a vision of the finished product. Providing you stayed loosely within the prescribed parameters you could be as creative as you liked. The more creative, the better it looks to the client- so long as you didn't stray entirely off the subject, as you've been known to do. But we won't go into that. I'm sure you've learned your lesson there. The plans often get changed several times before they're accepted. Sometimes we don't get the commission anyway, all too often that's the case. But the artist still gets paid. You could make a decent living doing it and still have lots of time to paint whatever else you wanted to. It wouldn't pay you a lot, but it would keep you going at least, until you established yourself in the fine art world. And you'd make enough of a living out of it even if nothing else turned up. What do you say?"

Agatha's face was itself a picture, glowing with hopeful excitement. She was almost levitating with all this talk of fine modern buildings in faraway places and her darling man having some part to play in their creation, and money to be had as well. And perhaps, eventually, his being a 'someone' in the art world, and painting her, just in her skin, like that Dora somebody, and being on display in art galleries. The very thought of it; she was almost fainting with excitement.

"That sounds great doesn't it, Padraig?" she said. "You know you could do it. Wouldn't you like to?" She was by now quite effervescent. Padraig was also more than a little interested.

"That sounds promising Da. I'd love to do it. Any chance of starting soon though. I'm getting desperate for money."

"There's every chance. I'll talk to my senior partners. There'll be no problem. And I'll let you have some cash to keep you going. Let's put the past behind us. We'll drink up and then take a walk around the city. And maybe later have a drop of something a bit stronger. We have things to celebrate, do we not? And can I take it you'll be calling on your mother whilst you're here? She'd like that."

"I'd love to, but I don't know if I can."

"Why not, why wouldn't you? She'd love to see you."

"Because she doesn't know I've left the clergy. She'll take a fit when she finds out."

"What? Do you mean she's no inkling of what you're doing? Does she not know about Agatha?"

"No. I've not had the courage to tell her. I write frequently to her, but I never tell her very much."

"Get in there Padraig, today. Tell her everything. I'll tell you how to do it. You know she has an awful temper – that's part of her loveliness. She'll scream and shout and throw everything she can lay her hands on at you. She always used to do that to me.

You'll have to duck and dive and dodge around the table like a cuckold dodging an irate husband who has a shotgun in his hands, telling her all the time the how and the why and the what will be of it all. Don't stop talking until you've said everything, and keep moving, quickly, else she'll knock your head off. Then dive through the door and run for it. I've done it many a time m'self, so I know how it is. Then, tomorrow, go back in with a big bunch of flowers and give her a hug. She'll be as good as gold to you, so pleased you've come back. She can be the most reasonable woman in the world after she's had her say. Sure, she's a grand woman, a wonderful woman. I love her still, tempestuous though she is. 'Tis a great pity we never got on.

"But going back to your position – yours and Agatha's I mean – if you take the work I'm offering you, you'll need a place to live in Dublin. I own a small house up an alleyway in one of the backstreets, not much more than a mile from here. I only use the upstairs of it, I rent out the ground floor to an old couple. It's suited me to have them there, as I've been abroad so much. They've kept an eye on the place, so to speak. You and Agatha can have it. And when the old folk drop off the perch – and I don't think that will be very far in the future – you'll have the rest of it. But you'll have to promise me you'll give them a hand when they need it. Is that a deal?"

Agatha was bursting with excitement; Padraig couldn't believe his ears.

"But what about you Da? Where will you live?"

"I haven't lived there for a while. I have a new companion. We've just bought a house in Ballsbridge. I'm not intending to travel much from now on. I'll live and work in Dublin. I've seen

*Two of a Kind*

enough of the world. I'd like a more settled existence. So, is it any good to you? It's not the most prepossessing pile in the city and it's not exactly what you might call a sought-after address, but it's served me well enough when I've needed it. I used to have a big place, as you know, in Sandymount, but being out of the country so much it seemed wasteful. The little place is cosy. If you began to make some money, in time you could pull it round, make it into something half - decent. Do you want it?"

"Of course I do! That would be terrific, wonderful."

The tears of joy running down Agatha's cheeks told her answer.

"I'll never be able to thank you enough."

"Forget about thanks. I owe it to you. It'll help salve my conscience. And anyway, I can well afford it. Now get around to your mother's, and give her my best regards. I want to keep in her good books in case there might be a wedding for us to go to. And let me say it again:keep your head down."

"Who is the lady you're going to settle down with in Ballsbridge Da?"

"She's a young widow, and a very beautiful one. Italian by the way."

"Then how did you meet her?"

"Oh, I've known her for a long time. We always got on well together. She was married to one of the younger partners, but he died suddenly, less than two years ago. He had a heart attack; I think she was too much for him. I'll have to watch out."

"Da, can I ask another favour of you. Would you look after Agatha for a couple of hours?"

"I will, of course, I'd be delighted to show her the sights. Leave her with me."

## Sean P. Gaughan

Padraig Nolan went off to visit his mother.

## CHAPTER TWENTY

Back in Glenowen, within a year or so a steady industriousness had established itself. The previous level of poverty had largely diminished, and an air of hopefulness now drifted about the place. A sizeable hotel had been quickly built to accommodate the many visitors, some of whom stayed long enough to be eligible to marry. People in the bigger houses were taking in paying guests, and were sometimes glad when they departed. When away from home standards sometimes slip a little. But overall, there was good money to be made out of cures and curiosity, out of wantonness and wedlock.

Darcy O'Neill's pub was always busy, and the travellers wanted food as well as drink, so he involved butcher Laffey in making pies to sell to his customers and employed Mary Flannagan to serve them at the few tables he set up at one end of the pub. Mary had not noticed any improvement in the shape of her breasts, but their size was still impressive, and the regular dowsing and massaging she gave them in the holy pool late at night had put her completely at ease with them and she welcomed the attention they attracted. The bit of money Darcy gave her made her more independent and disdainful of her husband Patsy's comments, as she now had plenty of compliments paid her by the customers she served. Her self-confidence increased enormously. Patsy became something of a 'has-been', just a lodger in his own house, but he was careful not to fall out with her these days. There were others who'd be glad to take her on.

Jonty McGarrigle had more than enough funerals to deal with. It was a good thing he'd had the foresight to buy Matt Laffey's van to use as a hearse. Business was thriving. The old horse – drawn contraption would never have kept pace. But he now had to pay out more to get his graves dug, as John Donohoe was worn out with digging and was always complaining about the hours, and the effort he was having to put in. This at least put money into Sean Mullarkey's pockets; he liked casual work and would turn up to dig a grave at a moment's notice. Being younger, and as strong as an ox, he could complete the work in half the time Donohoe would have taken – Donohoe still having other strenuous demands to fit in whenever he could, which, due to his declining energy, were becoming less frequent, much to the annoyance of several women. After half a day's work with the shovel had created a deep enough final resting place for Jonty's 'customer', Sean would collect his cash and then spend the rest of the day and half the night in O'Neill's bar, helping to line Darcy's pocket, whereas Donohoe would have retired to his bed.

Joe Murphy, having purchased McGarrigle's redundant horse-drawn hearse and converted it into a jaunting car, managed to eke out some kind of a living, but not a good one. But then he'd struggled to earn anything before. And when tourists did not require rudimentary transportation, he'd take the seats out of the car and cart turf from the bog for those who'd no means of shifting it other than with a panniered donkey, a time- consuming method of haulage. By such means he earned himself a shilling or two. These combined endeavours gave him just about enough money for O'Neill's products, so long as he didn't let Colm

Mullarkey talk too many drinks out of him. Mullarkey always felt that his friend Joe owed him a few, as Joe went into the jaunting car business only on his advice.

Father Tim ruddy – Nolan's replacement – didn't do so well out of it and was beginning to wish he'd been allowed to stay at his previous parish. He'd visited Glenowen some years previously, and had liked the quietness of the place, where nothing seemed to happen from one day to the next. It had seemed then a nice place in which to spend one's declining years. Now rather too much seemed to be happening. The inhabitants seemed to have a somewhat more ebullient attitude, and he was slightly afraid they could become ungovernable. Noel Daly, his erstwhile part-time breakfast chef, part-time town barber, was one of them. Now he had full- time work providing haircuts and shaves for the pilgrims, and was making good money from it. He was also listening to their stories about their own places of domicile and getting his head filled with preposterous ideas, particularly about setting up a proper salon instead of the scruffy kitchen of his cottage. Sure, weren't people getting above themselves now? The priest therefore had to pay more to get a replacement if he were to have his breakfast provided – unless he got it himself, which he was disinclined to do. Surely that was beneath any priest, wasn't it? And the best he could get in these unusual circumstances was the sluttish Norah O'Bryan, she of the over - brimming bosoms that had always terrified Nolan on the rare occasions when he had visited her. She still had little governance of them, indeed, she seemed totally unconcerned about their autonomous mobility, so the new man found them equally disturbing. He also found Norah's habitual use of profane language unsettling, and frequently upbraided her for it, but as it was to her all part of her everyday vocabulary, she took little notice of his complaints, nor, for that matter, anyone else's. Like several other women, she was becoming a little too sure of herself. Today the priest was complaining-yet again- about the fact that a seemingly indelible brown stain on his white-scrubbed deal breakfast table was still highly visible when Norah removed the tablecloth. "I've tried me best with it, Father; it won't be shifted. Sure, it's harmless enough; ye canan't see it when the cloth is over it."

"I still don't like it," said the priest. "It looks dirty."

"Well, it's not. I've cleaned it well," replied Nora, firmly. I'd be glad of a table as good as that m'self, stained or not. Sure, isn't a good big strong, well-made table. A bit of a mark on it doesn't hurt. Sure, you're bound to get marks on a table, what with putting your feet up on it and spilling tea or beer. All manner of things will put marks upon a table."

"I don't put my feet on tables, it's a disgusting habit. And I seldom spill my tea and I don't have beer in the house. I can't think what caused that particular mark."

"I know what caused it. It was the last man here, the quare fella who's just left. He done it."

"Will you not talk about a priest like that Nora. I don't like it at all, it's disrespectful. And how did he do it by the way?"

"It was some stuff he used to put on his feet. I know that for sure because I caught him putting his feet into a bucket of it one day when I called round here to tell him that Ned was knocking me about a bit too much. There's dabs of it all over the house, you'll find."

"He must have had strange coloured feet."

"Well obviously he did after he'd done that to them. I don't know what they'd have been like otherwise."

Father Ruddy was starting to wonder about the inhabitants of this place. What sort of lives did they lead? Why would their priest dye his feet brown?

"He was a white man, I take it."

"Well of course he was. Why wouldn't he be?"

"I just wondered if he might have been a coloured man, that's all."

"If he had been, he wouldn't have needed to colour his feet with dye, would he now?"

The priest could see that he was allowing himself to be drawn into an argument he'd be better to leave alone. "No Nora, I don't suppose he would."

"And we wouldn't have wanted one of those coloured foreigners amongst us anyway. They'd terrorise you."

"Now that's enough Nora. I'll have no more of it. They're human beings as good as the rest of us. You're not to speak ill of other people. It's unchristian."

"I'm sorry for that, Father."

Father Ruddy was looking to change the subject. He was finding Nora's logic somewhat perplexing.

"What sort of table do you have at home Nora?" He asked.

"I don't have a proper table. I only have a big upturned wooden box to put the stuff on."

"Why is that?" enquired the priest, his genuine surprise revealing how little he knew about the lifestyles of some of his parishioners.

"Because me feckin' useless husband has never got around to

putting a set of legs under it."

"Please don't use such deplorable language, Norah; sure, aren't I always after telling you about that?"

"Ye are indeed father; 'tis true. I'm sorry. But he's such a useless bastard I cannot help m'self."

The priest sighed in hopeless resignation. Inwardly, he had to concur that Ned O'Bryan was indeed a 'feckin' useless bastard.' He couldn't have put it better himself.

"Norah, I've decided. I'm going to buy a new table. Would you like to have this one?"

"Are ye serious father? Sure, wouldn't I love to have it! It's a grand table."

"You could cover the stain, I'm sure."

"That's no problem; I have an old shawl to throw over it."

"Do you not have a cloth?"

"No Father, I don't."

"Well take the cloth too. And if you have a shawl, would you bring it here and wear it over the top part of you? I find your present appearance somewhat distracting. Is that a deal?"

"It is so, Father. Amn't I so grateful to ye, y're so kind."

The priest considered the loss of a table he didn't care for in lieu of the concealment of Norah'sfree-floating breasts, which did, as he said, distract him considerably, to be a satisfactory transaction. He was well pleased with the deal. He'd have been better pleased if he could have found a less coarse-grained housekeeper altogether, although he felt that, in all probability, he'd have to make do with what he'd got, and slowly ameliorate her as best he could, and possibly do the same with several others of his flock.

## *Two of a Kind*

Norah couldn't get Ned out of the pub to help her carry the table home, but Joe Murphy and his jaunting car were enlisted for transport and two of her daughters were glad to lift it off the cart and carry it into the house. They could take their meals in a degree of comfort from now on. A few months later the dog died. He'd been losing weight ever since the table was installed.

*

Solly Axelrod found that whilst the tailoring trade was only slightly improved, he was now selling, in addition to suits and sports- jackets, quite a quantity of small stuff, and a few shirts, so he was well-pleased with the improvement that Mick Mullarkey's 'Saint Patrick' had brought to the town's commercial sector. However, this had to be weighed against the discord he'd caused by selling items similar to those stocked by Mrs. Maddigan at her drapery shop, and he'd had to endure her formidable wrath and daily vituperation, much of it unfairly conjoined to his Jewish ancestry. She had a bitter tongue. Eventually the new priest had to intervene and point out that the Jesus she worshipped had a similar pedigree to Solly's, and asked her to find a different language with which to castigate him. As she didn't give ground, it was Solly who eventually made the compromise necessary for peace to be restored. He now checked with her what it was that he should sell before he invested in any new stock, and so an uneasy truce was achieved

Theo McNally, the schoolmaster, did finally find his way out of the teaching he hated, although his hopes of developing a racecourse never materialized and his damaged ankle never improved, despite repeated immersions in the holy pool. He was beginning to lose hope in divine intervention. Then, in lieu of an unpaid bet with a tinker, he accepted a young horse which he knew had been stolen. Knowing more about its previous ownership than the tinker did he had every reason to believe it was the product of an unrecorded mating of a very ordinary mare with an outstanding racing stallion – the mare had been slipped into the same paddock as the stallion when its owners were abroad and its groom in the pub, where McNally had been plying him with drinks in order to gain 'inside information.' With a forged pedigree, McNally thought it could do well at stud, and so it proved. He trailed it around the countryside and he made good money helping it enjoy itself mounting mares throughout the land. It also took him away from the glen, where he'd never been happy, and put him into the forefront of the racing game, which he'd always enjoyed.

The only hint of sadness in this now thriving community, and it didn't sadden many, was the sudden death of Bridget Nelligan. Her heifer one day got out of the field and went to join Paddy Sullivan's cattle in a field a mile down the road. She'd mooed plaintively to join them for long enough. Now she was happy. Bridget went looking for her, and it was said that when she found her, she was being mounted by Paddy's new bull. Bridget collapsed on the spot. She never could countenance affairs of the flesh. Bridget's brother in Geesla was contacted by Miss Cronin and he came to the sparsely attended funeral. He found it difficult to express a great deal of mournful sorrow, as he was the only one in line to inherit the cottage, so his declining years were likely to be much more comfortable than he had hitherto expected them to be. The funeral was arranged, of course, by Jonty McGarrigle, now smartly attired in the navy - blue Saxony suit made for him by Solly Axelrod, although it was becoming too tight for him owing to the rise in his living standards, now that the town was more prosperous. Solly kept hinting to him that it was high time he was measured for a new one. Like everyone else, Solly knew that Jonty was 'in the money,' as the funeral business was livelier than it had ever been.

Every effort was made by Miss Cronin to trace Agatha so that she might attend the requiem mass conducted by father Ruddy. it was eventually established that she had departed Swinford for Dublin, but her address could not be traced in time for the funeral. However, reports eventually came back to Glenowen that she was living in bohemian harmony with some licentious artist who displayed pictures of her - totally naked - on the railings around Merion Square. She'd sometimes stand alongside of them, clothed, of course, just to demonstrate how realistic a likeness they were. (Although very few of the customers were making facial comparisons.) Apparently, they were selling well, and at fairly high prices, but, unfortunately, their artistic merits were not espoused by either the Gardai or the clergy, so some of the profit went into paying fines. However, the prices they were commanding seriously outweighed what the magistrates took off them, so they were living in splendid comfort, as Nolan was also being paid for producing artist's impressions of his father's architectural commissions.

\*

The new-found prosperity of the town lasted longer than did the holy figure around which it had been built. That came to an abrupt end.

There had been a week of continual torrential rain. Everyone was confined indoors for most of the time, stepping outside only when absolutely necessitous, such as going to church, where an end to the downpour was prayed for. Thatched roofs became sodden, some collapsed altogether. Roads were washed away as streams burst their banks. Currachs could not put to sea, so there was no fish to eat. The pilgrims and spouse seekers were confined to whatever lodgings they had found. The only person doing well out of it was Darcy O'Neill, whose pub was packed day and night, and some customers (as well as Mullarkey) were even sleeping on the floor. The deluge was considerable enough to cause small landslides on the higher slopes around the town. One of these led to some huge boulders on the mountain shadowing the glen being undermined, and rolling down, smashing the surface of the glen road before they rolled across it and down into the bog-land below.

The morning after the rain had ceased and a clearer sky was starting to emerge, Mick Mullarkey and Tim Murphy were walking through the puddles towards Glenowen. They came to the fallen rocks that were almost blocking the road. Then they saw the remains of the 'holy' figure. A huge boulder, bigger than itself, must have struck it from above, smashing away the head portion cleanly and completely at the point where the 'shoulders' of the figure had been, and also breaking the torso in two. What was left was now a form that resembled a headless eagle with two rounded humps for pinions. Mick and Tim stared at it in amazement.

*Two of a Kind*

"Willya look at dat, Tim," said Mullarkey. "What d'ye make of it?"

"What is there to make of it?" asked Murphy.

"Can ye not see it?" said Mullarkey.

"See what?"

"D'ye not see the wings of the Angel Gabriel in that rock Tim? Sure, It's another miracle."

Tim looked at Mullarkey as if he were mad, then turned his attention back to the broken rock. He studied the two humps, particularly salient because pale stone was now exposed on the base of darker, weathered rock, two buff- coloured humps, and said, "No Mick, no, I don't."

"Can ye not see anything in it at all?"

Murphy stared hard again for several seconds, wondering if he were missing something, his eyes on a level with the truncated rock. "I think I can see what you're looking at, Mick. But I don't see the Angel Gabriel.

"Well, what do ye see?"

"Well Mick, It's not the Angel Gabriel, that's for sure. In fact, it looks more like an arse to me."

Printed in Great Britain
by Amazon